*To Mary, my saving grace*

# THE DEATH STAR

Rockers have been mining teenage alienation—quite profitably—since Eddie Cochran's "Summertime Blues" in 1958. But Shirley's muse had a hard, bitter edge. In his lyrics, the grown-ups who ran the world weren't merely callous; they were malevolent. In a matter of weeks after his first music video was released, Shirley's ghastly face was splashed across the cover of every music magazine. All manner of rumors began attaching themselves to this bizarre new personality. One particularly persistent and piquant piece of gossip maintained that as a child, Shirley had murdered both his parents, a couple of dour Bible-thumpers, in their sleep.

All I know is that somewhere along the way, he had mastered stagecraft. The thing that impressed me most about his concerts was his uncanny sense of timing. I would see him launch into his performance often over the next few days and, each time, he nailed the moment that the crowd's enthusiasm climaxed.

But I wasn't following this tour to marvel at Shirley Slaughterhouse's showmanship. I was here to find out how—several nights before I first saw him perform—in an arena a hundred miles from Worcester, Shirley's only friend had met a very gruesome death . . .

# Killer
# SOLO

## DAVID HILTBRAND

AVON BOOKS
*An Imprint of HarperCollinsPublishers*

AVON BOOKS
*An Imprint of* HarperCollins*Publishers*
10 East 53rd Street
New York, New York 10022-5299

Copyright © 2004 by David Hiltbrand
ISBN: 0-06-054943-2
**www.avonmystery.com**

First Avon Books paperback printing: January 2004

Avon Trademark Reg. U.S. Pat. Off. and in Other Countries, Marca Registrada, Hecho en U.S.A.
HarperCollins® is a registered trademark of HarperCollins Publishers Inc.

Printed in the U.S.A.

10  9  8  7  6  5  4  3  2  1

# Killer
# SOLO

# CHAPTER

## 1

The house lights dimmed and the crowd erupted, a scalding howl of bloodlust and anticipation. The PA system began pumping out strange Sufi snake-charming music that became more insistent and penetrating as it gradually grew louder and faster. The audience, already stoked, got swept up by this swirling, modal sound—hypnotic music that seemed to climb and coil around your brain stem.

Roadies were leading band members out onto the dark stage, focusing hooded flashlights down at their feet. The people at the front of the arena were the first to notice the eerie processional and their cries of delight swept like a paper fire past where I stood behind the mixing board to the back of the floor and up into the tiers of balconies.

All the time, the crowd and the music continued to feed off one another. At the precise moment that the tension inside the arena crested, flash bombs exploded, clusters of spotlights began raking the hall and the wild dervish music segued ingeniously into the thunderous opening chords of "Blood Money." And Shirley Slaughterhouse was there. In fact, he was everywhere.

He stood in a merciless spotlight at center stage, inert and awkward, his head bent nearly to his shoulder, looking like a hanged man dangling from an invisible rope. A close-up of his face, his eyes wide and vacant, was splashed on a series of giant screens hanging above the stage and on every monitor and visual device around the Worcester Centrum Center, even, I noticed, on the big DiamondVision scoreboard suspended from the ceiling. Most rock acts won't use the arena's overhead board because the black-and-white reproduction is grainy and washed out. But it lent Shirley's face a spooky, haunted quality, like the Shroud of Turin. And the repetition of his image, everywhere you looked, created an immediacy and an inescapability, as if he had singled you specifically out of the audience.

His black hair was long and greasy. He never made an effort to push away the stray strands that dangled over his face like loose barbed wire. And what a face! Shirley Slaughterhouse had a pallor far beyond the bleached tint of Michael Jackson's. His skin resembled an eighteenth-century consumptive or a Kabuki artist in its startling whiteness. A thin sharp line of black makeup, like a blade, ran down the right side from his broad forehead to his concave cheek, bisecting his inert eye. Cinammon-brown lipstick covered and exaggerated his lips. When he opened his mouth, it appeared he had dyed his tongue black. Intricate, cuneiform-looking tattoos covered his arms and bare torso.

It was his eyes that grabbed you. Beneath plucked brows, the irises were two different colors—a blue so icy it appeared translucent, the other a ferocious horror-film red, flecked with yellow.

As the band continued to pound out "Blood Money," Shirley's head suddenly jerked upright, like a puppet's, and he screamed, "If we must burn, let us burn together!" The crowd went berserk.

Man and boy, I've been at thousands of rock concerts, from Blind Faith to Third Eye Blind, from Mungo Jerry to Smashmouth, from King Crimson to Kid Rock. But I have to say I've never seen anyone open a show as commandingly as Shirley.

That's quite an accomplishment for a guy who seemed to have emerged from nowhere. His first music video, released before he even had an album in the stores, created enormous buzz on MTV. "Ritalin Junkie," with its images of Shirley strapped into a jolting roller coaster, made him an instant icon.

Most adults probably weren't familiar with him, but among school-aged kids, he was an overnight sensation, with his macabre visage and his message of angry disaffection.

Rockers have been mining teenage alienation—quite profitably—since Eddie Cochran's "Summertime Blues" in 1958. But Shirley's muse had a hard, bitter edge. In his lyrics, the grown-ups who ran the world weren't merely callous; they were malevolent.

His vision was like Pink Floyd meets The *X-Files*. And the music was surprisingly good: rousing, body-slam rock with a chilling hint of techno. Mix and shake vigorously and you had a powerful package. In a matter of weeks, Shirley's ghastly face was splashed across the cover of every music magazine. All manner of rumors began attaching themselves to this bizarre new personality. One particularly persistent and piquant piece of gossip maintained that as a child, Shirley had murdered both his parents, a couple of dour Bible-thumpers, in their sleep, and that he had spent the last two decades in and out of foster care and lockdown.

All I know is that somewhere along the way, he had mastered stagecraft. The thing that impressed me most about his concerts was his uncanny sense of timing. I would see him launch into his performance often over the next few days and, each time, he nailed the moment that the crowd's enthusiasm climaxed.

After a sound check on a rainy afternoon in St. Louis I was hanging around with the tour's senior engineer, Terry Tisdale. I complimented him on his knack for gauging the audience so precisely. "It ain't me," Terry said. "It's Rocky." That snide nickname, short for *The Rocky Horror Picture Show,* was how the veteran crew members who had been hired expressly for this tour disdainfully referred to Shirley when he or members of his small retinue weren't around. And rock journeymen didn't come much more seasoned than Terry. He had started as a production assistant—which meant you fetched and carried things for the roadies—on a Savoy Brown tour back in 1970, dug the lifestyle and gradually worked his way up the ladder with Iron Maiden and Def Leppard. Now he spent his nights a hundred yards in front of the stage behind the console of a massive control board, as elaborate and multilevered as an old-fashioned church organ, coordinating and controlling the sound, lights and special effects for some of rock's biggest acts.

"The amazing thing," said Terry, flattening his gray hair and fluffing his ponytail, "is that the kid nails it from so far out. He signals me thirty seconds before he wants to start so I can cue the sequencers to make the transition to 'Blood Money.' Some nights I'm positive he's jumping the gun. Other times I got my finger on the switch for a minute or more—sure that he's blowing past it. But damn if he isn't always right on the money. I don't know how he does it. It's freaky, man."

But I wasn't following this tour to marvel at Shirley Slaughterhouse's showmanship. I was here to find out how—several nights before I first saw him perform—in an arena a hundred miles from Worcester, Shirley's only friend had met such a gruesome death.

# CHAPTER
## 2

When the call came, I was standing in the kitchen, waiting for the French roast to brew. It wasn't a long wait. I had one of those drip coffeemakers where you can yank out the carafe as soon as there's enough for a cup. I'm quick on the trigger. Not because I'm impatient. I mean, I am. But I happen to like that first mug bracingly strong.

I had a Jonatha Brooke CD playing. I can't listen to the radio in the morning. It's too damn raucous. Too much jabber. Too much forced hilarity. For the life of me, I can't understand why all the pop stations insist on being manic first thing in the morning when you're waking up. Then later in the day, the jocks get mellower and they let the music play. Shouldn't it be the other way around?

The local section of the newspaper was spread out on the counter in front of me. My attention had wandered away from an account of another acrimonious meeting of the board of supervisors. Outside, the morning fog was still skulking below the ridgeline, hiding from the gathering sun. Spring is always delayed here in northern Connecticut, like it's catching its breath before it moves north to take on the Berkshires.

A murder of crows was having a nasty debate of their own in an oak across the field. The birds were squawking at each other while hunching their shoulders up and down. It looked like they were reenacting the final courtroom scene from *A Few Good Men*. I was caught up in this rowdy Hekyll & Jekyll repertory company when the phone rang, startling me.

"Jim," said a booming voice, "it's Paul Roynton at Anderson & Finch. Please tell me you're available." So far, my plans for the day didn't extend far beyond a noon AA meeting and maybe shooting some jump shots at the outdoor court in town if the weather warmed up enough. The rec department had put in new chain-mail nets on the baskets and I loved the sound the ball made ripping through them if you swished it just right. I'd heave it up from behind the three-point arc, yelling, "Lloyd B. Free!" when the touch felt right. But I didn't think Paul needed to know the details of my busy itinerary.

Roynton didn't sound worried, but I could tell he was stressed. He had risen to the top of his insurance agency through sales. An inveterate glad-hander, he'd spend three minutes blithely shooting the shit with you before mentioning that you were standing on his Gucci. So the fact that he skipped the chitchat and got right to business told me that he was really concerned.

"What's up, Paul?"

"I need you to hustle up to Maine right away," he said. "We got a serious fuckup on one of the tours we're covering."

Not many people know it, but rock 'n roll is one of the insurance industry's biggest customers. Like movies, sports and other forms of big-ticket entertainment in this country, pop music plays for such giddy financial stakes, and the chances for unforeseeable reversals (overdoses, crowd disasters, loss of life and limb) and high-profile lawsuits are so rife, that no band ventures out on the road until it is covered by a hefty and exhaustive policy. Before you lease the sound equipment or decide which song will be your second encore, you have to get insurance.

You hear doctors complain all the time about how malpractice insurance is bleeding them dry. Believe me, they get off easy. Rock stars have a richly deserved reputation for debauchery, drug abuse, wanton destruction and volatile fans. Consequently they pay crushing premiums for their coverage. These days you really do have to pay your dues if you want to sing the blues. I guarantee if Keith Moon, the Who's Tasmanian devil of a drummer, had lived another ten years, he'd have his own personal insurance adjuster dogging his heels on every tour, busily clacking away on a calculator.

I wasn't in the protection racket—at least not usually. But some of my investigative assignments came from insurance agencies like Paul's. Anderson & Finch was a boutique firm that issued policies for full-scale stadium and arena tours. Usually it was like minting money: they'd extract a ransom from the rockers and if any lawsuits were brought, Anderson & Finch would move quickly to squash the bogus ones and settle all those with merit. But I could tell by Paul Roynton's brusque manner that he had his rep tie caught in the shredder.

"Have you heard of Shirley Slaughterhouse?" he was asking.

"I've seen pictures. He's the one who looks like Johnny Depp with dysentery."

Roynton snorted. "He's been out on the road for about two months. The kid is like a magnet for controversy. Protests and boycotts everywhere he goes, but the gate has been really solid. Most places. No major problems, really, until last night in Portland when one of his crew fell two hundred fifty feet off a catwalk. A real mess."

"During the show?" I asked.

"No. About three hours after the concert. The gear had already been packed. There was no reason for the guy to be up there."

"How are the police treating it?" As we talked, I was booting up my computer to do a quick periodicals search on Slaughterhouse.

"There are no obvious signs of foul play. I just talked on

the phone with Shirley's label president, Keith Fisher. You know him, right? He's up there trying to soothe the locals but they still don't want anyone to leave town until they complete their preliminary investigation, so we're probably going to have to cancel at least tonight's show in Montreal. Apparently Shirley hasn't been too cooperative with the authorities."

"What does that mean?"

"He's not real outgoing at the best of times. And the guy that died was a close friend, so Shirley's kind of in seclusion."

"What do you need, Paul?"

"Get up there right away and make sure we're not liable."

The insurance policies for these tours broke down into a rigid caste system. The talent was covered even if they got rug burn while screwing a groupie in the back of a limo. But the crew was only eligible for compensation while performing their duties.

Essentially, that meant I would have to reconstruct the events of last night. If the guy had climbed up on the catwalk for any reason that could be construed as work-related, then Anderson & Finch was going to be writing a big check.

After getting the name and number of the hotel the band was staying at, I asked if there was anything else I should know. I learned early on when I started doing freelance work for rock musicians and their labels to ask the wayward questions that pop into my brain, however vague or tangential. These throwaway queries often provide crucial information. It worked this time.

"There have been death threats in several cities the tour stopped in," Roynton said, "but apparently they started getting really menacing this past week."

"All right," I said. "I assume there's someone working security on the tour who can fill me in on specifics."

"Well, that's the thing, Jim. The dead guy, Jake Karn? He *was* security."

"Great," I said, marking a few Slaughterhouse profiles and recent concert reviews to be downloaded to my printer.

"Oh, and one other thing, Jim," said Roynton, trying to

pretend, not very convincingly, that this was a minor detail, hardly worth mentioning. "Before Fisher and his lawyers got there, Shirley told the Portland police that he knew Karn was about to die."

"What?" I said, with operatic dismay.

"Listen, amigo," said Roynton, his usual bulletproof bonhomie back in place, "I have to scoot into a finance meeting. Call me at home tonight. Let's get this one boxed and shipped in a hurry. 'Bye."

I started raising objections, but the dial tone wasn't listening. I looked over at the counter and cursed. While I was on the phone the whole pot had brewed. Watery coffee. Not even nine o'clock and already I wanted to start the day over.

# CHAPTER
# 3

I took a taxi from the Portland airport directly to the concert hall. The cab's heater was turned all the way up, but despite its annoying rattle and hum, it wasn't kicking out much warmth. At least none of it was making it to the backseat. My laconic driver, who looked like he was suffering from a bad case of cabin fever, didn't seem bothered by the chill. Of course, he was bundled up like a Kodiak prospector. I don't think I've ever seen anyone driving a car with mittens on before. Looking out the grimy windows, I could see ridges of gray snow still heaped along the curb.

I went right to the arena to scope out how far the guy had fallen and see how one got access to the catwalk. I didn't learn much. There was some action on the stage. A crew was setting up for a sound check. Death won't stop the show from going on and Alan Jackson was headlining that night. I wondered if he had winterized his cowboy hat.

Two policemen stood guard on the arena floor. I kept my distance, knowing my unofficial status wasn't going to impress them. But I could see that the scaffolding walkway was reasonably wide and definitely sturdy, with waist-high handrails. You'd have to be pretty clumsy—or pretty stoned—to tumble off that thing.

From there, it was a short ride to the Sheraton. Different cab but the windows were just as dirty and the driver looked startlingly similar to my first chauffeur. I thought of the watchcapped trio on *Newhart*. "I'm Larry; this is my brother Darryl and this is my other brother Darryl." Maybe these guys had cornered the taxi market in Portland. Good luck to them.

The fact that Shirley and his entourage were staying at the Sheraton told me the tour was doing good business. Status in rock music is always reflected in where you bunk. The Rolling Stones put up at the Four Seasons. Garage bands crash right in their van on the cold, rusty floor, contorting their bodies around their banged-up amplifiers.

The police investigation had commandeered the hotel's bright, vaulted lobby. Detectives were interviewing everyone from the musicians to the guys who drive the rigs with all the equipment from city to city.

It reminded me of those old British manor-house murder mysteries where the constable is questioning the weekend guests and the household staff one at a time. Only there was more green hair and tattoos milling about in the lobby than you'd see in a month of Shropshire Sundays.

Meanwhile business travelers were making their way from the registration desk to the elevators with their mouths hanging open, amazed that such armies of the night actually existed. The sight of all these bohos in a ritzy hotel was as startling as going for a run at the local high school and finding a herd of bison grazing placidly on the infield of the track.

I paused to soak in the surreal scene in the lobby when I took a hip check from behind, causing me to stumble over the carryall at my feet.

"Well, the police might as well pack it in," said a raspy and sarcastic voice. "Sherlock fucking McNamara has arrived."

Getting back my balance, I turned angrily to face Keith Fisher. He was one of those crass greedheads who are drawn to the music business like jackals to a carcass. To give the unscrupulous rat bastard his due, as a businessman he was sharper than an X-Acto knife and he had unerring instincts for the pop marketplace.

He had done well enough to start his own record label, Pound Ridge, the one Shirley Slaughterhouse was signed to. Fisher maintained a small and remarkably eclectic talent roster—from gangsta rappers to a Christian boy band, but in the past two years, the Pound Ridge artists had sold more records than all but two of the mega-corporate labels.

Standing in the lobby, Fisher was trying to project an image of hipness, not an easy task when you're built like a golf cart. He was dressed in a soft, silky suit—gray flecked with black. He wore ostrich-skin cowboy boots and a collarless Russian peasant shirt. His hair was pulled away from his knobby forehead and balding crown into a small, severe ponytail. And he was wearing enough cologne to make breathing difficult for anyone who wandered within ten feet of him.

We shared some harsh history. A few years before, he was promoting an oldies revue and one of the featured singers had a weight problem. I was hired to help him stick to his diet. It was an unusual gig for me. Mostly it meant convincing limo drivers not to take the guy through fast-food take-out windows late at night.

Anyway, at the end of the tour, Fisher held up my fee for months. When I objected, he spread rumors that I was demanding and irresponsible. Word of mouth is crucial in my line of work and I didn't appreciate him pissing in my well.

Ever since, whenever we met at industry functions, Fisher and I didn't bother with small talk. We immediately resumed hostilities.

This run-in was pretty typical. Both his juvenile nudge and his snide comment were intended to antagonize me. I'm the first to admit I have a short fuse, but it's hard to light. Keith Fisher was a human blowtorch. I cocked my fist and pulled back my arm.

The punch never happened. Something clamped my bicep. Firmly. I had forgotten about Nicky Hagipetros, the grim and enormous bodyguard who traveled everywhere with Fisher. I glanced over my shoulder to see Hagipetros looking down at me with evident hostility, like you would a bug who had crashed the picnic.

"Hello, Nicky," I said. The spark of anger I felt over Fisher's schoolyard shove vanished. I needed him to get to Shirley. And I have to admit, Nicky was a pretty effective deterrent.

"Let him go, Nick," Fisher said. "He's harmless."

I wriggled my wrist, trying to coax my circulation to resume, and turned to Fisher. "Have the police already spoken to you?"

"Never asked to," Fisher said. "*I* wasn't in Portland last night."

"Is Shirley somewhere in the crowd?"

"Nah," he said dismissively, his eyes darting around the lobby. "He's been squirreled away in his suite for hours. Probably won't emerge until it's time to go to the airport."

"I thought the police weren't letting you leave town."

Fisher shrugged. "I guess we can add that to the long list of things you don't know shit about," he said.

"Can I get five minutes with him?"

"Shirley? Oh yeah, he'll be thrilled," he said, smirking. "First he's questioned by the police. Now he gets to entertain some jerkoff from the insurance company. It's a real red-letter day for him."

"Why don't you let me do my job, Keith? Then I can get out of your hair. What's left of it."

Fisher nodded his head heavily at me, balefully biting his lip. "Talk to Shirley's publicist. She can set it up."

"Do you know how the cops are treating this?"

"Why don't you find out?" he said, stomping toward the revolving doors in his designer cowboy boots. Nicky was right on his augmented heels. "You're the fucking detective."

Fisher's parting insult happened to be true. Only two months before, my local newspaper, the *Winsted Gazette,* had written a story that made it official. There was a picture of me, looking startled and furtive, beneath the headline: "The Rock 'n' Roll Detective." The photo made my driver's license shot look flattering. Could have been worse. I could have had on the deerstalker's cap the photographer had brought along as a prop and tried to persuade me to wear. Sherlock McNamara indeed.

This sure wasn't the career path I'd intended to pursue. I had moved to New York City right after college. On the basis of a progressive radio show I hosted as an undergrad at Albert College, I got a job in A&R at a major record label. The initials stand for Artist and Repertoire. The high-end veterans of A&R have a stable of established acts, usually groups they "discovered" or lured away from other labels. Ostensibly, their job is to help their roster of performers select and develop their best material for recording sessions. But in actuality, they're responsible for keeping their performers reasonably productive and focused. It ain't easy.

Say you're representing an established star. You try telling some arrogant narcissist with three platinum albums, a house on the beach in Maui and a bad Vicodin habit that his new material is so flat-out awful, it sounds like a pack of dingos attacking a mule.

Or, conversely, imagine some nineteen-year-old who has just landed on the Fantasy Island of rock 'n roll—with more money, drugs and pussy than he can shake a drumstick at. Now you convince him to keep his nose to the grindstone. That's why rock 'n roll history is littered with the charred remains of one-hit wonders. That first giant step up to stardom is a doozy.

As I said, a few A&R agents are in it for the long haul. But most are like I was: young, smug talent scouts about as durable as ice sculpture. Your job is to sniff out fresh blood, haunting desolate clubs in search of the next Nirvana or Metallica. The headliners in these joints don't go on until after midnight. In New York, it's closer to three A.M. It's a job which demands a vampire's hours and Jack LaLane's stamina. The pay is lousy, but most of the recruits to A&R are so damned thrilled to be working in the music business, they'd do it just for the perks: a box of engraved business cards and an expense account that no one questions, even though it seems to have been assembled by six sailors on a frenzied shore leave from submarine duty.

If you do stumble onto some promising talent, then comes the hard sell. First you have to convince the band to sign with you. That's not easy given the fact that at most of these gigs you're standing shoulder to cheekbone in the mosh pit with your counterparts from three other labels; then, infinitely harder, you have to persuade your own jaded label executives to come out to hear the band and extend them a contract.

Still, I was drawn to the job because I had a good ear. (I like to think I still do.) But I was even more enamored of the lifestyle. Drinking to excess—that was expected. I had mastered that years before. It was the drugs that washed me overboard.

I had been a pothead since junior high. But I went from sharing a joint with the musicians in the dressing room between sets to snorting cocaine alone in putrid bathroom stalls to mainlining heroin in bombed-out shooting galleries on the Lower East Side. Eventually I spent more time scamming for money and searching for dealers than I did listening to music.

Fortunately, I worked for a guy who was acquainted with the symptoms of addiction and with the kick-in-the-pants method for dealing with them. I had stopped showing up for our weekly department meetings, my excuses growing more

and more outlandish; my appearance became grotesquely
wraithlike. I materialized in the office only late at night and
only to steal and pawn anything that would fit in a backpack.
Early one afternoon I was summoned to Hal Arrington's office, a meeting I was forty-five minutes late for.

He presented me with a plane ticket to Minneapolis and
the news that I was covered for a twenty-eight-day stay in a
rehab. "You don't have to go," he said. "But if you're not
checked in by seven o'clock tonight, you'll be dismissed
immediately and without severance." I started to object
about what a busy guy I was, all the responsibilities I had to
attend to.

He quickly interrupted my line of bullshit. "Son," he said,
"it ain't easy being an addict, but if you don't take advantage
of this opportunity, it's going to get a whole lot harder. This
is it: last gas for two hundred miles. If you got any brains
left, you better pull it over."

Let me tell you, getting sober is no Jimmy Buffett concert. Once you get through the roaring hell of detox, which
is like being tortured during a sleep-deprivation experiment,
then the painful stuff starts. You have to face a gauntlet of
unpleasant truths about yourself and root out a dizzying array of ingrained bad habits. Sometimes I think I stayed sober
just to avoid going through rehab again.

When I got back to New York, Hal Arrington did me another favor. He fired me. Gently. "This isn't a healthy environment for you, Jim," he said. "I'll keep you on the payroll
for a month, but I suggest you spend that time going to a lot of
AA meetings and looking for a job where you're not spending every night in the clubs. You stay clean for a year and I'll
rehire you at the label if you want. In another department."

We never made it that far. Hal was fired in December
when the latest release from the label's pop diva tanked.
Merry Christmas. But about ten months into my recovery I
was working in Hedgehog's, a record store in Greenwich
Village. The year before, when I was still with the record
company, I used to come in there, furtive and twitchy, trying

to sell them boxes of CDs I had swiped from the office. Now I was behind the counter.

Anyway, in walks George Fontana, a band manager I had met a few times. We chatted for a while, and the next day he called me unexpectedly at the store. "You got sober, right?" he asked. "Listen, my band Spontaneous Combustion is in town recording an album at Electric Ladyland."

"Can't wait to hear it," I said. "I liked their first album. Grunge without all the maudlin self-pity."

"Yeah, well, at this rate, there ain't going to be a second album. My singer, Tommy Malthus, is a stone junkie. He treats New York like it's some kind of outdoor drug bazaar. Can you help?"

"Help? What can I do?"

"I want to hire you to be Tommy's bodyguard."

"George," I said, "I weigh about a hundred and forty pounds when I get out of the shower." (This was seven years ago; I haven't missed a lot of meals in the interim.)

"You're not going to be sumo wrestling, Jim," George said. "I just want you to protect Tommy from himself."

Two factors overwhelmed my doubts: George offered me a daily wage that was as much as my biweekly take-home at the record store. And my AA sponsor thought it would be a good reminder of why I was fighting to stay sober. "Think of it as twelve-step work," he said. "Just make damn sure you get to a meeting every day while you're doing it."

I took the job, never thinking it would lead to anything. But like most businesses, rock music is a pretty hermetic world. Word got around that I would sheepdog the real hard cases. My overall won-lost record stayed fairly low. But I got a lot of work. I didn't blame myself for the many who flamed out and I didn't take credit for the few who turned it around. I made damn sure *I* stayed sober.

Overall, the labels and managers who paid me were happy if I was able to throttle back the self-destructiveness enough to keep their artists on the stage or in the studio for a time. Gradually, I was hired for other chores besides babysitting addicts and drunks. Soon I was getting calls from the musicians themselves when their personal lives got particularly messy.

Oh, and Tommy Malthus? He made it through that recording session but then he hit a rough patch: moved to New York, took up residence at the Chelsea Hotel and was arrested for possession so many times he became personally acquainted with nine-tenths of the law. At a certain point I guess the night-court judge got tired of arraigning him. Tommy is serving time in a facility in upstate New York.

By the way, that second Spontaneous Combustion album really sucked.

# CHAPTER
## 4

I should have been looking for Shirley Slaughterhouse's publicist, but I couldn't tear myself away from the wild scene in the lobby. Guys who hadn't been awake at this hour since their Clearasil days were splayed across every piece of available furniture. The lucky ones had sunglasses. The rest were squinting like moles in the bright daylight. Most had cigarettes dangling loosely from their fingers. It looked like the S.S. *Ozzy Osbourne* had struck a reef outside the hotel and these were the shipwrecked survivors.

I was wishing that some latter-day Norman Rockwell could be here to capture this tableau when Shirley's publicist found me. "Hello, there, stranger," she said, in a deep, smoky voice that always reminded me of a young Kathleen Turner. I knew before I turned that it was Paula Mansmann.

Publicity is one of the hardest and most thankless tasks in the music business. You have to mediate between the thin-skinned, hemophiliac talent and the cynical, bloodthirsty rock press. It's like guiding a balloon through a porcupine convention. Paula made it look easy.

I had seen her turn down requests from the most prickly writers at *Rolling Stone* and *Time*. But after five minutes of her subtle ego-rolfing, they'd leave her office convinced that not doing the story was their idea.

Paula relied on technique (she was part matador, part pickpocket and part Geisha) and a whole lot of charm. She could make the busboy at an International House of Pancakes feel utterly fascinating and witty. I must have asked her out ten times when we were working at the same label, and every time she made me feel like she was saying no only with the most profound regret. She stood there in the Sheraton lobby, smiling brightly, her glossy black hair pulled back tightly. One thing was for sure: she looked a lot better in a ponytail than Keith Fisher did.

"Hey, Paula," I said, blushing with pleasure.

"Hey, Jim," she said. "Keith told me you were on your way. I'll tell you, seeing you is the first good thing that's happened today."

"Rough morning?" I asked.

"I'll say. I had to go roust all these guys out of bed. Could have used a cattle prod for that. Then I had to assemble them in the parking lot and ferry them over here."

"Not everyone is staying in the Sheraton?"

"Nah. Only Shirley, the band and a few other guys. Most of the crew and staff were at the Motel 6 over by the interstate. Then I had to tell my happy little campers I was taking them all to be interrogated by the police. They loved that."

"What was the reaction when you told them Jake Karn was dead?" I asked.

Paula shrugged. "Pretty muted," she said. "Of course, most of them are all but comatose at this hour. You could tell them you'd harvested their kidneys overnight and it wouldn't get a rise out of them. But Jake wasn't real popular anyway."

"No? Why not?"

She leaned in and spoke quietly. Muting her husky voice made it sound even more sexy. "Shirley is pretty reclusive," she said. "And Jake was sort of his mouthpiece to everyone on the tour. It was a bad chain of command. A lot of people resented taking orders from some small-town guy who had never been out on the road before."

"Do you know if the police have turned up anything?"

"I don't think so," she said. "So far, no one has copped to seeing Jake after midnight last night. Most of the interviews have been short and sour. This crowd doesn't tend to be real cooperative with the police."

"When did Keith Fisher get here?"

"About ten o'clock. He had Nicky with him and a couple of lawyers—one who flew up with him from New York and a local guy they called from the plane. Keith just left to plead with the police chief to let the tour move on to Montreal tonight."

"You think that's going to work?"

"Keith can be pretty persuasive," she said, smirking. "The lawyers went over first to pave the way. They seemed to think that the police would let us move on as long as Keith agreed to make everyone available for additional questioning *and* if he agreed to pay the airfare for the Portland detectives to fly in and visit us whenever they needed to. Of course, that's only if the coroner here sees nothing suspicious. If he spots any red flags on Jake's body, we're not going anywhere."

"What do you make of all this, Paula?"

She paused, her brown eyes widening. "Why don't we continue this in the lounge?" she said, flicking her head at a saloon across the lobby, obscured behind a barrier of hoar-frosted glass. I gave her the after-you hand flip.

As we walked into the executive watering hole, I spotted a guitar wrangler named Billy O'Connor who used to work for Stevie Ray Vaughan. Billy was slumped over in a booth with his usual bad posture. His flannel shirt had the sleeves rolled up and he leaned on the table, the veins snaking across his Popeye forearms like coaxial cables. His most distinctive feature, though, was the eye patch he wore cinched around his rusty-colored shoulder-length hair.

There was nothing wrong with Billy's eye. He had started

wearing the patch after working as a roadie for Dr. Hook in 1978 and he liked the look. Sitting across from him was Legs Turkel, a wizened lighting tech who always wore a once-colorful knitted wool beanie. I think it was Legs's tribute to late-era Marvin Gaye.

Sitting with them was Sandra Blanchard, an effusive makeup artist with hair so flyaway she looked like the poster child for the static electricity display at the Please-Touch Museum. She had on a pair of blue oval Janis Joplin sunglasses that she never took off. About twice every minute she'd let loose with her piercing birdcall laugh.

The three of them were drinking tequila sunrises and loudly dissing Madonna. "God, she is soooo desperate," said Legs.

"Those poor kids," said Sandra. "Can you imagine? 'Don't play in mommy's lingerie closet, Lourdes. That bra will put your eye out!'"

"I'd rather have Nico for a mother," said Billy.

"I'd rather have Courtney Love," trumped Legs.

"I'd rather have Kathie Lee Gifford for a mother than her," crowed Sandra. At this they all began laughing so hard they almost fell off their stools.

Paula ordered an iced tea and I got a club soda as we settled in at a table. "How long you been working for Pound Ridge?" I asked her.

She thought for a second. "Can it only be six months? God, it seems so much longer than that."

"I don't mean to offend you, but why would you go to work for Fisher?"

She poured a blue packet of sweetener into her tea and stirred. "I'm not insulted. I know you don't get along." At the end of the bar, a guy with a weather-creased face and a flowing ponytail drained the last in a series of Bloody Marys, wiped his droopy mustache with a cocktail napkin and shoved off. As he passed us, he flicked his head at Paula and gave her a crooked grin. She smiled back and wiggled her fingers at him. "Roadie?" I asked.

"No, he drives one of the big rigs with all the stage sets." At least he didn't have a to-go cup.

"Anyway, to answer your question," Paula continued, "I took the job at Pound Ridge because Keith offered me a chance to head up my own department. Of course, on days like this that's not such a treat."

"Have you been traveling with the Slaughterhouse show?"

"Only sporadically," she said. "I wouldn't be here today except Shirley is supposed to be making his first appearance in Canada. There's a media event scheduled after his sound check this afternoon. I came up for that."

"What was your take on Jake Karn?"

"Only met him a couple of times, and briefly at that," she said, swirling her lemon wedge around in her glass with a red plastic swizzle stick. "Not a bad guy, but he got a little full of himself on this tour. Always bossing people around."

"You said people resented that?"

"Yeah," she said glumly, then brightened. "Remember when your grade school teacher would have to leave the room and she'd appoint some unpopular kid the class monitor? Help build up their self-esteem? Jake was that kid. Took the job a little too seriously. He could be annoying. But not enough to make someone throw him off a catwalk."

"Was he a stoner?"

"About average, I guess," Paula said. "My impression was that he liked to get a buzz on but he was usually pretty functional when I saw him. *But* . . . I heard recently he was hitting it pretty hard."

"Hard enough to stumble off a catwalk?" I asked. She shrugged.

"What was your first thought when you heard about his fall?"

"Well," she said, cocking her head as she pondered the question, "it wasn't shock."

"Why not?"

"This whole tour has been such a nightmare. Something

bad was bound to happen. Shirley is one of the most vilified artists I've ever worked with."

"Yeah, well, when your roadshow is named the Triumph of the Antichrist, you're going to draw some heat."

Paula laughed. "I know, but this kid has really been a lightning rod. Protests outside every arena, death threats, bomb scares. City councils and mayors have forced us to cancel almost a third of the itinerary so far."

"Boy, you just can't buy that kind of publicity, can you?"

"It's been more eventful than a Partridge Family reunion," Paula replied, smiling.

"How is Shirley taking Karn's death?"

"I only saw him for a few minutes," she said. "But he seemed all right. I really don't think it's hit him yet."

"Can I get an audience with Shirley?"

She consulted her watch. "He's got a charter to Montreal scheduled in an hour," she said. "I'll try to get you in his suite before the flight. Of course, if the police don't wrap it up soon and let the crew hit the road, we're not flying anywhere."

"I'd appreciate it if you could get me a few minutes. It sounds like Shirley was the person who knew Karn best."

"Don't expect too much in the way of illumination," Paula said. "Even in the best of times, Shirley's not a real linear talker. The more stressed out he feels, the more opaque he gets." She raised an eyebrow. "Did you read that interview in *Rolling Stone*?"

"Yeah, I did," I admitted. "It was like listening to Commissioner Gordon try to interrogate the Riddler. I felt like I knew less about Slaughterhouse *after* reading it."

"Incredible, isn't it?" she asked. "He's a self-erasing artist."

"What about the death threats, Paula?"

"Humph," she snorted, and frowned, working the lemon again. "He started getting hate mail a couple of days after his first video was played on MTV and people got a look at him. But we disregarded that, because the letters were coming in to the address listed for his fan club on the CD. And guess who handles all that correspondence? Two interns in my office.

"But since the tour began, the notes are a lot more personal and threatening. And the scary part is that they're waiting for us at the front desk when we check in at every stop on the tour. Whoever is sending these letters is operating with some pretty good information."

"Can I see the threats?"

"Sorry," Paula said, lifting her shoulders, a gesture which drew my attention to the front of her blue-silk blouse. "Keith had me turn over the whole sheaf to the police. I'll show them to you as soon as they're returned."

"Did anyone ask the hotel personnel who was dropping off these notes?"

She laughed and swiveled in her chair, recrossing her legs. My eyes drifted to her skirt and shifting thighs. I reflected on how automatically men respond to visual stimuli and how adept women are at choreographing that response. "You have to remember that Jake Karn was in charge of security. At least that was his title. He and Shirley thought it was all a big joke. They laughed at the notes."

"One more thing," I said. "I understand Shirley told the police he *knew* something bad was going to happen to Jake. What's up with that?"

"I wouldn't put too much stock in it," said Paula. "You'll see when you meet him. Shirley affects this ominous manner—half Old Testament, half Psychic Hotline."

"It just occurred to me: When you're talking to him, do you address him as Shirley?"

Paula smiled, slid off her chair, stood up and then leaned over toward me. "Always," she said, then headed for the lobby.

I wandered over to the trio in the booth, who were now heatedly discussing which singers were closet gays. I had overheard them arguing about various members of 'N Sync as I wrapped up my chat with Paula, and now as I approached, Sandra was asking, "What about Julio Iglesias?"

"Get out!" exclaimed Billy. "With all the girls he's ever loved?"

"I'm sorry," said Sandra, "I just don't think a straight man would devote that much attention to his tan."

"What about George Hamilton?" asked Legs.

"Thank you for proving my point," said Sandra.

"Did any of you know Jake Karn?" I interrupted.

"Well, there's one guy we *know* wasn't gay," said Billy.

"Why do you say that?" I asked.

"He must have been the happiest man on the tour," said Legs. "He was the gatekeeper."

"The gatekeeper?" I repeated, puzzled.

"Yeah," said Legs. "That's a job description that was coined back in the glory days of Led Zeppelin."

"Bullshit," said Sandra, "it probably goes back further than Bill fucking Haley."

"Anyway," said Legs, "the gatekeeper is the guy on the tour who screens the girlies who want to meet the band after the show."

"Some girls will do *anything*," said Billy, opening his eye wide for emphasis, "to get backstage or into the star's hotel room."

"It's like being appointed harem-master," said Legs, "except you don't have to have your tally whacked."

"Does Shirley really get a lot of groupies?" I asked skeptically. I couldn't locate the sex appeal under the death mask.

"Oh yeah," said Billy. "And not all of them look like Morticia Addams, either. A lot of them are real hotties."

"Karn would lead them on, tell them he could get them into Shirley's hotel room," said Legs, "but after he auditioned them, he'd tell 'em to get lost."

"No one hangs with Rocky after the show," said Sandra.

"Or before, for that matter," said Billy.

"He's a fucking recluse," agreed Sandra.

"If I was looking for who killed Karn," said Billy, "I'd

start with all those pissed-off girls who gave head to the ugly little puke and then realized they'd been had."

"Well, I think Julio Iglesias killed him," said Legs, "in a fit of jealous pique." They all raised their glasses to toast this notion.

Before I could pursue any more of their theories, a crowd of tour personnel flooded into the room. They stampeded toward the bar like early birds at a garage sale. The police had obviously concluded their inquiries. Through the throng, I could see Paula gesturing to me from the lobby.

# CHAPTER
# 5

As the elevator ascended to the hotel's top floor, Paula cautioned me not to expect too much. She said if I tried to press Shirley for information, he'd clam up and have me escorted out. "If you get two coherent sentences out of him," she said, "consider that a victory."

Shirley's suite was easy to spot. Two bulky guys in bad suits stood at either side of the door. They eyed me like they had just turned around in a luncheonette to find half their club sandwich missing and I was the guy on the next stool with no plate in front of him but a dab of mayonnaise on his chin.

I knew that look. I had worked security one summer at a club called Tut's in Chicago. Me and another guy stood directly in front of the stage riser, facing the audience. The performers—bands like Pere Ubu, the Cramps and Robin Lane and the Chartbusters—assumed we were there to shield them from any overzealous fans. Actually, our only responsibility was to protect the PA system in the event of a riot. Mostly we just stood there like cigar-store Indians, arms folded on our chests, spoiling for trouble, glaring at people who were trying to have a good time.

Paula informed the boys that I was expected. That didn't do much to lighten their expressions. Paula opened the door with a key card and told me she'd wait outside. The suite's outer room was standard hotel opulent, but the bedchamber was fashioned like a sultan's tent.

The overhead lights were off and all the lamps were wrapped in fabric. Music was playing—a breathy, effeminate singer over plinky acoustic music. Orange and black batik sheets were pinned to the ceiling, hanging down in concentric semicircles. I had to push my way through the seams, like a character in a play hesitatingly making his way onto center stage.

Just outside the innermost sheet was a low-slung altar with five sticks of incense burning in an engraved brass cylinder. It was surrounded by a collection of plastic dolls' heads with their hair in various stages of distress or mutilation. All of them were the sort with eyes that close when you lay them down. Propped upright, their sparkling striated blue eyes all stared out vacantly. In front of them on the rug sat a portly, smiling Buddha statue. Tattooed on his bicep was a truculent-looking Cupid with a skanky cigar butt hanging from his lip.

I parted the final sheet and saw Shirley and a girl sitting on the bed. Something about their postures and their gauzy white cotton outfits made me flash back to John and Yoko, giving interviews to flustered newspaper reporters from hotel room beds.

The girl, spectacularly pale, had long, oily black hair, an aquiline face, a horsey mouth and, by quick inventory, three blotchy birthmarks running from her neck up to her cheek. She briefly noted my entrance, then went back to staring fixedly at the foot of the bed, a smirk on her lips.

Shirley had his legs wrapped around her, with his feet—long, thin, the toes dotted with tufts of wiry black hair—locked together. He was hunched forward with his chin on her shoulder, his lips near her ear. He never looked up at me as I approached the bed.

"Thank you for seeing me," I said. Shirley said something to the girl I could not hear and her snotty smile became a little more pronounced.

"I'm really sorry about what happened to Jake," I said. More whispering resulted in another smirk. "Did he usually stay at the venue so late after a show?" I was slowly working my way around the bed trying to catch his eye, but the girl's hair shielded him from every angle.

"Look," I said, "I know you've had a lot of people intruding on your privacy today. If you could just clarify a few things for me, I'll leave you alone."

No whispering. No response at all. I felt like we were making progress.

"Is that the Incredible String Band?" I asked, gesturing with my head at the music coming out of the sleek portable stereo by the bed. Shirley's gaze slowly swung around toward me. Even though I was prepared for them after seeing his face on so many magazine covers, Shirley's mutant eyes still startled me. I actually winced. But at least I had his attention.

"Did Jake say or do anything out of the ordinary yesterday?" I asked.

I was surprised when he finally spoke. "I suppose that depends on how you think about death," he said. His voice, ghostly and strained, sounded like wind whisking through a Skid Row alley. "I'm sure Jake would consider it to be an unusual day."

"Did you pick up on any hints that something bad was about to happen?" I asked, circling over the same ground.

"Fate, in my experience, always walks in his own shadow," he said.

I wanted to pursue that cryptic statement, but remembering Paula's warning, I moved on.

"Can you tell me when you last saw or spoke to Jake yesterday?"

He swiveled his head back to the girl's ear. It was a dismissive gesture. I fought an impulse to grab this spoiled freak by his hairy toe and drag him off the bed. Paula was right: exactly two sentences. Maybe Shirley was working with a quota. But I was angry that my best and only source on this case talked in riddles. So I fired a shot across his bow. "Has his family been notified?" I asked.

That brought him back, this time with a wounded look on his emaciated face. "Don't the police . . . Christ, I really should call Jake's mother," he said. "Would you ask that publicist to come in?"

"Yes, I will," I said, pleased to have located a nerve beneath Shirley's studiously inscrutable facade. "One last question before I go: What do you think happened to Jake?"

Shirley's gnostic demeanor was already back in place. "He became," he said, turning back to nuzzle the girl once again, "the man who fell to earth."

I backed out of the room, wondering if it would be appropriate to execute a series of bows as I retreated. Paula was out in the hotel corridor jollying up the hired muscle. "He wants to talk to you," I said.

"How did it go?" she asked.

"He was pretty damn enigmatic," I said. "I should talk to the detective who interviewed him. I doubt he let Shirley be quite so evasive."

"You might be surprised," she said. "Keith was by his side the entire time running interference. He can be pretty intimidating. Did you ask him point-blank what happened to Jake?"

"Oh, yeah," I responded.

"What did he say?" she asked.

"He quoted David Bowie to me."

# CHAPTER
# 6

The police permitted Shirley and his ragtag army to take off for Montreal. I didn't bother to follow the circus up there. I hadn't thought to pack my passport but I figured whatever problems they had would still be waiting for them when they came back to the States the next day. So would I. Flying directly to Pittsburgh, the next stop on the tour, I checked into a hotel, requesting a businessman's suite with an ISD phone line.

I called down to room service for a fruit basket, two large bottles of sparkling water and a pot of coffee, popped an old Terry Reid tape in the stereo, plugged in my laptop and sent a few search engines out scouring for Shirley hits. The first wave was all fan shrines, most of them cannibalizing each other's content and PIFs. They were written in a curious no-gloss style. These kids obviously idolized Shirley but it wouldn't be cool to fawn, so the enthusiasm was buried under a patina of slack indifference.

After room service arrived, I began springboarding around, using suggested links. I quickly left the proselytes behind and the mood turned ugly. There were all kinds of angry and strident manifestos, decrying Shirley's grotesque appearance and his evil influence. No pictures on these pages but excessive punctuation. Exclamation points are clearly the mark of the righteous.

One page offered this sentiment—straight from the Cotton Mather school of music criticism: "His very appearance is an abomination!! His 'music' is nothing but the baying of hellhounds!! Some brave Christian witnesses who have attended one of his shows report that this monster openly performs Satanic rituals right on the stage!! He must be stopped!!!"

Another writer shared a pragmatic strategy for derailing the Shirley juggernaut: "Our congregation was (praise God) alerted to this pestilence early on. We organized a picket of the local Kmart and within two days the store agreed to pull Slaughterhouse's CD from the shelves. That is by far the fastest we've gotten the store to banish offensive material! Obviously even the merchants recognize how dangerous this heretic is. And when it was announced that this sacrilegious singer's tour would take him to Indianapolis, we traveled to a city council meeting with several other prayer groups that Reverend Isaacson put us in touch with to protest. The show was cancelled! Better to light one light, brethren."

I put Reverend Isaacson in the search box and found a number of entries. He was the minister of an Adventist church in Sandusky, Ohio, and the founder of an advocacy group called the Christian Decency Coalition. The curious thing I noticed about the CDC as I scrolled through their literature was that their take on most of the hot-button issues, from sex to politics, was fairly moderate and well reasoned. But when it came to Shirley Slaughterhouse, the tone grew rabid. Reading Isaacson's broadsides about Shirley was like stumbling upon Ahab on the foredeck in the middle of the night, fulminating to the waves. "He is a cynical and calculated affront to Christian values," read one sermonette, "a demonic contagion, the ugly epitome of our decadent society, a herald of pure evil. And where does he peddle his poisonous notions? To our impressionable young people!"

Following the reverend's urging, I posted him an e-mail, asking if it would be convenient to visit him to talk about Mr. Slaughterhouse. I stayed a little vague about my affiliation, but then again, my status was rather undefined. I wasn't in either camp; I just wanted to sit by the fire.

I quickly flashed through the on-line editions of some of our nation's more distinguished newspapers, skimmed the entertainment news services and peeked into a couple of rock music salons, but the references to Jake Karn's death were scant and unspecific. Most of the squibs didn't even mention the poor guy's name. They merely reported that a member of Shirley Slaughterhouse's road crew had fallen to his death after a show in Portland. A "spokesperson" for Shirley's label (probably Paula) was quoted, expressing the grief shared by the artist and his entourage at this tragedy. Most accounts followed the quote with a dry observation that the tour itinerary would be uninterrupted, with tonight's show in Montreal going off as scheduled.

I was surprised at the lack of coverage, but I guess this was a story without any juice. Some behind-the-scenes schlub dies. Yawn. It's not like J.Lo had a new lover or another one of the Backstreet Boys checked into rehab. The most prominent mention was a brief notice on *MTV News,* and that was only so they could flash pictures of Shirley on the screen.

I went back to where I started: the fan bulletins, to see if there were any new postings with information or even speculation about Karn's death. I figured even gossip would be an improvement over what I knew now, which was nothing.

Taking up an investigation mid-tour was always frustrating. The insurance company wanted me to get them off the hook but they didn't want me to upset the artist. The rockers were by and large pampered and arrogant. I didn't have any real leverage with them unless the musician's management was willing to provide it, and that wasn't about to happen with Keith Fisher calling the shots. All I could do was troll for news and gossip and hope to ask the right person the right questions.

I stumbled across one intriguing entry: a home page from a guy who tagged himself Virgil 62. In a casual but authoritative tone, he talked about Jake Karn being friends with Shirley since they were children, back when Mr. Slaughterhouse was still going by his given name: Irvin Ostertag. (This contradicted the record company bio and most of the articles I had read—all of which identified Shirley's preshow biz name as Pete Turner. I tended to believe Virgil's version. Who would make up a name like Irvin Ostertag?)

Jake and Irvin had grown up together in Catoga Falls, a blighted industrial town in western Pennsylvania. A spindly outsider, Ostertag had been a favorite target of verbal and physical bullies all through his school years. Karn, not a real popular kid himself, was at least chunky. He provided what protection he could to his skinny friend. The two boys had experimented with alcohol, drugs and, according to Virgil, masturbatory sex together. Karn's loyalty had been rewarded with a series of jobs when Ostertag changed his name and morphed into a shock rocker just after junior college. Karn worked for his buddy right up until his dying day.

At the bottom of the page was a picture I had never seen before. According to the caption, it showed an adolescent, acne-splattered Ostertag, looking sullen and pained in a ridiculous, ill-fitting school marching band outfit and spangly smokestack hat. He looked like the lead in a cheap road version of *The Music Man*. But it made me a believer. Even though his hair was much shorter, there was no question this was the kid who grew up to be Shirley.

Standing next to him on a football field with players and parents milling in the background was Karn, heavyset but smiling and comfortable-looking in a black Quiet Riot T-shirt and baggy jeans.

Virgil 62 had a theory: Karn was killed because he had

supported and encouraged Shirley in his desire to abandon
rock in order to found and run a rehab center that would use
music therapy to treat troubled youth. In this scenario, Karn
was murdered for his undue influence on Shirley by greedy
record executives who didn't want their golden goose to
leave the nest.

I bookmarked Virgil 62's page, got up, stretched, poured a
cup of coffee and then tried to call Chris Towle, my AA
sponsor. I wanted to bounce some ideas about Shirley off
him and also just check in. The alcoholic part of my brain
likes quick, conclusive results and this case was already beginning to frustrate me. Chris had a way of calming my
mind and putting things in perspective. But all I got was his
answering machine.

I glanced at my watch. At this hour of the evening, Chris
was probably at a meeting. I realized I should be following
suit. So after leaving a message, I hauled the phone book out
and began looking up Intergroup to get the location of a
meeting convenient to the hotel. (One of the great serendipi-
ties of AA: It's always easy to find at the front of the phone
book, even if you're three flaming sheets to the wind. Your
fingers can't be too drunk to do that walking.)

Just as I found the listing, my computer beeped, indicating I had mail. It was a message from the Reverend Isaacson, inviting me to visit him at his tabernacle in Sandusky
the next morning at eight A.M. The minister was clearly not
on the same time clock as the rock tour.

# CHAPTER
## 7

I got an early start, pointing my rental car across the river and onto the Ohio Turnpike. I cranked up one of my favorite Todd Rundgren tapes, *Black and White,* to combat the depression I usually sink into driving on our major highway arteries by first light of day. It's the heedless hum of commerce gearing up, the acrid taste of bad coffee, the stench of low-hanging diesel fumes. Maybe my mind still associates the hour with hangovers, but being on the highway at that catching-the-worm time of the day always makes me feel blue.

Arriving in Sandusky about forty-five minutes before my appointment, I quickly located Isaacson's Church of the Divine Light, a grassy campuslike complex set outside of town. I backtracked to a Dunkin' Donuts, ordered coffee and killed some time sitting at the counter flipping through the local paper. I still walked into the church about ten minutes before eight.

The nave was gleaming and expansive, with vaulted windows over the entrance pouring light down onto the polished floor. A second set of doors led into the arena-sized worship area. A maintenance man in lime-green coveralls directed me to the reverend's office around the rotunda.

I knocked on a crenellated wooden door with a plain brass cross affixed to the middle panel and a voice asked me to enter. From behind a large, uncluttered desk rose the Reverend Isaacson—slender, boyish and impeccably groomed, from his short but wavy honey-brown hair to his manicured fingernails that emitted a peachy, glowing halo of light. He glowed like a young Tony Franciosa. His suit was expensive and perfectly tailored but not showy. His smile was dazzling. The first thought that came to mind was, He's so *tidy*. Then, for some reason, as he stepped across the room with his arm extended, I saw an image of one of those wrapped drinking glasses that are sitting next to the foam ice bucket when you check into a cheap motel: Sanitized for your protection.

"Ah, Mr. McNamara," he said, shaking my hand and gesturing me to one of the three high-backed leather chairs arranged in front of his desk. He went back to his seat. "You're more than punctual, a trait we share. I am often early for appointments." His smile was almost blinding. "What brings you to my church?"

"Well, Reverend, it's Shirley Slaughterhouse," I said, watching for a reaction. He was looking at me intently, his fingers steepled beneath his chin. "As you may have heard, a friend of his was killed the other night after a show in Maine. I've been hired by the insurance company that underwrites the tour to look into that man's death."

Isaacson continued to regard me expectantly. I just let my statement hang there for a minute. Finally, he tilted his head in a birdlike gesture and said, "And what can I do for you?"

"I thought you might be able to shed a little light on the subject," I said.

"I still don't follow you," he said, narrowing his eyes.

"Can you tell me anything about this incident?"

"Are you suggesting I had something to do with this man's death?" he asked, cocking an eyebrow. I had to suppress an urge to smile. He was so damn cute, so doll-perfect.

"You have been a very impassioned critic of Slaughter-house," I said.

He settled back in his chair and I noticed his shoulders take on a little starch. "Yes, Mr. McNamara, I have been," he intoned. It was a small room, but he was playing to its far-thest reaches. "And I will continue to be. I consider that to be my righteous duty. Slaughterhouse exerts a profound and pernicious influence on young people."

"How far would you go to stop that influence?"

He gazed at me steadily for a few seconds. "I would never advocate or condone violence, Mr. McNamara." His gaze drifted up beatifically to a point over my head. "I merely try to alert people to the threat Slaughterhouse represents and urge them to shun him."

"I understand, Reverend. But surely you're aware that there are people who hear a message as strong as yours and feel the urge to lash out or punish."

He turned his palms over in a gesture of acknowledgment.

"Do you know of anyone who might go that extra step? Who might try to harm Mr. Slaughterhouse or his employ-ees?"

"No, sir, I do not," he said without hesitation.

"Were you in Maine on the night of this young man's death?"

"Yes," he said, sighing and rejoining his hands in a pious pose. "I was leading a prayer vigil outside the arena that evening."

"Wow. You drove to Maine? You must really have it in for this guy."

"Do not confuse what this man does with entertainment," he said, his voice taking on a sermonizing cadence. "Are you aware he calls himself the Antichrist, Mr. McNamara?"

I nodded.

"Your Mr. Slaughterhouse is promoting a sick lifestyle, sir. He is poisoning the minds of impressionable young peo-ple. I would travel a good deal farther than Maine to oppose that!"

"You've been to a lot of his shows?"

"I have been *outside* a number of his performances," he said, straightening a desk blotter that did not need straightening, "with other good Christians. But we leave quite early—shortly after the concert begins. As was the case that night in Maine."

"Why?"

"Why what, Mr. McNamara?" he said, his impatience mounting.

"Why do you leave early?"

"Because at that point generally the only people left outside the arena are pretzel vendors and parking lot attendants."

"And there are people who can vouch for your whereabouts that night?"

He looked affronted by the question, as indeed I had assumed he would be.

"My word is usually sufficient. But yes, there were any number of people with me on the bus that night. We drove from the vigil in Portland directly back here."

"And everyone was on board? No one from your group stayed in Maine?"

"Not as far as I know," he said, making no attempt to mask the irritation in his voice. "We always take a head count before we leave. I'm sure we did that night in Maine."

"Have you ever actually met Shirley Slaughterhouse, Reverend?"

"No," he said, shaking his head. "Nor would I want to. And I doubt very much that I ever set eyes on his friend, the unfortunate young man who died."

"Okay," I said. "Just a few more questions."

"No, Mr. McNamara. I see no point in continuing this conversation. I have other duties to attend to."

"I can tell I have offended you, Reverend. I apologize. I'm just trying to get to the bottom of this, turn over some rocks."

"I am not a slug burrowing in the dark, sir," he said. "I do my work, God's work, in the bright sunlight."

"Well, thank you for seeing me," I said, rising to hand him my business card, which he frowned at but accepted. "If you do, in your ministry, come in contact with anyone who seems to pose a real physical threat to Mr. Slaughterhouse, please e-mail me."

The reverend was already reaching for the phone when I got to the door. "God loves you, Mr. McNamara," he called to me in parting.

On impulse, I turned right outside his office, away from the entrance to the church. Down the corridor, I tried a pair of double doors and walked into what appeared to be a small warehouse area. Along the far wall was a bank of cubicles where crisp young phone solicitors who looked like they had their hair cut three times a day chatted away animatedly on phone headsets. In the open area nearer the door, a crew of women were filling and addressing padded mailing envelopes with pamphlets, books and tapes.

I had taken in this thriving enterprise for only a few seconds when my shoulder was grabbed from behind and I was spun around. At the other end of the arm that still gripped me was a bruiser in a buzz cut. He had that nasty smile that bullies sometimes wear to let you know they could stuff you in a Dixie cup if they wanted.

I've put on some weight since my junkie days. I go big now—just under six-foot-two and 190 pounds—and this guy made me feel puny. So did his companion, standing beside him in a matching blue suit, his arms crossed on his chest. They looked like a matched set of battering rams.

"We don't tolerate visitors in this part of the church," came a voice from somewhere behind the rhino twins. A pair of hands wiggled fretfully between them and the hardy boys parted. Out stepped a gaunt man with stringy hair and pock-marked skin. "Allow us to escort you to your car," he said.

"Who are you?" I asked.

"I'm Simon Jones, deacon of this church."

"No kidding, huh?" I said. "Deacon Jones?"

Jones made a small Cardinal Richelieu–like gesture with

two of his fingers and the muscle-boys clamped me. I looked around for cameras as they propelled me down the corridor, one holding on to each of my biceps. I didn't see any, but judging by how fast they grabbed me up in the mail order room, they had to have a pretty extensive surveillance system set up in the church.

Deacon Jones remained on the church steps as the power-pair, with no prompting from me, swept me right to my car. Talk about efficient—they even knew my ride. Obviously, I had been under observation since I entered the parking lot.

They stuffed me behind the wheel, slammed the door and smiled down at me. These boys seemed to be enjoying their job way too much. I wondered why Isaacson, the boy Baptist, needed leg-breakers. He certainly didn't seem so damn cute to me anymore.

# CHAPTER
# 8

**B**ack in Pittsburgh, I used the hotel health club for a workout and a sauna to burn off some of the static in my head. I had spent my formative years being slapped around in Catholic schools, so I had no problem reconciling clergy and violence. But I was having trouble coming up with a scenario in which the reverend would have his holy rollers snuff out Shirley's friend.

I could imagine some fanatical attack on Shirley himself. That would make a statement. But why Karn? Whatever went down, I couldn't see Isaacson himself pushing Karn to his death. He wouldn't want to get those immaculate hands dirty.

Of course, with Hans and Franz around, that wouldn't be necessary anyway.

By midafternoon, the Slaughterhouse entourage had checked into the Hyatt. I walked over to the hotel, called Paula from the lobby and went up to her suite. She answered the door in a silky paisley print dress. Her hair was brushed down and she was holding a sheaf of faxes.

"How was Montreal?" I asked.

"Great show. Sold out. No incidents," she said, smiling

wanly and gesturing me into the room with the papers. The day was overcast but the view of Pittsburgh was spectacular. With its steep hills, network of rivers and heavy industries, the city looked like some dystopian Hollywood vision of our future.

"You seem distracted." I perused through her fruit basket, pulling out a pear. "Bad news in the faxes?"

"No, not all," Paula said, putting the papers down on a glass-topped coffee table and sitting on a couch, gathering her legs under her. "It's research confirming how popular Shirley is in France, Belgium and Scandinavia. We released the album in Europe before we did in the States. He's scheduled to tour over there in a few months."

"So what's wrong, Paula?"

She nibbled her lower lip before answering. "There was another death threat when we checked in here. They even knew the name Shirley checked in under: Alistair Crowley."

"Can I see the note?"

"It's on top of the bar over there."

I pulled a single sheet of legal-sized yellow-lined paper out of a plain white envelope with *A. Crowley* inscribed on the front. The note was brief, written in blocky capital letters with a black Magic Marker:

> *YOU'RE NOT FOOLING ANYONE,*
> *YOU SMELLY PECKERHEAD!*
> *YOU WILL DIE PAINFULLY!*
> *AND SOON!*

"Is this consistent with the tone of the other death threats?"

"I suppose so," said Paula, wrinkling her forehead with concentration. "They all seem to accuse him of being a phony. Then they say his end is near. This is the first one, as far as I know, that makes any reference to his body odor."

"Hmm," I hmmed.

"Why do you ask?" she said, reaching over the suite's wet bar to snag a glass.

"It's just that the phrasing is so vernacular." I said, putting the too-hard fruit down on the coffee table after a test bite. It was like chewing particle board. "I assumed these notes would be full of religious language, real fire-and-brimstone stuff."

"Nah. This one was pretty typical," she said, lifting a bottle of Evian. "You want some water?"

"No, thanks. Listen, Paula," I said, hunching forward to rest my forearms on my thighs, "there's something else about Shirley that's bothering me: All the press clippings say his real name is Peter Turner and he grew up in a Pittsburgh suburb. But I read a pretty convincing account on the Internet last night that says his name is Irvin Ostertag and that he grew up in some tiny Rust Belt town an hour north of here."

"Shit, that's out there? I *hate* reality."

"You mean it's true—his name is Ostertag?"

"Yes, it's true," she said, settling on the couch, her feet crossed at the ankles. "But it's so dreary, don't you think? I prefer my sweetened version."

"Wait. You concocted this fictitious history for Shirley? How did it get repeated over and over in print? Didn't anyone dig into his background?"

"Actually, Shirley came up with his own history. I just helped him dress it up a little bit."

"And no reporter ever bothered to confirm it?"

"Your naïveté is showing," she said, laughing. "Rock 'n roll has always been a carnival where you get to reinvent yourself. Like the French Foreign Legion, with groupies. But this is the golden age of the publicist. You can make up the most outrageous lies about an artist's background and see them repeated in a newspaper two days later.

"It used to be a feature writer would spend a month profiling a musician. They'd really root around. Now they're doing three or more a week. It's all hit-and-run, quickie bios. They're writing from press releases, for God's sake! Journalists today like having their stories prefabricated for them. Then they can just plug in the quotes. It's all about pictures and feeding the hype. And once a story has been repeated a couple of times in print, no one questions it anymore."

"I've never seen this cynical side of you, Paula."

"But it's true. It's almost become too easy to put stuff over. I would never say this to a journalist, but I can tell you because you're inside the tent."

"Yeah, but if I stumbled across his true history ten minutes after going on-line, surely some reporter will get wind of it."

"Right," she said, lifting her palm in a so-what gesture. "Then there will be two versions of Shirley in circulation. That will only add to his mystique. I mean, it didn't hurt Alanis Morissette when that story circulated that she grew up in a gypsy family, traveling around in a caravan."

"Really? I heard she was from circus folk, some famous acrobat family from Manitoba."

"See what I mean?" said Paula, her laugh jingling like a charm bracelet. "These things take on a life of their own."

"For a while people were saying that Eddie Van Halen was the grown-up kid from *The Courtship of Eddie's Father*."

"You can make up anything," she said. "And the Internet carries these crazy stories like spores."

"So did you make up the rumor about Shirley killing his parents?"

"I wish. We got so much mileage out of that. But Shirley's mother is very much alive. I think his dad passed away *a long* time ago." She shot me a look. "Natural causes."

"Well, since we're so close to his hometown, I think I'll take a trip up there tomorrow," I said, sitting back. "See if I can dig up any helpful background on Irvin and Jake."

"Can't help you there," Paula said, peering down at the LED display on her buzzing beeper. "I saw Shirley's mom once briefly before a promotional appearance. In fact, it was here in Pittsburgh. But I never talked to her. She didn't strike me as the outgoing type, Jim."

"Maybe you can help me make some progress here this afternoon," I suggested. "Who on the tour, besides Jake, is close to Shirley?"

She considered the question for a few seconds. "No one. Except his girlfriend Jacinda. She and Shirley are joined at the hip, but she's real, um, laconic. Come to think of it, I'm not sure she can even talk. Maybe they communicate telepathically."

"How about the other members of the band?"

"All hired guns. Shirley met them all a few months ago at the first rehearsal for this tour. And as far as I can tell, he doesn't spend any time with them off the stage. He even demands a separate dressing room before the shows. I can arrange for you to talk with them, but I'm not sure how much insight they'll be able to provide."

"This kid is a real enigma, isn't he?" I said, smiling and standing up.

"And I think he's determined to keep it that way," Paula said, dialing on the house phone.

I started with the guitarist, Tommy Freeze. He answered the door in a silk dressing gown, uncinched, revealing only bright red thong underwear. He had a big mane of frizzy hair, dyed undertaker black, which he continually reached up to scratch vigorously, as if he had lice. Drug paraphernalia was lying on the bar in his suite—a syringe, a blackened spoon with a dot of cotton sitting in its bowl and a rubber tube to tie off his arm.

"How you doing?" Tommy asked, flinging himself on the couch and making no effort to close his robe. His pupils were contracted but he seemed fairly lucid. *Pinky and the Brain* was playing loudly on the TV set.

"I'm all right," I replied, nodding but not sitting down. "How about you?"

"You don't remember me. But we met before. I was playing with a band called the Razors. We opened for Stone

Temple Pilots. You were hired by their manager to try and keep Scott straight." He paused and smiled. "Guess that didn't work out too good, huh?"

I shrugged. "If someone doesn't want to get straight, nothing in this world is going to keep him from using. But I imagine you know that."

"Yeah," he said, roiling his hair. "I almost called you once myself in a real fucking dark hour. Guess I wasn't ready."

"Well, the help is there when you decide you want it. The blue pages in the phone book are full of resources. And you can call me anytime."

"Yeah, I'll keep that in mind," he said, suddenly bored, his attention returning to the TV. "So what'd you want to talk about?"

"Jake Karn."

"Who put you on to me?" he asked with alarm.

"I'm talking to everyone in the band, Tommy."

That assurance seemed to settle him down. "There's nothing to say. Good riddance. The guy was a fucking leech." Tommy reached inside his thong and began idly scratching his scrotum.

"What did he do to you?"

"He liked to fuck with people's heads, the sneaky little cunt. And it wasn't just me. Everyone in the band hated him. He was Shirley's messenger boy, always bossing around us lowly musicians. But we figured out he was goofing on us, making up bogus instructions just to bust our chops."

Tommy scoffed and continued. "One night after a show in Gainesville, he told us Shirley wanted us to start wearing women's underwear onstage because our playing lacked—what was that word he used?—empathy or some shit. None of us believed that one."

My eyes drifted down to his red silk thong. I didn't see how that wardrobe demand would pose much of a problem for him.

"Anyway, I guess he loosened up as time went along. He

sure was having a blast being on tour. Reminded me of what this was like before it became a job."

"Did you see him the night that he died?"

"No," said the guitarist, reaching over to a table to grab and light a filtered cigarette. He inhaled noisily. "I remember that for sure because it was unusual. Right after the show, Karn would go into Shirley's dressing room and they'd close the door. Then he'd come out and deliver some bullshit critique of our performance. Every fucking night. 'Shirley says your solo on "Suffer the Children" was sloppy' or 'Shirley says don't ever share his microphone again. He says it smelled like a shit sandwich all night.' But that night in Portland, everyone noticed that he didn't come backstage, so we didn't have to listen to his load of crap."

• "Did you see him later that night?"

"Nah, I didn't know shit until Raul told me and Mike he was dead that morning."

"Who's Raul?"

"Raul Porto. He's the stage manager."

"You remember what time that was?"

"Around six."

"He woke you both up?"

Tommy looked at me like I was insane. "We were still up," he said.

I moved down the hall to the bass player's suite. Mike Denny had long brown hair framing a boyish face that years of devoted dissolution had coarsened. His looks always reminded me of Rick Derringer, the "Rock 'n Roll Hoochie Coo" guy. Mike was an energetic performer, but I hated the way he primped and postured, jerking forward his head and pushing out his lips with every note he slapped on his bass. Obviously he was imitating the great rock bantams—Mick Jagger or Michael Hutchence—but it was like watching some giant land bird—an emu or ostrich—pecking away determinedly at a grapevine.

I knocked on Mike's door and seconds later it flew open.

A young bellboy brushed past me, avoiding eye contact, a look of guilty exultation on his face as he scurried down the hall. I strolled into the suite. Two girls who appeared to be about sixteen but were tarted up to look far older sat hunched over on the couch, laughing loudly and waving champagne glasses. The acrid smell of sinsemilla hung in the air.

The girls, wearing short skirts, ripped stockings and enough mascara to caulk a boat, glanced up at me briefly and went right back to their revelry. "Have you girls seen Mike?" I asked.

"In the flesh," giggled one, and they both began to laugh, their heads coming together and their shoulders heaving.

"He's in there," said the other, pointing at the bedroom. More merriment ensued.

I could hear loud headbanger rock playing from the other side of the door as I knocked. After three tries without any response, I opened the door and stuck my head in. The music (I think it was the Cult) was deafening.

Mike was standing on the bed, his eyes shut and his head thrown back, naked except for a white cowboy hat, alligator boots and a holster around his waist holding two pearl-handled pistols. The plump girl who was kneeling in front of him scrambled for the floor when the door opened, yanking desperately on a bedspread to cover herself. Mike opened his eyes, saw me and, despite his state of arousal, greeted me easily. "Hey, man," he said with a goofy grin, "how's it going?"

Off to the left by the window was Billy O'Connor. The roadie had his eye patch folded up onto his forehead to squint into a video camera on a tripod. When the girl dove out of the frame, O'Connor took his face away from the lens and saw me. "Get the fuck out," he shouted.

I did.

As I closed the door I heard Billy calling above the music, "Don't worry about it. Let's just pick up where we left off. You're doing great."

**D**on't ask me why drummers always come last but they do. I continued on to Gram Hesh's room more in the interest of being thorough than in any real hope of finding out anything useful about Jake Karn's death. Gram answered the door quickly, looking startled. "Hey," I said. "My name is Jim McNa—"

"I know who you are. Paula told me."

"Can I talk to you for a minute?"

"Yeah, come in," he said, pulling back the door and gesturing me in.

His suite looked like a dorm room: clothes strewn around on the floor, CDs piled up outside their jewel boxes all around the stereo, music magazines and comic books lying everywhere, the bed unmade. You had to admire a guy who could get a room this messy in three hours. He really knew how to make himself at home.

Gram was a tall, rangy kid from Tulsa. He had long white-blond hair, startling blue eyes, a boxy chin and swimmer's shoulders. He always played with his shirt off onstage, not out of vanity, but for the freedom of movement. He had a fast, eloquent style of drumming that often reminded me of Ginger Baker.

I removed a wet towel that was hanging on the back of a chair, swept a *Raygun* and a *Gear* off the cushion and sat down. "How's it going?" I asked.

He shrugged, his fingers drumming rapidly on the armrest of the chair as he stared at me. I didn't read too much into his hand jive—I had noticed that one or more of his limbs was usually in motion, registering a beat only he could hear.

"Did you have much contact with Jake Karn?"

"Not too much," he said, his knee beginning to jerk. "Did you talk to Shirley? That was his best bud. They go way back. But they weren't getting along lately. Jake was kind of on thin ice with everybody."

"Including you?"

Gram shook his head. "Nah, we were cool. We hung sometimes. He wanted to write songs."

"Did he play an instrument?"

"Not so's you'd know it. He could pick out chords on a guitar, but mostly he was interested in writing lyrics. He had a funky little laptop he would keep his ideas on."

"Were his lyrics any good?"

The drummer shrugged again, a gesture I interpreted as: *How the fuck would I know?*

"Jake wasn't a bad guy," he said. "People made out like he was a parasite hanging on Shirley. He was really loyal."

"Did you notice any differences in Jake's behavior in the last few days?"

Gram's shoulders rose up again. "I wasn't that chummy with him, man. You should ask Tommy. Him and Jake were partying a lot near the end." I wondered why the guitarist hadn't volunteered that information. He sure hadn't tried to hide his own drug use.

Gram's thumb was thumping the armrest and his pupils were starting to dart around. I knew I had just about tapped out his attention span, but I tried one more question.

"Did you see Jake that last night in Portland?"

"Yeah," he said, narrowing his eyes and nodding his head. "I came offstage last as usual. I play off the rest of the band to the finale of 'Ritalin Junkie.' I saw Jake headed backstage to talk with Shirley like he usually does . . . or did. I assume that's where he was headed. Then that guy with the beanie grabbed him and told him something and Jake went tearing off back toward the crowd."

"Legs? The lighting tech?"

"Yeah."

"Legs Turkel?" I asked, just to rule out those countless other guys named Legs that I know.

Gram nodded.

"And that was the last time you saw him?"

He nodded again.

"All right," I said. "Thanks for your time."

I stopped by Paula's suite, but she wasn't in, so I left a message for her using the house phone in the lobby and headed back to my hotel. The message light was flashing in my room. Paul Roynton, my employer, had called, as had Chris Towle. I called my sponsor first. Staying sober is all about priorities.

As far as I'm concerned, Chris is a musical giant. But most people wouldn't recognize him if they bumped into him on the street. He was the lead singer and songwriter for Risen Angels, a band that in the late seventies put out three of what are widely regarded as the most sophisticated and durable albums of the rock era.

Actually, to call them a band is a misnomer. Risen Angels was Chris, his writing partner Jon Polier and a circle of accomplished session musicians they liked to work with. Their lyrics were elliptical and evocative and the music contained all kinds of eclectic influences, but it smoked. One reviewer likened their style to "Dave Brubeck meets George Clinton."

The group created its magic in virtual anonymity. This was back before there was an MTV, back when Kurt Loder actually worked for a living. There are no pictures of the band on their album covers; they shunned interviews and toured only once at the very beginning of their career. I have a ticket stub from that tour that I keep in my pocket. Bought it at a flea market in Soho for a quarter: Risen Angels opening for the Kinks on Halloween night in 1973 in Chicago.

The band broke up without fanfare at the height of their popularity. Four years later, Chris put out an intriguing solo record, *Cold Crush,* and then seemed to vanish.

I met him when I was first trying to get sober and he was a regular at an AA meeting on Perry Street in the Village. I had no idea who he was but I was always drawn to what he shared at meetings. He came up to talk to me one Friday afternoon at the end of the hour. I had been grousing to the group that I needed to get a job but the only thing I really knew was the music business. I was worried about people, places and things dragging me back into my addiction. He gave me some sound advice about how, in recovery, things work out the way they're supposed to, but rarely within the time frame we might like. It took me a couple of days to get up the nerve, but I asked him to be my sponsor.

Chris really carried me through my first year, giving me a foundation in living sober that still serves me well. I didn't know about his previous life for the first six months he sponsored me, even though I had been to his loft several times. There were no gold records hanging on the wall, no pictures of him carousing with John Lennon, no clues to his former existence at all. For a guy who had put out two of the best rock albums of all time, *Looking for Trouble* and *Cumulative Effect,* he was just incredibly humble.

About a year later, he grew tired of New York. He had lived in Greenwich Village since he was a teenager and he hated what the new money class was doing to the neighborhood.

His next move was pretty radical for a rock star/city boy: He took a job as a counselor at the Caron Foundation rehab in rural Pennsylvania and bought a small farm in nearby Sinking Spring. No doubt influenced by him, I moved to Connecticut five months later, but I still spoke to him on the phone two or three times a week and stopped in to see him whenever I could.

Chris answered the phone on the fourth ring. "Hello?"

"Hey, boss," I said.

"Hey, Jim. That 412 area code—is that Pittsburgh?"

"Yes, it is. I'm impressed."

"You shouldn't be. We don't have all that many area codes in Pennsylvania. Doesn't take long to master them."

"How's it going?" I asked.

"I'm fine. How about you? You working out there or just sightseeing?"

I filled him in on Jake Karn's suspicious death, my run-in with Keith Fisher and the fact that I was now touring with Shirley Slaughterhouse. To my surprise, Chris was familiar with my curdled client.

"You can't watch MTV for half an hour without seeing his kisser," he explained. "He leaves a rather indelible impression."

"He's wild, isn't he?"

"Welcome to the midway, kid. Rock has always had a lot of freak show in its blood."

"I didn't think you watched MTV," I said.

"I don't. Not at home. But the kids in the adolescent ward at Caron always have it on in the lounge. When I go in to talk to one of them, I get secondhand MTV. I bet Shirley puts on quite a show."

"I haven't seen him in concert yet. But he sure riles people up." I filled him in on the Reverend Isaacson's crusade.

"Whoa, that doesn't sound right," Chris said. "The guy travels to *Maine* to protest outside an arena? That's obsessive. In fact, from Ohio it's about four states beyond obsessive."

"Plus Shirley's been getting death threats," I added. "That's my immediate focus—seeing if this guy's death is related to those threats."

"Well, I'm no criminologist," Chris said—and I have to admit, I missed the rest of his point because I flashed that those four words would make a pretty good opening line for a Risen Angels song. Later, I tried to fill out the rest of the first verse. Hey, if Jake Karn could write lyrics, so could I. But I gave up after ten minutes of frustration. The only rhyme I could come up with was *herpetologist*.

"You know what kind of freaked me out?" I said to Chris. "Shirley's girlfriend. I assume he can have his pick of women, but he spends all his time with this chick who looks like Alice the Sea Hag from the old Popeye cartoons."

"Not unusual," Chris replied. "The cliché about rock stars and models really isn't true. It's like working in a candy store. When women are throwing themselves at you, the thrill of conquest evaporates. You end up gravitating back to your most basic and essential taste in the opposite sex, which was probably fully formed before you hit third grade. It's only those hard rock and big haircut guys you see ending up with the pneumatic Playboy bunnies. And that's because they have no inner lives. Their imaginations were shaped entirely by porn."

That got us reminiscing about first crushes for a while. I hadn't thought of Jan Potchtar in years. I doubt I would recognize her if saw her today, but back in second grade, she made my heart swell. Just before we hung up, I mentioned my plan to visit Shirley's hometown out in the boonies of Pennsylvania.

"I'm always bragging to my friends about the natural splendor of my adopted state," said Chris. "This will give you a chance to see it firsthand, to commune with nature."

Neither of us knew it, but I was about to get a good deal closer to nature than I would have liked.

# CHAPTER
## 10

I had already turned in the car from my Ohio jaunt, so the next morning I rented another sedan and headed north to Shirley's hometown.

Catoga Falls was a broke-down factory community in Venango County, moldering away on the eastern bank of the Allegheny River. Two-tiered wooden houses badly in need of paint were bunched on the slope. It looked as if a bowling ball, released from the right spot on the hill, could topple the whole village. Closer to the water, I could see a few big factories, now shuttered and empty. Across the river, a bluff rose up sharply, discouraging development and blocking out the sun from midafternoon on.

From the air, the street layout must have resembled a big tic-tac-toe board. I cruised around for a few minutes, then parked by the only grocery store I found. Walking up to the manager's pulpit, I asked the aggravated-looking man behind the bars if he knew where I could find the Karn household. He gave me explicit directions. He waited until I had thanked him and started to walk away to add, "She's not there."

"Pardon me?" I said, turning back.

"Judy Karn. She's not there," he said, looking up from his invoices. "Went to stay with her sister in Altoona. Believe they have a family burial plot there. That's where they shipped her boy's body. Terrible thing."

"How about *Mr.* Karn?"

"Hasn't been one in more than twenty years."

"Could you tell me how to find Mrs. Ostertag?"

"You a reporter?"

"No, nothing like that." He seemed disappointed to hear that but his directions were once again easy to follow. Of course, in a town this size, I could have just started knocking on doors and I would have found her pretty quick.

The house was on the upper of the two cross streets that paralleled the river. It was a two-story wood frame building with gray paint peeling in spots and a mottled tin awning over the doorway. I pushed the bell a couple of times but couldn't hear it ring inside so I tried knocking.

A frail woman wearing a sweater over a print dress and flesh-colored stockings edged into the front room and looked at me apprehensively through the window. Opening the door a crack, she stared at me like I had antennae on my head. I surmised that they didn't get much foot traffic in Catoga Falls.

"Mrs. Ostertag?" I asked. Her head nodded almost imperceptibly. "My name is James McNamara. I work for a company that helps put on your son's concerts." She didn't respond. I was beginning to think that maybe refusing to engage in conversation was an inherited trait in the Ostertag family.

"I came up to Catoga Falls to speak with Judy Karn, but I understand she went out of town. Is that right?" This time there was no doubt. She nodded. "I'm sorry I missed her. I wanted to pay my condolences." Receiving no encouragement, I barged on anyway. "I thought since I was in town, I'd stop by, see how you're getting along."

Having exhausted my opening statements, I decided to

wait her out. A long, uncomfortable silence followed. Finally, she spoke. "They had a special Mass for him, you know."

"Who's that, ma'am?"

"Judy's boy, Jake. Father Sindoni held a vigil at church last night."

"Jake and your son went way back, I guess."

"To kindergarten," she said. "I called Junior today."

"Pardon?"

"To tell him the funeral is tomorrow."

"Junior?"

"My son," she said and then the corners of her lips curled. "I guess you know him as Shirley."

"We're not that close, ma'am," I admitted.

"Would you like to come in?" she asked, opening the door wider.

"Sure."

She led me into the front room and gestured to a rather dispirited-looking mustard-yellow couch. I sat. She stood over me, her shoulders hunched inside her dark cardigan. "Tea?"

"Yes, thanks." While she was in the kitchen, I surveyed the room. There were a few religious images scattered around the room, but almost no family snapshots—except for one strained portrait in a cheap frame on the mantel. It was clearly a school photograph of young Irvin, the same tortured face I had seen on the Vigil 62 website.

Once we were settled in, sipping from our mugs, Mrs. Ostertag said, "I always feel funny around the people Junior knows from his work. I just can't call him Shirley."

"A lot of performers take on stage names," I said.

"Sure. Like, Kirk Douglas and Charles Bronson. But *Shirley*?" she said.

"It's a little unconventional," I allowed.

"I think I know where he got it from," she said slyly.

"Where's that, ma'am?"

"When Junior was growing up, there was a Shirley Temple movie on TV every Saturday. We used to sit in this room every week and watch them. Back then, we only got three stations. Two, really. The third one had too much static to watch. When Junior got successful, the first thing he wanted to buy me was cable service. You know they invented cable TV right here in western Pennsylvania?"

I raised my eyebrows and pushed out my lower lip. Everything I know about being an encouraging listener I learned as a kid from watching Johnny Carson.

"I told Junior I got rid of the TV a few years ago. It only reminds me how fast the world is spinning nowadays." She mused on that, then continued. "Maybe I should have gotten the cable. Junior might come to visit more."

"I'm surprised he hasn't moved you into a new house."

"Oh, I don't want to move. This has been my home for nearly thirty years. Too many memories. Besides, Junior isn't making a lot of money."

"He isn't?"

"No-ooo. He told me he owes a bundle to Mr. Fisher. Junior signed a contract two years ago. All his expenses—making his record, traveling from city to city, even his spending money—are written off against his future earnings. The more popular he gets, the more he owes."

I was surprised at how informed Mrs. Ostertag was about her son's financial matters, but the scenario she was describing wasn't unusual. Lots of bands at the beginning of their careers are so eager to get a shot that they sign contracts that are shockingly disadvantageous to themselves. In a matter of months, they end up owing their labels hundreds of thousands of dollars. They don't see any profits from the first album; even if it charts, they're lucky to break even. Then, if the second one tanks, it's time to get acquainted with old Chapter 11. I'm sure Keith Fisher had Shirley wrapped up tighter than a boa constrictor.

"I have to say, though," Mrs. Ostertag continued, "that

Mr. Fisher has been very kind with Judy. He's picking up all the funeral expenses." Keith, no doubt, was expecting a hefty insurance settlement to more than compensate him for his generosity.

I nodded.

"Those Shirley Temple matinees were a good time for us," said Mrs. Ostertag wistfully, fidgeting with the doily on the arm of the couch. "We both enjoyed them." She frowned. "It was the calm before the storm. Junior's dad spent Saturdays down at the tavern. Never knew what kind of mood he was going to come home in."

"Is your husband working?"

"No. He died when Junior was twelve. Heart attack." Catoga Falls: Home of a Thousand Widows.

"Oh, I'm sorry," I said. She scrunched up her face in a bland expression of resignation. I took it Mr. Ostertag wasn't greatly missed.

Another silence settled in the room. I tried to dispel it.

"So," I said, "you told me about the Shirley part. Where do you suppose he got the Slaughterhouse?"

"I know Junior had a bad experience once in a meatpacking plant," she said, blinking several times in succession. "Maybe it comes from that. His Uncle Joe used to work over at Hanratty's Meats near Oil City. When Junior was thirteen, Joe took him to the factory. My husband had recently passed and Joe was trying to spend time with the boy. He took him on a tour of the plant. It didn't go well. When they got home, Joe was frowning and Junior was real pale. Wouldn't talk about it. Wouldn't eat his dinner either. To this day, he rarely touches meat."

"Mrs. Ostertag," I said, "when you talked to Junior, did he say anything about Jake's death? Anything at all?"

"Only that he was glad they had these last few months together," she replied. "He said that being in charge of the show was the happiest Jake had ever been in his life. Junior said he was real glad he got a chance to see that."

Later, when I thanked her for her hospitality and walked back to my rented Sable, darkness had fallen. I considered driving over to the high school to learn more about Jake and Irvin in their youth, but I decided it would be a waste of time. They were the type of kids who, even in a small school, probably slid through the system without leaving much of a mark.

I started the engine, trying to figure out if I had enough time to make it back to Pittsburgh for the show that night. Heading south, I noticed the road sign: "Rte. 62." That made me think that Virgil, the cyber-diarist, was either very close to Shirley or he had done his homework.

About two miles outside of Catoga Falls, as the road traced the bends and curves of the river, a van came roaring up behind me. He pulled up so close I couldn't see the driver in the rearview mirror, only his grille looming over my bumper. On a long curve, the van crossed the double yellow lines and pulled up parallel to me. The side windows and panels were tinted black. The van edged ahead and began to weave over into my lane. Not wanting to play Ben Hur with this idiot, I eased over to the shoulder and stopped.

The driver stood on his brake and the van shimmied to a halt about eighty yards up the road. The brake lights went off and I heard, even from that distance, the cat-scream of the gears as he backed up rapidly. Almost immediately, a hand holding a gun came out the driver's window pointing back at me. The van wobbled back and forth as the gunman, twisted around awkwardly in his seat, tried to steer while backing up and aiming. I was thinking that Annie Oakley couldn't hit this shot on her best day when I heard two quick pops and the windshield collapsed. A pistol at that range? Had to be a lucky shot. But that didn't make me feel a whole hell of a lot safer.

I flopped onto the seat, which was covered with crumbs of glass, and flung open the passenger-side door. Crawling out,

I crab-scrambled desperately about twenty-five yards down the embankment toward the river, my heart clattering in my chest. Trying to hide behind a clump of underbrush, I slid into a bog, sinking down almost to my waist into mud, mud that was both slimy and icy cold.

The van pulled to a stop just behind my abandoned car. The passenger-side window came down but the dash and dome lights were out and all I could see was a silhouette in the front seat. The seconds ticked by with excruciating slowness. If the shooter climbed down the hill to look for me, I knew I couldn't extricate myself from the deep muck in time to run. I was a propped-up target.

But the door never opened. Instead the pistol poked out the window. Two shots rang out and I heard one bullet whack through the leaves in the bushes about ten yards to my right. I sank lower in the bog, trying to keep my weight spread as widely as possible.

Then a hoarse baritone bellowed, "Fuckin' asswipe!" The window rolled up and the van tore off down the road. A pair of headlights swept by on the other side of the road. The approaching car had probably scared off the van.

I waited a couple of minutes to be sure he wasn't coming back, then started the laborious process of clambering out of the bog. I lost a shoe and got mud all over the upper part of my body as I struggled.

While the van was racing backward toward me, I had memorized a partial from its Pennsylvania plate. I debated heading back into Catoga to file a police report, but then I pictured what the sheriff of Catoga Falls would be like and all the stupid questions I'd have to answer. That seemed like another kind of quagmire I didn't want to wade into.

There was no way of knowing if my attacker was local— someone who heard I was poking around Catoga Falls—or if he had followed me up from Pittsburgh, waiting for an opportune moment. Either way, I was certain this little ambush was somehow related to Shirley.

Even with the heater turned all the way up, it was a long, frigid ride back to the city without a windshield. I was covered in cold muck and the wind was funneling in over the hood at a brisk seventy miles an hour.

# CHAPTER
## 11

I turned quite a few heads as I stomped on one shoe through the lobby to the elevators. Splotched with freeze-dried mud, I looked like a Maori tribesman who had barely survived a monsoon. If nothing else, Shirley's tour was providing some memorable spectacles for America's business travelers.

My hands were still cramped in the position of grabbing the steering wheel, so it took some awkward fumbling to extricate my key card from my pocket, open the door, take off my stiff clothes and turn on the water. After about twenty minutes in a hot shower, I was shivering only with fear and anger. Since I don't handle either emotion particularly well, I called my sponsor and told him about my attacker.

Chris let me vent and then offered to fly to Pittsburgh to be with me, which I gratefully declined. He thought I should have contacted the police right after the incident so at least there would be a report on file. We theorized about who the gunman might have been working for. I liked Keith Fisher—a lot. Chris favored the church angle. I reminded him of the van driver's parting profanity. He didn't strike me as the religious type. Before we hung up, Chris suggested maybe I should hit a meeting.

Of course, that's usually the substance of Chris's advice, whether I've endured a near-death experience or a broken shoelace. And it always works. For the chemically dependent, meetings are the universal panacea, an hour in the decompression chamber.

First I left a message for Paula, then I called Intergroup in Pittsburgh and was pointed toward a speaker/discussion group that started in just under a half hour. Leaving my ventilated car in the garage, I grabbed a taxi. The cabbie knew right where the church was. In every town, the hacks are usually pretty familiar with AA haunts. A lot of rookies in recovery have had their licenses suspended for DUIs, so they depend on taxis to take them to meetings. Then too, a disproportionately high number of cabdrivers are drunks.

When I got back to my room, I was in a far better frame of mind, mellow enough to dig out an old Tom Rush tape from the bottom of my music kit. I was listening to "Merrimac County" when the phone rang.

"Hey, Jim," said Paula. "I just got in from the concert. How you doing?"

"Not bad for a guy who spent the first part of his evening dodging bullets."

"What? What are you talking about?" she asked anxiously.

"Remember I told you I was going up to Jake and Shirley's hometown?"

"Yeah?"

"Well, while I was there, some guy in a van drove me off the road and took four shots at me."

"Oh, my God! Are you all right?"

"I wasn't hit. But it scared me shitless."

"Jesus."

"This wasn't road rage, Paula. It was meant to stop me from looking any further into Jake Karn's death."

"What did the police say? Did they catch the guy?"

"I haven't called the police. I wanted to talk to you first."

"Me? Why?"

"Because you're the only person who knew I was going up to Catoga Falls."

There was a pause before Paula said, "You're not . . . Jim, you know I could never be involved in anything like that."

"No, it must have been someone you talked to. I want you to think carefully: Who else did you tell where I was going?"

She hesitated for a moment. I wasn't sure if she was searching her memory or deciding what to tell me. "Just Keith," she said finally.

"There's a surprise."

"He asked last night if you were going to be at today's show. I don't think he likes you too much."

"You mean there are people he does like?"

"Anyway, I told him you were going to Catoga Falls. But before you jump to any conclusions, I want you to know I just spent the last three hours with him. He was backstage the whole time. Stayed through the show."

If jumping to conclusions were an Olympic event, I'd be Carl freakin' Lewis, but her alibi didn't change my mind. Keith may not have been in that van but I still thought it was one of his flunkies.

"Come on, Jim," Paula said when I didn't answer. "You don't seriously think Keith would—"

"Paula," I interrupted. "I don't think there's anything Keith Fisher *wouldn't* do. But why would he come after me? I don't pose any threat to him. Unless . . ."

"Uh-huh," Paula said. "They didn't always get along but for the most part Keith was glad to have Jake on the tour. He thought it kept Shirley focused. Besides, he wasn't even in Portland the night Jake fell." Then she blurted, "Oh, gosh."

"What?"

"Jake's autopsy results," she said. "They were issued this afternoon. That's why I called."

"What was the verdict?"

"The fall killed him. He died as the result of massive

trauma. There was no evidence of prior injuries, although the coroner couldn't rule it out. What she did find was a whole shitload of chemicals."

"Like what?

"Ecstasy, meth, cocaine, pot and booze. No one thing at lethal levels. But Jake was definitely partying the night he died."

"Did the police issue a statement?" I asked.

"Yes. It said that since there was no evidence of foul play, they saw no need to commit any more resources to the investigation. They declared it an accidental death."

That ruling wouldn't sit well with my employer, since it didn't get Paul Roynton's company off the hook for liability. However shit-faced Jake may have been, we still needed to prove that his presence on the catwalk was unrelated to his job.

"Is Fisher still around?" I asked.

"Yeah, he's right down the hall. He's going to Jake's funeral in Altoona tomorrow with Shirley. Then he's flying him to the next stop on the tour."

"Cincinnati?"

"Uh-huh. Keith's jet is taking me to Cincy in the morning with a writer from *Spin*. Then it's circling back to pick up Shirley and Keith. You want to go with me?"

"What time?"

"We're supposed to leave at eleven. Why don't you come to the hotel around ten and we'll have breakfast?"

"I'd like that."

"I have to admit, I'm seeing you in a whole new light." There was a voluptuous Mae West purr to her voice. It provoked an immediate response in me, like a flock of monarch butterflies were migrating through my chest.

"Oh yeah?" I said, hopefully. "How's that?"

"Hmmm," she breathed. "Man of mystery, man of action."

"There are facets to me, Paula, that you've never dreamed of."

"Really?" she said, humping the word.

"There's no time like the present to start exploring them," I said.

She laughed and her voice slipped back to neutral. "I'll see you at breakfast. And, Jim? I'm really glad you weren't hurt tonight."

"Me too."

I was tired—I guess because my adrenal glands got such a workout coming back from Catoga Falls. Before I turned in, I called up the Virgil 62 site. It had been updated that afternoon with a tribute to Jake Karn along with a recent picture that showed him standing on a bare stage in some arena, smiling down at the camera.

It was the first good look I had gotten at Jake. He was on the plump side but he didn't appear self-conscious about it. In fact, he seemed pretty damned pleased with himself. Based just on appearances, he resembled a small-town forklift driver more than he did the supervisor of a major rock tour.

I wondered again where Virgil was getting his material. The essay under the picture extolled Jake's qualities: loyalty, diligence and a sly sense of humor. It also claimed that Jake had been an integral part of Shirley's creative process. According to Virgil, Jake was the inspiration for the song "The Hunted" and he had helped Shirley with lyrics from time to time, including the chorus to "Children's Crusade": "Like lambs to the slaughter/ Your sons and daughters/ With hearts like rocks/ You kill the clock/ You kill the clock."

Okay, it wasn't exactly Cole Porter. But I checked the credits on Shirley's CD: Jake hadn't gotten a writer's credit either.

# CHAPTER
## 12

That morning I returned the rent-a-car, fibbing a little—okay, fibbing *a lot*—about what had happened to the windshield. If I mentioned gunplay, the Avis agent would have demanded a police report and I didn't have one. I pleaded vandalism.

Then I lugged my bags over to the Hyatt and met Paula in the lobby restaurant. She gave me a long, comforting hug, then searched my face with her eyes and asked if I was all right. As we ate, I recounted the story of my ambush again, embellishing the menace because of the way it flared up Paula's concern. By the time I got to me cowering in the bushes while bullets zinged by my head, she was clutching my hand tightly.

I know, I'm shameless. But how many times do you get to sit at a table with three flavors of pancake toppings and brag to a beautiful woman about how you narrowly averted death? Not nearly often enough.

After breakfast (Paula had yogurt and fruit; I had eggs and sausage—two links for me and two in honor of the sausage-abstemious Shirley), we talked about the funeral and the day's itinerary. I asked her where the *Spin* writer was. "I called him to see if he wanted to have breakfast. I get the impression he's not a morning person. He said he would meet us at the airport van," she said, glancing at her watch, "in five minutes."

Fifteen minutes later, Paula and I were still waiting outside by the hotel shuttle when a skinny guy in his twenties slingshot out of the lobby's revolving doors, scuttled sideways and tumbled over some suitcases sitting on the curb. I couldn't believe he hadn't seen them, since he seemed to be having trouble lifting his head up. I would have thought anything below knee level, like the luggage, would have been right in his line of sight.

"Adam?" Paula called out. "Are you all right?"

He scrambled spastically to his feet and came over, a pale, scruffy kid with unruly, Whoville hair, poorly fitting thrift shop threads and orange Keds high-tops. Maybe that's why he stumbled. The sneakers looked to be about four sizes too big. "Adam," Paula said, "this is Jim McNamara." He jerked his head in acknowledgment without meeting my eyes. "Jim," she continued, "this is Adam Buckman."

"I've read your stuff," I said. "It's very good." It was true. Buckman specialized in these long, rambling articles that grew out of him spending a few days with a band or singer. He would hang with them, encourage them to carouse and then spill it out on the page, in pieces that were exceedingly revealing, well observed and usually quite funny. I couldn't believe this was the author of those stories. He didn't seem to be taking in anything.

All the way to the airport, despite Paula's efforts to draw him out, he sat hunched over, occasionally scratching his forearm. I thought I heard him muttering to himself once or twice. He seemed about one outburst shy of a locked ward, reminding me of a couple of guys I grew up with who ended up orbiting in and out of mental hospitals, zonked out on Thorazine.

At the airport we circled past all the big commercial terminals to a small, separate building where the private jets loaded. Paula went to talk to the pilot, Adam disappeared into the men's room and I was reading a newspaper I had spread across a deserted counter when someone squeezed my shoulder.

I turned to see the scrutinizing eyes and warm smile of Don Henley. "Hey, Jim," he said. "How goes the battle?"

"Taking on a lot of shrapnel lately, man," I said. "How you doing?"

"Good, man. Good." We clasped hands. "What are you doing here?"

"I'm following the Shirley Slaughterhouse tour," I said. "We're on the way to Cincinnati. How about you?"

"Just flew in. Pittsburgh tonight," he said. "City of Brotherly Love tomorrow."

"Is this an Eagles' tour or solo?"

"I'm talkin' to you, ain't I?"

I nodded, acknowledging the lack of a royal entourage. If Don had been traveling with the Eagles, he would have already been whisked away in one of a fleet of armored Suburbans. The fact that we were having a quiet conversation meant he was on his own.

"How's the family?" I asked.

"Outstanding. The kids have probably grown a foot in the month I've been away."

A group of people were huddled by a limo outside the glass door we had come through. One of them, in a satin team jacket and sunglasses, was gesturing to Don. "Gotta go, man," he said. "If you're in Texas in May, come by the farm. We'll slaughter a side of veggie burgers."

"All right, man. Good to see you."

I waved as he climbed into his car, then turned back to the paper, noticing Paula standing by the entrance to the pilots' lounge, staring at me.

"You know Don Henley?" she asked.

"Yeah."

"Where from?"

"He lost something valuable a few years ago," I said. "I helped him recover it."

"You have to tell me that story sometime."

"Ah, the man of mystery," I said. "So many stories." She punched me playfully in the shoulder.

At that moment, Adam came caroming out of the bathroom and we went outside to board the jet. While we were still on the tarmac, Adam raided the galley for copious amounts of imported beer and chocolate donuts. I've never tried that particular nutritional mix, but it seemed to work wonders for him. He went from catatonic to voluble during the short flight, telling outrageous stories about a plane ride he had recently taken with Limp Bizkit and peppering Paula with questions about Shirley.

"What do you mean, you don't know if he likes Jagermeister?" he asked incredulously as we started to descend.

"I'm his publicist, Adam," she said. "I don't party with him."

"You must *observe* the man," he said.

"Shirley is something of a recluse," she said, chuckling, "as you will shortly find out."

"You really have your work cut out for you, Adam," I added, "if you think you're going to get all palsy-walsy with him."

"Palsy-walsy?" he said, echoing my phrase with added italics. "I think you've been watching the Little Rascals too long, man."

On the ground, a shuttle was waiting to take us to the Westin. Adam sat up front with the driver, restively flicking around the radio from station to station. Paula and I sat way in the back, leaning against each other, talking quietly. "I'm surprised he hasn't asked anything about Jake's death," I said.

"Not his speed," she said. "He knows the kind of article he wants to write. It involves decadent, backstage antics, drunken boasting and outrageous quotes. Adam is a professional star-fucker. He wouldn't touch the death of a roadie with a mic stand."

"But still," I said, "it's got to be the most controversial thing that's happened on this tour. Wouldn't he ask, even out of curiosity?"

She patted my hand and looked at me like you would a dim cousin. "There haven't been any press inquiries about Jake since we got to Pittsburgh," she said. "Not one. Just that flurry of first-day notices. You're the only one riding this mule, cowboy."

I told Paula I needed to talk to Legs Turkel. She said she would get the name of the motel the crew was staying at, but in all probability, Legs would be among the contingent that went directly to the venue.

I checked into the hotel, stretched out on my bed and watched *All My Children*. Pine Valley was in turmoil. Adam was really raising cane. Afterward I walked down the street to a diner and had some soup, then hailed a taxi over to the arena. I had him drop me off around the back of the building, by the loading area. At that time of day, security is pretty lax. I walked inside unchallenged and found Legs sitting on the edge of the stage, disassembling a spotlight that he had cradled in his lap.

"How's it going, Legs?"

He distilled his enthusiasm for seeing me down to one word: "Shit."

I squatted down in a catcher's stance next to him anyway. "I need to talk to you."

"Why me?"

"Because as the concert in Portland was ending, you came up to Jake Karn and said something that made him tear off back into the crowd." Legs glared at me, worry and hostility fighting for control of his expression. "I need to know what you told him that night."

"I don't have to tell you shit, man," he said, snarling.

"It may be important, Legs."

"Fuck you."

"I'm not trying to jam you up here. Even if it's something . . . personal, if you tell me, I can keep it confidential. You refuse and I have no choice but to call up the Portland PD and tell them you have information about the night of Jake's death."

"You wouldn't," he said pleadingly.

I looked off into the empty mezzanine and shrugged.

"You're an asshole; you know that, man? . . . If any of this comes back to hurt me, I'm going to fuck you up," he said, pointing a screwdriver at me for emphasis. "The guy I'm about to tell you about, he can't know you got his name from me. And I don't want to be questioned by the cops about any of this—now or later. I tell you and that's the end of it. Got it?"

I nodded.

"All right, Karn kept hassling me to help him get some drugs," Legs said, frowning, then screwed up his face for a whiny imitation. " 'I don't know anyone. You've been touring for twenty-five years. You have all the connections.' So I called up a guy I know in Boston and he drove up that night. I met him by the concession stands and then after the show I told Karn where he was waiting. Karn went running off and that's the last I saw of either of them."

"What's the guy's name?"

Legs flattened down his beanie with both hands and puffed out his cheeks as he exhaled with exasperation. Finally he said, "Joey Stamps."

"Is that his real name?"

"I think it's Joey Stampinato."

"All right, Legs, one last thing: Joey's phone number."

"No way!"

"Listen, Legs, this guy may have been one of the last people to see Jake alive. I'm not going to accuse him of anything. I call him once, ask him a few quick questions and that's it."

"Jesus," he said, shaking his head. Then he stood, yanking his tool belt straight, reached in the back pocket of his jeans and pulled out a small, well-thumbed address book. I stood up too. He shook the book at me. "My name stays out of this. Understood? If he asks where you got his number, tell him . . . Make up some shit but do not mention me. All right?"

I nodded. Jake opened the book. I got out a notepad and took dictation.

"If this comes back on me . . ." he said, letting the threat hang in the air. He returned the book to his pocket. "That's it. Me and you are fucking finished."

Legs exited stage left, his tools rattling angrily.

I returned to the arena that night about a half hour before the show was scheduled to start. This time I had the taxi drop me off far from the building, about where the concert traffic was starting to tie up and crawl. All around me, kids in Goth regalia were hopping out of minivans and streaming toward the illuminated venue like black moths. They didn't want to be seen getting dropped off by their parents right in front of the doors.

I thought about how the mothers and fathers must feel, waving goodbye to their babies who are dressed like horror movie extras. Being a parent isn't easy. Of course, neither is being a teen.

As I walked through the parking lot, I paused to watch the protest being conducted by the Christian Decency Coalition. A small but vocal group of marchers walked in a flat oval, holding placards. Most of the signs were plastered with blown-up pictures of Shirley and legends that said: "The Face of Evil" or "Antichrist?/Antimatter." (That last one made me do a double-take. It seemed so—I don't know—deep.)

They chanted, "It ain't rock 'n roll if it poisons your soul."

The Reverend Isaacson and several others of the committed stood off to the sides and tried to pass pamphlets to the concertgoers. I didn't see any takers.

I wondered what this demonstration was supposed to accomplish. Anyone who ventured this close to the building almost certainly had a ticket. Most of the kids hurrying past ignored the protesters or treated them with outright derision. But Isaacson and his pamphleteers responded to the insults and even the curses with smiles and blessings. They weren't converting any Shirley fans but I supposed it was a form of moral victory for them to be out here waving their flag right by the mouth of the devil's lair.

I glanced around the parking lot. A bus from the Church of the Divine Light was parked about thirty yards away. Standing in its shadow stood Deacon Jones, staring Ginsu knives at me. I held his glare for a few seconds, until he lifted up a walkie-talkie and spoke into it. I couldn't imagine who he was talking to. Maybe no one. He could have been trying to impress me with his authority.

That struck me as an apt metaphor for most organized religion: a guy speaking into the static of a solitary walkie-talkie.

Closer to the entrance, I saw a pack of burly men move quickly around the corner of a building and fall like bounty hunters on a skinny guy wearing a watchcap. Draped over his arm, he was holding up a black T-shirt with Shirley's picture above the slogan "Triumph of the Antichrist Tour." Printed on the back were all the cities and dates. A box of the shirts sat by the guy's feet.

He was facing the arriving concertgoers, hawking his shirts for $20. So he never saw the goons approaching. They were brutally efficient, knocking him to the ground without warning, barking something at him while one waved a laminated half sheet in his face. One of the attackers scooped up all his shirts and stuffed them in a tote sack. They lifted the guy to his feet and roughly shoved him away from the building. After making a few last threatening gestures at him, they set off at a quick clip, continuing their double-time circuit of the building.

You can witness this smash-and-grab scenario repeated outside almost every rock concert. I've even seen it, albeit staged less violently, in the floating hippie bazaar that surrounded Grateful Dead stadium shows. I'll bet there are scavenger squads prowling the perimeters of Phish performances.

It's all because T-shirts and other paraphernalia are big business. A vendor purchases the rights to create and market gear with the band's likeness during a tour. The official goods are sold inside the gates for exorbitant prices at the ubiquitous concession stands. Meanwhile the vendor fiercely maintains his monopoly against the bootleggers who follow the tour like seagulls coasting alongside a ferry. These street entrepreneurs are outside, selling indistinguishable knockoffs of the clothing at a discount.

To protect his obscene profit margin, the licensed vendor hires a band of enforcers, often supplemented with off-duty cops, to manhandle the competition and confiscate their goods at every stop. (If the expropriated shirts are of reasonable quality, they'll end up lying on the concession stand tables the following night.)

Of course, running off the bootleggers is like trying to keep squirrels away from your backyard bird feeder. The guy I saw roughed up that night in Cincinnati probably walked to his car, pulled another armful of Shirley Slaughterhouse shirts out of his trunk, and was back in business within five minutes. Usually they worked in pairs, one operating as a lookout. As soon as the shirt sheriffs storm into sight, the peddlers take off into the parking lot as fast as their sneakers will carry them. That's why the bootleg bouncers circle the building at a brisk trot—hoping to maintain the element of surprise.

Thanks to Paula, I had an all-access pass waiting for me at the VIP entrance. Once inside, I walked for what seemed like a mile through the arena along a narrow cinderblock passage painted a nauseating aquamarine, before I came to the band's lounge. This low-ceilinged bunker was crowded, smoky and very loud.

It was the usual mix: radio contest winners, regional representatives from the record label, a couple of drug dealers, some guys from the beer company that was sponsoring the tour and a bunch of people who knew somebody in the promoter's office. They were all standing around, bright-eyed, hyper-alert, trying to pretend this was what they usually did on a Thursday night. Everyone was talking too loud, even considering the fact that a boom box on the table with the cold cuts was blaring out an AC/DC CD. I spotted Adam Buckman, the *Spin* writer standing over by the tub of iced beer, talking animatedly to a pissed-off-looking woman who appeared to be a weight-lifter.

The various band members and their cliques had commandeered the couches in the room. The guitarist Tommy Freeze was dressed in distressed jeans, a loose-fitting Moroccan shirt and some heavy eyeliner. He looked wasted, as did the two guys on the sofa with him. They were all lying back, not looking at each other, not looking at anything, just sensually smoking Marlboros and laughing easily. Tommy kept jangling the array of silver bracelets he had on his arm.

Mike Denny was also in his element. The bass player was waving around a bottle of Heineken as he chatted with two girls who sat on either side of him, leaning in to catch his every word. The girls looked thrilled and Mike seemed pretty happy too. Every once in a while, his eyes would sweep the room. I wasn't sure if he was trolling for more girls or making sure that everyone was taking in just how studly he was.

Gram Hesh appeared to be trapped. He was sitting, doing a fast drumroll with his thumb and pinky on the arm of the couch. He had the wide-eyed look of a horse that smells smoke. Two beefy guys in their thirties were standing over him, working hard to engage him in conversation. Gram would glance up at them nervously, then his eyes would shift to his lap or across the room and he would sigh, at times huffing his cheeks like a trumpet player. He looked so forlorn, I decided to rescue him.

"Hey, Gram. How's it going?" He jerked his head in acknowledgment. "How you guys doing?"

"Hey, all right. How you doing?" said one of the men, proffering his hand. "Brad Hayes." I shook. "This is Bobby Lawrence." Another hand to shake. "We're in sales over at WSGI. We were just talking to Gram about bringing Shirley over to the station early tomorrow. We have a really fun morning show. They could pop in for a few minutes, maybe cut some promos—"

"You should talk to the publicist. She's that strong-looking gal over by the beverage tray," I lied. "I need to talk to Gram about tonight's set."

"Sure thing," said Brad. "Hey, good talking to you, Gram." He and Bobby held out fists to be one-potatoed, two-potatoed. "Have a good show."

Gram exhaled deeply as they walked away. "That guy was really grinding my nerves," he said.

"Why didn't you tell them to fuck off?" I asked.

He shrugged and twisted up his lips. "He never stopped to take a breath. Salesmen."

"I meant to ask you," I said. "You know that laptop you said Jake used to jot down lyrics?"

"Yeah."

"Have you seen it since?"

"Naah," he said, puckering up his face. I jumped to another track.

"Have the shows been different since Jake is gone?" I wondered.

"Yeah," said Gram, pounding rapidly on his knees. "Now we don't have any contact at all with Shirley. Not even secondhand."

At that moment, the stage manager, Raul Porto, entered the room and lifted the mouthpiece on his headset away from his lips. "Five minutes to show, people," he said. He walked to a door at the rear of the room, knocked and moved halfway in, presumably to deliver the same message to Shirley. Gram began stretching and limbering up. Mike Denny and Tommy Freeze didn't alter their activities at all.

The door to Shirley's inner sanctum opened and Keith Fisher came out, followed shortly after by Shirley's girlfriend, Jacinda. She was wearing dark lipstick and her fingernails were painted a matching color. Jacinda looked angry. Almost immediately she got involved in an intense conversation with Keith. I couldn't hear what they were saying over the music. But it looked like each was trying to convince the other of something and both were growing more frustrated. Finally she scowled at him and held up her middle finger right in front of his nose. Then she spun around and walked out of the room, passing Raul as she went.

"Musicians up, please," Raul said. Again he went to the interior door, knocked and opened. "It's time, Shirley," he announced. The room grew quiet as Shirley emerged, shirtless under a red-silk robe with an ornate dragon stitched on the back. There were three nasty scratch marks on his neck that disappeared under the robe. Tonight's tinted contacts made his irises look coal-black and forest-green. He looked neither right nor left as he moved through the throng. Trancelike, he followed Raul, who was whispering into his headset, toward the stage.

Keith Fisher started to follow, joining the general exodus from the room. I stepped in his path. "I want to talk to you," I said.

"Your timing sucks. As usual," he said, trying to walk around me. I moved to intercept him. "I need to support my headliner," he said, beady eyes narrowing. "He's had a rough fucking day. He just buried his best friend."

"You'll be there before the first song is over," I said. "But first, Keith, I want you to tell me why."

"Why what, numbnuts?"

"Why did you send someone to shoot at me yesterday in

Catoga Falls?" I demanded. "What is it that's worth killing me for?"

"First of all," he said, cocking his bullet-head and leaning in close, like a Marine drill sergeant, "I didn't sic anyone on you, you paranoid fuck. If I had, you wouldn't be standing here. Second of all, there's nothing I'm afraid of you finding out. You couldn't find your limp dick with both hands.

"And while we're at it," he said, bringing his thick index finger near my chin, "you just officially wore out your welcome. In case you didn't hear, the case is closed and the body is in the ground. I don't want you hanging around anymore. I'm gonna call your boss, Paul Roynton, tonight and tell him you're a fucking liability I will no longer put up with."

I stared at Fisher for a few seconds, then asked him the question I really wanted answered. "What happened to Jake Karn's personal effects?"

"What?" he sputtered, caught off guard. "They were packed up and shipped to his mother."

"All of them?"

"Yeah, we made sure she got his complete collection of porno magazines," he said. "Shirley went through his room and picked out the things Karn's mother might like and that wacky chick who does makeup boxed the shit up. The rest got thrown out."

I stepped aside and Fisher rumbled toward the exit. At the door he turned. "Just so's you know, McNamara," he said, "when I want you dead, I won't hire someone to do it. I'll fucking kill you myself."

It was a good exit line. A real dipped-in-Bourbon detective would have hit him with a snappy rejoinder but, truth is, I couldn't think of one. So I set off to look for Sandra Blanchard instead.

It didn't take long. She was leaning against the wall right outside the door, smoking a cigarette and twisting a strand of her frantic hair around a finger on her other hand. "Hey, Sandra," I said, more than making up for my lack of cleverness with Fisher.

"That asshole," she said, with feeling. "This is the third of Fisher's acts I've worked for in the past two years. The people he signs always need a lot of makeup. And he still doesn't know my name. 'That wacky chick'? What a schmuck." Obviously, someone had been eavesdropping in the corridor.

"Yeah, he really inspires loyalty in his workers," I said. "Listen, Sandra, when you were going through Jake's stuff, did you see a laptop computer?"

"Yeah. It had decals of bands and comic books plastered all over it."

"What happened to it?"

"Shirley took it."

"Thanks," I said. I started to move down the hall toward the crash and thump of the music, distorted down here in the bowels of the building. But Sandra grabbed my arm, her nails sinking into my bicep.

"Wait a minute," she said. "That's not what I wanted to talk to you about."

"You got my attention," I said, looking down at her talons.

"Legs is really pissed at you," she said. "He says you tricked him into giving up a name this afternoon by threatening to turn him in to the Portland police."

"Yeah?"

"Then we heard the case was already closed. The police no longer give a rat's ass what happened to Jake." Sandra paused to take a pull off her menthol. "Legs says you mindfucked him, and if he didn't have to work the lights, he'd be down here kicking your ass right now."

"Anything else?"

"Yeah, Legs said to tell you don't bug his friend in Boston if you know what's good for you."

I nodded solemnly, waving away the spume of smoke she blew in my face. I drafted a memo to myself: Don't forget to call Joey Stamps.

# CHAPTER 14

The show that night in Cincinnati was one of the best I saw during my time with the tour. Shirley was clearly more subdued than usual but for some reason, his detachment only made him seem more mysterious and otherworldly onstage. It was his voice that grabbed me. He sang even the angriest songs with a poignancy that was uncharacteristic of him, as if he were desperate to get his message across.

Even though he appeared preoccupied, he still threw himself into the macabre theatrical set pieces scattered throughout the evening. During "Missionary Position," for instance, he mounted the giant gnarled pulpit that had been wheeled out onstage and punctuated his musical sermon by tearing pages out of an outsized gilded Bible as big as a cot, pages which burst into flame as they fell through the air.

On "Brain Damage," he was strapped onto a gurney by two stage hands wearing mad-scientist wigs, thick glasses and lab coats. As they lowered away their prop ten-foot hypodermic and activated the plunger, Shirley went into convincing convulsions as the emerald fluid was injected into his chest. (Actually it was antifreeze fluid and it drained into a tube Shirley had braced in his armpit.) And he carried off the show's most physical moment with aplomb: donning a military uniform for "Cold War" and doing the old Soviet goose step, his leg freezing at its belt-high apex with each tin-soldier stride.

There was a scary moment early in the set when a moon-faced guy with a patchy ginger beard and a Nepalese knitted cap scrambled over the barricade at the front of the crowd and threw himself up onstage.

Two members of the security detail in front of the stage converged on him too late. They were quickly joined by a handful of their co-workers. They stood there in a knot, all wearing yellow parkas emblazoned with "Security," yelling at each other and pointing in different directions. A couple of them made painful and unsuccessful attempts to clamber over the stage apron.

Meanwhile the guy made a beeline for Shirley. I was impressed with Shirley's composure. He saw the overzealous fan coming but he never flinched, never missed a note, never stopped playing to the crowd.

From the wings, I watched as the guy skittered to a stop just to the left of Shirley's microphone stand. He wavered there for a second, his mouth open, his eyes ecstatic. It would have really disrupted the song had he shouted something at Shirley, which he seemed on the verge of doing. But after a second, as Shirley continued to perform—not ignoring him, but not allowing himself to be distracted—the guy bobbed his head, his face breaking open into a big, silly grin. He began mirroring and exaggerating all of Shirley's expressions and movements.

I glanced all around me, amazed that no one had jumped in to haul off this wild-eyed intruder. I could see all the crew members were tensed, holding their breath. It's a spooky moment when someone bum-rushes the stage and looks like he's going to assault your meal ticket. A couple of backstage people took a step toward Shirley, then hesitated and looked around as if imploring someone else to *do something*. From the crowd buzz, you could tell that the audience was also getting uncomfortable. I watched Keith Fisher, who stood with his arms folded, frowning but impassive.

The band had reached the third chorus of "Suffer the Children." At this point, as he always did, Shirley took the mic in his hand and began leaping and twitching, like a steelhead salmon fighting up a waterfall to spawn. In the process, I noticed he was also subtly putting some distance between himself and his shadow. The stage crasher seemed delighted with Shirley's frisky new motion. He leaped behind the singer and wrapped him tightly around the hips, that goofy, rapturous grin still on his face.

And Shirley kept jumping. Or trying to. Every time he would get a few inches off the ground, jerking the intruder up with him, the guy would tighten his embrace. You could hear him faintly over Shirley's microphone as he grunted and laughed with the effort of tethering the singer. His expression suggested that he was involved in some wonderfully tricky and terribly important game.

Something in me snapped. I really didn't want to go out on the stage, but I couldn't watch this ugly spectacle anymore. And I was furious that none of the people on Shirley's payroll were acting to help him.

I looked around me one more time, hoping someone was going to step up. Then, inhaling deeply, I took the plunge. As soon as I sprinted onto the stage, the wall of sound and lights overwhelmed me. I wavered, throwing up a hand to shield my eyes. I must have looked like a convict getting caught in the tower searchlight as I tried to escape from prison.

You can't imagine how bright it was out there. I felt I was having a religious experience.

Continuing on, I started peeling the stage crasher off Shirley, one tentacle at a time. I was afraid we were going to get into a squirmy third-grade wrestling match, but to my relief, he submitted without much struggle.

Holding him from behind by the biceps, I started to march him away. Still singing, Shirley scampered over to the other side of the stage

The audience began cheering and clapping over the music. The bearded guy assumed the applause was for him. He twisted around in my grip, freed one hand and began waving triumphantly.

Two burly guys in yellow came running toward us from the wings. I guess they had given up on the frontal assault and finally circumnavigated the stage. They seized the fan roughly and began dragging him away.

He turned back to me. "Did you see?" he shouted ecstatically. "Did you see? Me and Shirley, man. We were like totally locked in!" He was still yelling something as they hauled him off, but the music drowned it out.

I noticed Mike and Gram exchange anxious glances when the guy had first rushed across the stage at their front man. But they had kept a steady bass and drum bottom going throughout the incident (although Mike had prudently moved over to the far side of the drum riser). But not Tommy. Initially he stood there, slack-jawed, still strumming, trying to figure out what was going on. But when the fan grabbed Shirley from beyond, like a man trying to wrestle a large dog into a tub, Tommy stopped playing. He stood with his hand on his hip, cackling.

Tommy's recess made little difference to the aural texture of "Suffer the Children." The primary sound—all of the orchestral touches and keyboard flourishes—was delivered by sequencers. Tommy's primary job was to establish the opening riff and then plug a guitar solo into the middle of each song. The synthesizers did most of the heavy lifting. But Shirley noticed Tommy's amused reaction. As he ran across the stage after being freed from his fan, he crossed right behind Tommy. It didn't take a lip-reader to detect that Shirley angrily spat out "Asshole" as he moved past the guitarist. It was the only acknowledgment Shirley made of the disruption. Tommy quickly resumed strumming.

Even that strange interlude didn't detract from a superb show. And because of Shirley's intensity and commitment to the material, it was quickly forgotten. There was one other significant alteration to the usual set.

Usually the incendiary "Classroom Carnage" was the encore and final song. But as the band jogged offstage, Shirley paused. He called over Billy O'Connor, the guitar wrangler, and whispered to him. Shirley stood in the wings, drying himself with a towel, breathing deeply and listening to the crowd clamor for more. Billy returned with an instrument, the house lights went down and Shirley stepped out on the stage bathed in a single spot. The audience roared its approval.

Shirley brushed the strings of the black-lacquered guitar to make sure it was in tune. He stepped up to the microphone and announced, "This is for the ugly angels." He began plucking the chords to "The Hunted," a song he never performed in concert. (Hell, I didn't even know Shirley could play guitar.) The forlorn acoustic version he delivered in Cincinnati was vastly different from the strident recorded arrangement.

Virgil 62 had claimed this song was inspired by Jake and that seemed manifestly true as Shirley sang it with plaintive abandon. Cigarette lighters flickered on all over the arena, the rock audience's traditional gesture of empathy.

Shirley even reworked some of the lyrics for the occasion. One verse, for instance, went:

> *You don't dress like we do,*
> *And you'll pay for that too.*
> *You are the hunted.*

> *You're a painful reminder.*
> *A lost leaf from our binder.*
> *You are the hunted.*

But on the night of the funeral, Shirley revised it:

> *We made you an outsider,*
> *But you turned into a fighter.*
> *Now we are the hunted.*

> *You scared us, we scorned you*
> *But your spirit adorned you.*
> *Now we are the haunted.*

At the end of the song, Shirley kissed the fingers holding the guitar pick, and held that hand aloft, his head hanging down. The lone light went out, plunging the building into darkness. The crowd was completely silent. But even odder, after the light was extinguished, for several long, stunning seconds, I swear you could still see Shirley clearly onstage, frozen in his stance, as if he were illuminated from within.

**"W**e got one," Paula said.

After making sure she was in the lobby, I headed downstairs. I had left a message for her, before we left for Memphis, the next stop on the tour, asking her to let me know if there was a death threat waiting when Shirley's entourage checked in.

Paula was sitting in a high-backed chair near the front desk. She was wearing a dress that looked like it was part of the Wilma Flintstone collection. It was electric-blue and black in a cheetah-skin pattern. She was tapping a white business envelope against her knuckles, an envelope she handed to me as I walked up.

On the front, written in a black felt-tip pen were two words: *EDGAR CAYCE.*

"Is this the name Shirley used to register?"

Paula nodded, biting her lower lip. I opened the envelope (which had never been glued) and pulled out a single sheet of lined paper:

*ASHES TO ASHES*
*CRUMBS FROM CRUST*

*YOUR TIME'S GROWING SHORT*
*IN YOUR DEATH WE TRUST*

"Poetry, huh?" I remarked.

"I don't know if I'd go that far but it does rhyme."

We crossed the lobby to continue our discussion in a chop house called Casey's Dugout, which was decorated in a century-old baseball motif. The waiters all wore gray cotton uniforms and flouncy faux-period sports caps. The menu featured items like Casey's Clout (eighteen ounces of prime rib and a potato) and the Mudville Medley (a rather unappetizing designation for a mixed grill). It's hard to get a bite to eat these days without running into some garish theme or other. Half the time you can't tell if you've entered a chain restaurant or just the fevered brainstorm of some local guy who took a few too many marketing courses.

"Bold outfit," I said to Paula, as we took a booth. "You look like you're going on a mastodon hunt at Betsey Johnson's salon."

"That's the good part about being out on the road with an act," she said. "I finally get to wear all those clothes that are stuffed in the back of my closet, in the section I call 'What Was I Thinking.'"

"That dress isn't quite loud enough to cover up the fact that you look tired. Tough night?"

"Didn't I tell you?" she said. "Some crazed fan got in Shirley's suite last night. The guards never saw her. Maybe she climbed in the balcony. I don't know. But she woke Shirley up and spooked him real good. She was babbling something about how he had to stop giving away the secrets of their mystic tribe."

"I bet he was scared. After that guy tried to squeeze him to death onstage. Must have been a full moon in Cincinnati last night."

"They always say it's Cleveland that has the crazies," mused Paula.

"Maybe they're migrating. Was Jacinda there with Shirley?"

"Yeah," said Paula, chuckling. "Shirley was cowering in the bed, but Jacinda dragged that girl out of the bedroom by her hair. The two of them were clawing and screeching at each other in the front room. The guards heard them but wouldn't come in. Apparently you don't last long in the security business if you burst into a rock star's room just because you hear a woman screaming. But Jacinda had the presence of mind to yell, 'Fire.' That brought the guards in and the person took off."

"Took off where? They didn't catch her?"

Paula shrugged. "Apparently not. Maybe when you're a member of the mystic tribe, you learn how to vanish."

I shook my head. "Are we buying this?" Paula widened her eyes but didn't say anything. "Are the same security guards working today?"

"No," Paula said. "It's cheaper just to rent a pair in each city than to fly them around. I'm sure I can get you the number of the service we used in Cincinnati. Why do you ask?"

"It's such a bizarre story. An unhinged fan gets into and out of the hotel room without the guards stopping her? Doesn't make sense."

"You get used to that no-sense thing, working with Shirley," she said. "What do you think of the note?"

"I'm not sure what to make of this. 'Ashes to ashes/ Crumbs from crust'? It's like a nursery rhyme. Hard to take that seriously. It doesn't sound all that threatening."

"The tone is more frivolous than the earlier notes."

"This is the second note since Jake died, right?" Paula nodded. "But neither made any reference to Jake," I continued. "So I don't think whoever is writing these notes had anything to do with Jake's death."

"You mean otherwise he'd be bragging about it?"

"Yeah." I tapped the paper. "I'll follow up on this anyway. How did you get the note?"

"What do you mean?"

"Well, if it has Shirley's name on it, or at least the name he's registered under, why didn't they give it to him? I'm assuming he checked in before you."

"Everyone does," she said. "I'm usually the last one to get my room key."

"So why did they give the envelope to you?" I asked.

Paula shrugged. "The rooms are all part of the same booking. I'm sure the hotel clerk knew that I was a member of Shirley's party. Why don't you ask him? He's still behind the desk."

"I think I will," I said, rising. "Could you order me the Mutton Chop and a diet birch beer?"

As I crossed the lobby, someone called my name. It was Shirley's guitarist, Tommy, coming off the elevator in a loose V-neck blouse with long sleeves and stone-washed jeans. I don't know how he saw me, or anything else, with his eclipse-dark sunglasses.

"Hey, Tommy. What's up?"

He stood next to me so we were shoulder to shoulder, leaned toward me slightly and began speaking out of the side of his mouth. Everything about him was a billboard screaming, *We are passing secrets.* All we needed were decoder rings.

"Hey, man. We have to talk," he said. His words were a little muffled. I think he was trying not to move his lips.

"Okay," I said, with a trace of skepticism.

"There's some things you should know. Things I should have told you right away."

"About Jake?"

He turned and made bug eyes at me, as if I had just blown it by mentioning the name out loud.

"The guy was pulling some bad shit," he said, again out of the corner of his mouth.

"Let's talk now, man," I said.

"Can't," he said. "Have to see a man about some horse." I didn't try to stop him. If he was on his way to cop heroin, he would gnaw his way through my rib cage and out my back to get there. "Come see me later—before the show."

I nodded. "What room are you in?"

"1522," he said in his strained ventriloquist's voice. Then he strode toward the exit in his awkward pigeon-toed gait. I turned toward the front desk.

The desk clerk was a thin man in his late twenties with a follically challenged mustache and a cocoa-dusted Southeast Asian complexion. His name tag read "Rajesh Prabhakar." He was frowning down at his computer screen as I approached.

"Excuse me," I said.

"Yes, sir. May I help you?" he said, looking up and offering me a luminous smile.

"My name is Jim McNamara. I'm looking at some security concerns for the Shirley Slaughterhouse tour." The name clearly didn't ring any bells with Rajesh. I tried again. "Pound Ridge Records?" He shook his head. I pulled out the envelope. "Did you give this letter to Ms. Mansmann a little while ago?"

He studied the envelope warily, not wanting to step in something that might get him in trouble. Then he settled for the truth. "Yes, I did."

"Just a few questions," I said. He nodded warily. "Why did you give it to Ms. Mansmann?"

"She was giving me instructions on Mr. Cayce's privacy concerns and phone restrictions."

"Pardon?"

"She had a list of people whose phone calls could be put through to Mr. Cayce," he said. "She said he was not to be disturbed and if the staff had any questions to call her room first. So I asked if she would mind delivering the letter to Mr. Cayce."

"Okay," I said. "But why didn't you give the envelope to Mr. Cayce when he checked in?"

"First of all, I wasn't sure which one was Mr. Cayce," he said. "A group came in from an airport van and Ms. Mansmann collected all their key cards from me at once. She went upstairs with them and then came back down to get her own room and to give me special handling instructions for Mr. Cayce."

"So you gave her the envelope when she returned?" I asked.

"Yes, sir."

"Why? Why did you wait?"

"Because I didn't have it when they first came in. The letter was delivered afterward."

"Gotcha. Did you see the person who dropped it off?"

"Yes, sir," he said, gazing over my head as he recalled the details. "A young woman, maybe twenty-two, about five-seven, with long black hair. Red poplin top and blue jeans. And she had a deep cut on her face that looked quite fresh." He traced a line with his finger from inside his eye, across his cheek to his jaw. "The lady in question?"

"Yes?"

He pointed over my shoulder. "That's her."

I spun around. There was Jacinda scurrying across the lobby from the newsstand to the elevators, clutching a stack of magazines. Even from a distance, I could see she had a nasty slice across her face.

# CHAPTER 16

When I rejoined Paula in the restaurant, I didn't mention that it was Jacinda who had left the note. I don't know why. I guess I wanted to make sense of it myself before telling anyone else.

I spent the rest of the afternoon making phone calls. First I checked in with my boss Paul Roynton. His secretary kept me on hold for about three minutes before Paul picked up the phone. A maddening elevator-music version of some Kenny Rogers song played in my ear the whole time. Talk about adding insult to injury. That was one of my good memories of working at a record company. When you put someone on hold, at least they were listening to cool music.

"Hey, Jim. You have anything for me?" Paul said, as soon as he came on.

"No. Still poking around. But I must have hit a sore spot. Someone tried to shoot me the other day outside Pittsburgh."

"Who?"

I recounted for him my experiences as a clay pigeon in Catoga Falls.

"My God. This really happened?"

"What do you mean, really happened?" I said. "You think I'm making it up?"

"No. It just explains that long, pissed-off message I got from Keith Fisher last night."

"He told me he was going to call you."

"I'd say you're definitely stirring things up," Paul said with a mirthless chuckle. "Keith told me in no uncertain terms that I had to get you out of his hair. Pronto. He said you were bothering his staff and the crew, disrupting the tour. Claimed you were instigating trouble just to see how people reacted."

"Oh, bullshit, Paul. Fisher is such a—"

"*And* he made a point of telling me that you've gotten paranoid, that you're making up stories about people trying to kill you."

I took a deep breath before speaking. "The bullets were real enough to shatter the windshield in my rental," I said. "You'll see that when you get my expenses."

"I believe you, Jim," he said. "And it worries me. I didn't think this assignment would pose any danger. I want you to promise me that you'll be careful from here on out."

"You hear the coroner's verdict?"

He sputtered his lips. "Yeah."

"What do you want me to do?"

"Stay with it," he said. "I'll try to hold Fisher off. I don't want to antagonize him unduly. He brings me a lot of business. Even though I'm losing my shirt on this tour."

That statement flummoxed me. "Look, Jim," said Paul, "the clock is ticking. Fisher faxed me the claim for Jake Karn's death benefit the same day as the funeral. I need you to arrive at some conclusions quickly."

"I thought the autopsy established that the guy was on more drugs than a Mexican racehorse."

"And we could plead that as a contributing factor if we wanted to fight this in court," Paul said. "Of course, all they'd have to do is put Karn's poor, widowed mother on the stand and we'd be cooked. The jury would probably double the settlement. And she told Fisher something that really bolsters their case."

"What?"

"Turns out Jake had an intense fear of heights. Stoned or not, she's saying there's no way he would have gone up on that platform unless he had to."

"That's a new twist."

"A few days, Jim," he said. "That's all I can promise you. Figure this out by then or we're going to fold up the tent."

I called the security agency hired to protect Shirley in Cincinnati. Actually they were across the river in Covington, Kentucky. I had to go three rungs up the company hierarchy before a supervisor reluctantly gave me the name and number of one of the guys assigned to stand outside the rock star's suite.

The man who answered the phone managed to make "Hello" sound like an insult.

"Is this Stan Harris?" I asked.

"Who is this?" he said truculently.

I identified myself and asked him to tell me about what had happened in Shirley's room.

"Not much to tell," he said in a calmer voice. "Those people are fuckin' crazy."

"You mean Shirley?"

"And his kookie girlfriend."

"You heard the sounds of an altercation from out in the corridor?"

"We heard sounds," he said. "Put it that way. It was pretty muffled."

"But you heard Shirley's girlfriend arguing with another woman?"

"We heard *her* voice for sure. She was screeching all night. But we never heard no one arguing with her."

"But you heard her yell 'Fire' and that's when you entered the room. Correct? What time was that?"

"About quarter to three."

"And what did you find?"

"Nothing. Just him and his girlfriend. Looked like they had gone about fifteen rounds. Offered to get her medical attention. She had a nasty cut."

"What did they say caused it?"

"They didn't. He walked off all mad as soon as we came in. She said nothing happened. Said she yelled 'Fire' to see if we were asleep."

"And you left it at that?"

"We get paid eight-fifty an hour, pal," he said. "The client tells us to leave? We leave."

"Wait a minute. I thought you saw an intruder."

"Bullshit. We didn't see nothing. That's some crock they made up later that day. They called our supervisor and tried to get us in hot water. Said we let some woman who attacked them run right past us."

"Didn't happen?" I asked.

"No," he said emphatically. "I'm telling you, man, no one went in or out of that room all night long."

I pondered Stan's story for a few minutes. Then I dialed Joey Stamps, the dealer in Boston whose number Legs had given me. I got his machine three times. "It's Joey," said a bored voice. "Leave a message."

I had just hung up on another futile attempt to reach out to Joey when my phone rang. It was Paula.

"Hey," I said. "If you're heading to the arena, I'll go over with you. I just need to make a quick stop first."

"No, Jim," she said. "I have some terrible news. Tonight's show got canceled. The city council held an emergency session an hour ago and pronounced it a dangerous gathering."

"I'm sorry, Paula."

"That's not the bad news," she said. "Tommy Freeze just OD'd."

**"Y**ou mean OD'd . . . like *dead* OD'd? Or like rushed
to the hospital?"

"He's dead," Paula said, her voice quavering. "Could you
come up? Room 1522."

There was a bottleneck at the door when I got there. Gram
Hesh was just leaving with Raul, the stage manager. The
drummer looked up at me sadly and shook his head as he
passed by. I saw Tommy's body as soon as I entered. He was
curled up at the foot of the bed, almost in a fetal position. He
had on blue jeans but was shirtless and shoeless. The needle
was still in his arm. The flesh-colored surgical tube he had
used to tie off his vein was laying by his thigh. His skin was
tinted blue, his posture appeared petrified and there was a
slightly surprised expression on his face. In fact, he looked
like Leonardo DiCaprio in *Titanic* when he starts to drift
down under the icy water. Reflexively, I made a sign of the
cross and said a quick prayer for Tommy.

Across the room, a beefy guy with blond wavy hair wearing an orange hotel-staff jacket stood watching and frowning, his arms folded across his chest. I flashed on how much

the guy looked like the old baseball player Rusty Staub. Paula was over by the window, looking out through the gauzy curtain. As I turned to her, the sadness in her face bubbled over into tears and she moved quickly into my arms. "Poor Tommy," she said as I hugged her.

After a moment, I asked if the police had been called. "Should be on their way up," said the hotel guy. As if on cue, two uniformed officers walked in, followed by a crusty-looking character with slitted eyes. He was wearing a blue windbreaker that had "Coroner" printed on the back.

"Who found the body?" asked one of the cops.

"I did," volunteered the hotel man, raising his hand. The other cop approached Paula and me with a notepad and pen. He asked who we were and what we were doing here. After ascertaining that we had arrived postmortem, he took down our room numbers and asked us to leave. The coroner had taken a cursory look at the corpse, tilting his head like a bird as he stared at Tommy at various angles from close range. He was nosing around in the bathroom when we left.

Paula asked me to come back to her suite, which was just down the corridor. We settled on the couch in the sitting room, Paula throwing her head back against the cushion so her trembling chin was pointed up at the ceiling. I watched her gulp down some deep breaths trying to settle her feelings. She had an elegant neck. She reached over without looking and took my hand.

"It's so sad, isn't it?" she asked. I agreed. "I met Tommy like seven years ago at the South by Southwest conference down in Austin. He came down from, I think, Reno, or someplace in Nevada with this blues trio he fronted. He wore a sweatband around his head when he was onstage." She smiled at the memory.

"He was such a sweet kid. Then he moved to L.A. and got involved in the club scene." Paula's face half turned toward me but her eyes stayed on the ceiling. I wasn't sure if she had said "club" or "drug." "Some local rock band called the Razors lost their guitarist to a drug OD and they recruited

Tommy to take his place. He stepped right into the guy's shoes."

At that point, Paula seemed sufficiently composed to answer a few questions, so I plunged ahead. "I saw Gram and Raul leaving as I came in. Were they in the room with Tommy?"

"No," she said, sitting up and letting go of my hand to dab at her eyes with a tissue. "They were here with me when the hotel manager called to say Tommy was dead. I had just gotten through telling them tonight's show was canceled. We went down to Tommy's room together."

"Do you know what happened?"

"Other than the obvious?" she asked. "No."

"Was someone with Tommy when he was shooting up?"

"I don't . . . Yeah, someone must have been."

"Why do you say that?"

"Because someone phoned the switchboard and said the guest in Room 1522 was going into cardiac arrest," Paula said. "The operator said the call originated from Room 1522. She sent up someone from security to check it out."

"She didn't call an ambulance immediately?"

"I asked about that too," she said, nodding. "But they told me it's hotel policy not to summon emergency medical personnel to a guest's room until they have confirmed the situation. Apparently all their security workers have CPR training. So he got up here and when no one answered his knock, he used his pass key and found Tommy. Whoever was with him, left."

"When was the last time you saw him?"

"Down in the lobby just after we got in from the airport," she said. "I've taken on some of Jake's chores just until we can hire a tour manager Shirley can live with. So I handed out the room keys and the per diems. Tommy took his and went up to his room."

Like professional athletes, touring musicians receive a generous cash stipend every day they're on the road. The money is intended to pay for meals, toiletries, impulse buys and all other incidental expenses. Of course, if you're a junkie like Tommy, it's a wonderfully efficient way to finance your habit. Per diems have killed more rock musicians than swimming pools, car crashes and jealous girlfriends combined.

I had to restrain myself from jumping into the circumstances surrounding Tommy's death. After all, the insurance company wasn't on the hook for this one. Shirley's backup band were essentially day laborers. Even if the musicians were covered away from the stage—which they weren't—putting a needle in your arm is tantamount to suicide.

But it seemed far too coincidental that Tommy was dead a couple of hours after promising he was going to come clean about Jake. And death by needle was the easiest murder to stage. I wondered who was in the room with him and if they had arranged the dose for him.

"Where is Fisher?" I asked.

"Back in New York," Paula said. "Right now he's desperately trying to recruit guitar players for the audition we're going to hold in Nashville tomorrow morning."

"You're going to try and replace Tommy?"

"Canceling the tour is out of the question."

"But you're not canceling *any* dates?" I said. "You're planning to have some guy come in cold and play tomorrow night's show?"

"I know it sounds callous," she said, "but as Keith pointed out, it's not like the Stones losing Keith Richards. This wasn't an organic band to begin with. Shirley hired all these guys just a few months ago. If we find a guy with decent chops, he can rehearse with the band all afternoon and play tomorrow night. It may be ragged, but the crowds aren't turning out for the guitar playing anyway."

"So how does that work?"

"Keith is working from a short list of young guitarists in New York and Los Angeles," she said, putting up her legs on the coffee table. "If any of them show an interest, he messengers over a copy of Shirley's CD and a round-trip plane ticket. Other people at the label are spreading the word too and it's going to be posted on the Internet. Anyone can audition, but if they're not invited, they have to pay their own way."

"Where's that writer from *Spin* magazine?" I said. "I haven't seen him all day. He may not have been interested in Jake Karn's death but I'm sure he's going to jump on Tommy Freeze's. When the lead guitarist overdoses in the middle of a tour—that's catnip for a feature writer."

"You haven't seen him because he's not here," Paula said. "He flew back to New York from Cincy. He tried a couple of times to hang with Shirley, get him to open up. Apparently it didn't go too well. The last words he said to me before he left for the airport were, 'The guy is a fucking hermit.'"

"We warned him," I said. "Shirley is not the chatty type."

"Yeah, well, here's a shocker. I almost forgot in all the craziness surrounding Tommy. But that notorious hermit asked if you would have dinner with him tonight."

**D**inner, it turned out, was in Shirley's bedroom. I wasn't expecting us to chow down at Casey's Dugout, but I thought he might at least make the effort to come out in the living area, where there was a perfectly good dining table. Instead we stayed in his bedroom the whole time.

Even without the harum-scarum soft contact lenses Shirley wore during his shows, his eyes were still startling—a pale, grainy blue. His hair was pulled off his face in two wings which were fastened at the back of his head with a red ponytail tie. As far as I could tell, he wasn't wearing any makeup, which made him seem more vulnerable. He had on black leather pants that Jim Morrison would have admired and a billowy, diaphanous saffron shirt. His collar and chest were plainly visible. Either those scratches I saw below his neck in Cincinnati had already healed or he had put makeup on them. The gash on Jacinda's cheek, however, was not so easily hidden. She sat atop a chest of drawers against the wall, eyeing Shirley and me with the wary disapproval of a cat.

A compact electric keyboard was hooked up to a portable computer on a desk over by the window. The laptop's screensaver was flashing through a rapid-fire montage of urban rush-hour stampedes—throngs of grim office workers sluicing to work, or maybe on their way home. It looked like George Orwell's nightmare. On top of the TV, there was a large brass ornament adorned with orange fingernail polish. It was shaped like those bulbous spaceships from the old Flash Gordon serials. Smoke from burning cones of incense drifted up from a chamber inside it. Shirley's gleaming boom box was playing at a remarkably reasonable volume. Most rockers listen to their music at punishing, Spinal Tap levels. That's because after years of standing in front of amplifiers, their ears are shot. Hearing loss is an ironic occupational hazard of the modern musician. Roll over, Beethoven.

"Do you know who that is?" Shirley asked, pointing his chin at the CD player. I knew this was a test. He had been impressed that I recognized his obscure musical selection the first time we met. He wanted to see if I could pull a rabbit out of my hat again.

I recognized the band, or I was pretty sure I did. But I spent a few long seconds pondering the music—punk attitude overlaid with a cohesive melodic sense and a whiff of sensitivity—trying to give Shirley the impression that I was sifting through vast archives of rock 'n roll styles. "Hüsker Dü?" I ventured at last.

He stared at me and then bobbed his head slightly, betokening, I hoped, a measure of respect. I felt luckier than a Powerball winner. He had challenged me at the one thing I have any appreciable talent for: identifying a rock group from the last thirty years from a snatch of their music. I may not know a hack from a handsaw, but I can tell the difference between Foghat and Foreigner in an instant.

I breathed another sigh of relief when he tossed me the room service menu and asked me what I wanted. I had imagined Shirley to be on some ghastly, bland macrobiotic diet served up by a pale, skinny personal chef. I had been dreading a supper consisting of some swampy mix of seaweed and bean curd. Instead Shirley requested popcorn shrimp for an appetizer and barbecued chicken as his entrée. Jacinda grimaced and made a hissing sound as Shirley phoned in his order. Maybe she didn't approve of his choices—or maybe it was the fact that he never offered to get anything for her.

After Shirley hung up on room service, the conversation bogged down. We made a few fitful attempts at idle chatter but kept hitting the ball into the net. I decided to wait him out. After all, I was the guest. I wasn't here to entertain him. Once the waiter had wheeled in the cart and departed, Shirley made a subtle head signal and Jacinda, with evident resentment, slunk out into the living room, closing the door behind her.

"My mother told me you came to visit her," Shirley said, pulling his shrimp off the cart and leaving me to fend for myself.

"Actually I just dropped in on her," I said. "I went up to Catoga Falls hoping to see Mrs. Karn but she had already left for Altoona." Shirley was focusing on his food, not even looking at me. "Your mom was real nice, though."

"She give you her Shirley Temple rap?"

"Sure did," I said. "She have that right?"

He scoffed. "I hated those stupid movies. The only reason I sat there with her is I was afraid to go outside."

"So how did you pick your stage name?"

"Alliteration," he said, tossing a battered nugget up in the air and catching it in his mouth.

I stood up to get my food and instead, on an impulse, walked over to the door and pulled it open. Jacinda tumbled into the room. From her knees, she glared up at me with un-bridled hostility.

Shirley got up from the bed, put his plate back on the cart, walked over and lifted Jacinda up roughly by her arm. "Ex-cuse us," he said, pulling her into the living room and shutting the door. I sat back down on the mattress. They were arguing, her voice raised louder than his. I heard her shout, "Since when do you give a shit about that?" There were a few more muffled exchanges, then I heard the outer door slam and a moment later Shirley returned, grabbing his chicken on the way back to the bed.

"That's a nasty scratch she has on her cheek," I said.

"We had a visitor last night," he said, settling down on the bed with his chicken.

"I heard. Must be scary when someone tries to push their agenda on you like that."

He gave a false laugh, a bitter you-don't-know-the-half-of-it hoot.

"Still," I said. "I was a lot more concerned about your safety this morning." Shirley looked at me quizzically. "Those threatening notes you keep getting. I thought maybe they were related to Jake's death. Then, today, I found out who was sending them."

He hesitated for a moment. "A little too obvious, I guess," he said, with a tight smile. "It doesn't matter now. It was all a goof anyway." He put the plate of chicken aside. There was a smudge of barbecue sauce at the corner of his mouth.

"I don't understand."

"Me and Jake started writing the notes months ago," he said, going over to the stereo. I suspected by the way he shielded me from seeing him change CDs that I was in for another pop quiz. "Like two weeks into the tour, Keith Fisher was really ragging on Jake. He said things were all fucked up because Jake was an amateur. He didn't know jackshit about running a tour." He turned to face me, as strident guitar riffs began bulleting out of the boom box. "And he was right. Jake was fucking hopeless." Shirley laughed at some private memory of Jake's malfeasance. "But I didn't care. I didn't want some industry hack who didn't know my music running the show. Orderliness is way overrated anyway.

"But Keith wouldn't let up. He insisted Jake had to go. He said if I wanted to keep him on the payroll, it had to come out of my end." Shirley's voice grew sarcastic. "Like I have an end. So we decided to make Jake indispensable. We wrote the first death threat that day. After we had a few in the bank, I told Keith that I was really rattled, that I only felt safe with Jake around. Without him, well, I just wasn't sure I could go onstage anymore."

"And that worked?" I marveled.

"It was a gamble," Shirley said. "You don't want to extort guys in the record business. They wrote the book on the subject. Fuckin' sausage men."

"Excuse me?"

"I noticed that all these music executives look like the butchers I grew up around. All you have to do is throw a bloodstained apron on them. Anyway, Keith was pissed. Really pissed. I think he probably saw through it. But after he fumed for a while, he backed down. Jake kept his job."

"Why did you keep writing them after . . . ?"

"Because it would have seemed too obvious if they stopped when Jake died," Shirley said, flopping back on the bed. "And these last few were kind of a tribute to him. But I think it's over now. Jacinda and I both tried our hand at it, but Jake really wrote better notes. His you believed. I think he must have had a lot of latent hostility toward me."

Shirley tried to arrange himself in a lotus position and winced. His leather pants wouldn't cooperate so he stuck his feet straight out on the bed. "Okay," he said animatedly. "You're two for two. Now we'll test your mettle." Or maybe, considering the music, he said metal. He gestured like a *Price Is Right* spokesmodel at the stereo.

"I was stumped," I said, "*until* I heard the vocal. There's only one Lemmy. He sounds like a full cement mixer trying to climb Pikes Peak. That's Mötörhead. But I can't tell you which album."

"Yeah, Lemmy is pretty distinctive," Shirley said. "But I figured a guy who's familiar with the Incredible String Band couldn't possibly get Motorhead. You have eclectic tastes."

"Turnabout is fair play, Shirley," I said. "Now I get to quiz you." He frowned. "Have you had any more thoughts about what might have happened to Jake?"

I could actually feel Shirley retreating into his cryptic

shell. It was like a cold front moving through the room. He shook his head decisively.

"I understand that night in Portland, he didn't follow his usual routine of coming back to see you after the show." I waited briefly for a response but Shirley was staring at his feet. "Do you know why?"

"A lot of rituals were disrupted those last weeks," he said without looking up.

"Would it surprise you to know he didn't come to your dressing room because he was meeting a drug dealer?"

Shirley didn't look up or answer.

"Did you hear the toxicology report?" I asked. "Was Jake always such a druggie?"

"No. He only fell into that at the very end."

"What changed?"

Shirley's eyes slowly came up to meet mine. I could sense I was very close to being sent away without dessert. He didn't answer.

"Terrible news about Tommy, huh?" I said.

Shirley lifted his eyebrows noncommittally. "Heroin is a harsh mistress," he muttered.

I thought of Jacinda prowling around the hotel angrily and it crossed my mind that he must know a thing or two about harsh mistresses. Instead I said, "You seem to have a cavalier attitude about people dying."

I could see my suggestion made Shirley seethe. He took a couple of deep breaths before responding. "Don't presume to know my feelings. Just because I don't wear them on my sleeve like some people."

"I'm sorry. That was presumptuous. Listen, do you play chess?"

He looked at me warily and after a moment nodded.

"Would you like to have a game? I have a portable set in my room."

"No. I want to do some writing." He gestured with his head at the keyboard hooked up to the computer.

"Is that Jake's laptop?"

"No," he said, as if I were accusing him of something.

"But you do have it?"

"Yes."

"May I borrow it?" I asked.

"Help yourself," he said, his patience gone. "It's in the closet over there." I located the computer on the floor among a pile of strewn clothes. The laptop was an old dinged-up Toshiba without a carrying case. Almost every inch was covered with decals for bands like Brad, Radiohead, Gomez and Fountains of Wayne. I rooted around among the gaudy clothes, which looked like the droppings of a theater troupe, until I found the power cord for the computer. I wrapped it around the shell and was standing up to leave when I noticed a couple of rolled-up posters leaning against the wall.

I looked over my shoulder. Shirley was already absorbed in his computer screen, his back to me. I unfurled the posters out of curiosity. They were definitely not of commercial quality, more like prototypes. Both featured spooky images of Shirley—one a head shot, one full-body, bracketed by the text: "He killed his own parents. . . . Imagine what he'd do to yours."

I laid them back down, closed the closet and headed for the door. "Goodnight, Shirley," I said. "Thanks for dinner."

"It was a promise to my mom," he said without inflection and without turning around. "She said I should get to know you. Now I have."

When I opened the door, Jacinda didn't tumble in this time. She was leaning against the doorjamb, glaring at me like I was a prom-night pimple.

# CHAPTER 19

The audition for Shirley's new guitarist began at ten the next morning. The place was packed. I was shocked that this many viable candidates could be rounded up so quickly. Guess there are a lot of out-of-work musicians.

The tryouts were held in a rented nightclub in Nashville. It was a zoo: all manner of exotic animals on display, a few of them pacing, most sprawled out in grumpy indolence. The odor in this confined space was abrasively rank. And the food service was crappy. The catering consisted of a succession of hideously doughy pizzas sitting under a heating lamp and a limited variety of canned beer and sodas in a corrugated tin tub. But no one complained about the cuisine. Journeymen rock musicians are on the frat-boy food plan anyway. Every meal ends up being a bleary brunch.

The musicians complained about everything else, though: the short notice, the inconvenient locale, the time of day, the acoustics, the brevity of actual playing time allotted to them. All of these were legitimate gripes—particularly the abbreviated nature of the audition. Some of them didn't even get through the opening chords to "Children's Crusade" before getting the hook. Raul, following a peremptory signal from

Shirley, would bark into his microphone: "Okay, that's enough. Thank you for coming."

No one complained as loudly as the pros who were here by specific invitation. If I counted right, there were a dirty dozen of them, guys who had flown in on red-eyes from Los Angeles and New York and been shuttled over to the club. They were easy to spot by their plumage: They sported by far the most tattoos in the room, dense swirls of designs that covered their arms and, in many cases, boiled up their necks almost to their chins. Not coincidentally, almost all their shirts had the sleeves hacked off, the better to display their livid body art. They sat in a pungent group near the stage, snapping gum and pissing and moaning about everything. It looked like the methadone clinic at Folsom Prison.

No one in that assemblage presented as outlandish an appearance as Shirley. He was wearing a flat, wide-brimmed black hat that had been fitted with an honest-to-God black veil covering his face. He looked like a flamenco dancer who had suddenly been widowed. When he lifted the veil to drink his bottled water, I saw he was powdered and had that black exclamation point of grease paint bisecting his left orb. He was wearing a braided orange jacket with stiff, extended epaulets and no shirt underneath and puffy silk paisley harem pants. He even had silver sequined genie slippers with the toes curled up. I wondered how he managed to borrow Michael Jackson's Sunday-go-to-meeting outfit.

The man was definitely in full Shirley mode that morning: introverted and aloof. I worried that maybe our dinner the night before had provided him with too big a dose of normalcy, that all that barbecue sauce and polite conversation had driven him deeper into his sulky self-absorption. Of course it could have been the stress of facing a room full of strangers, all of them counting on him to make their dream come true.

And some of these guys really were dreaming if they thought they stood a chance of joining Shirley's band. Among the thirty-five walk-ons, there were porcine guys with buzz cuts who looked like they had just gotten out of the Navy; some good old boys (I assumed locals) in cowboy hats, even one paunchy guy with a big bushy beard and a tropical shirt. Believe me, it didn't matter if they were the next Hendrix. They simply didn't fit the image.

In rock bands, it's important to keep up a united front. I always wondered how pudgy little Mickey Mars got in Mötley Crüe. He seemed like he had teetered into the wrong comic book on the ludicrously elevated six-inch heels of the moon boots he wore. I suppose it's possible that when the band was first forming, Mickey's parents were the only ones who would let the boys practice in their basement.

Or take Mick Taylor, the best guitarist the Stones ever had. He was doomed from the start. He played like an angel. Unfortunately, he looked like one too. Standing onstage with the rest of that death-warmed-over lineup, Taylor always came across as a rose in a crack house. He had to go. Order was restored when the Stones hired Ron Woods. He had a face like a wood-boring insect and an aura of decadence. Fit right in.

For pure talent, the best guitarist at the audition was a fresh-faced kid named Danny Clifford. Actually he reminded me of Mick Taylor with his long, flaxen hair and strawberries-and-cream complexion. Played like him too. The kid got a beautiful tone out of his hollow-bodied Stratocaster. He had fast hands and let loose some searing solos on the two songs he got to play before Raul, on a signal from Shirley, sent him packing. At that point, Shirley was merely flicking his pinky, which struck me as unnecessarily disdainful.

I approached the kid afterward. "Hey, Danny?"

"Yeah," he said, looking up from his knees. He had wrapped a dish towel around the neck of his guitar and was laying it back in its case.

"My name is Jim McNamara," I said. "Just wanted to tell you how much I enjoyed your playing."

"Thanks," he said, standing up. He wiped his hand on his

jeans and shook my hand. Not a lot of guitarists will do this. They claim they're protecting their hand but I suspect most of them just don't like to be touched.

"I'm sorry I'm not in a position to help you here today," I said. "But you're terrific."

"You should hear me when I haven't spent the night on a bus," he said, chuckling. Turned out he had taken a Trailways down from the Twin Cities when he heard about the audition. He had only picked up the guitar two years before, when he was seventeen. He had spent most of his waking hours since then sitting in his bedroom in Eden Prairie, playing to records.

"You a big Shirley Slaughterhouse fan?" I asked.

"You work for him?" he asked in return. I shook my head. "Then, no. I'm not really into him." He glanced around. "I guess I don't have to watch my words. I'm not going to get this gig anyway, am I?"

"Probably not. But you got to play longer than most of the session guys they brought in from the coasts."

"Ah, I knew it was a long shot," he said. "But I thought it might get me some exposure."

By far the seediest-looking guy in the room was one of the tattooed elite near the stage, a skinny, scabrous alley cat from Los Angeles who went by the name of Slab. He was repulsive, with tendrils of braided hair hanging down over his unshaven, cadaverous face. Slab's most noticeable feature was a permanently curled lip, the kind it had taken Billy Idol years to cultivate.

All through the morning, Slab and the rest of the pack of pros kept up a caustic running commentary, making fun of the walk-on auditioners. In part it was a status thing, but I think it was also a way of intimidating the competition. At one point a tall, gawky guy who looked like Bruce Hornsby stumbled as he took the stage. One of the hotshot guitarists heckled him, shouting something that made Slab laugh. At that moment I wondered if maybe his lip was curling like that to escape from his teeth. He had some of the most gnarled and stained choppers I've ever seen. I assumed from his atrocious dentition that he was British. Turned out Slab grew up in Modesto.

The winner of this bake-off was never announced. I saw Keith confer with Shirley at the back of the room. Keith nodded and began to walk toward the stage. Raul announced over the PA system, "Thank you everyone for coming. There are two vans outside. One will be doing a loop to the airport. The other can ferry people around the city—to the bus station, hotels, wherever. Just give the driver your destination. No more than ten people at a time in the vans, please."

No one was listening. Every eye in the place was on Fisher. The suspense reminded me of a beauty pageant. Fisher milked it for all it was worth, pausing and changing direction, never giving away the winner with his eyes. Finally he walked up and put an arm around Slab and said something to him. Slab snarled at Fisher—or maybe he was smiling. Hard to tell.

Forty-five other guitarists exhaled disappointedly. Some of them gathered around the beverage tub, trying to stuff as many beers as they could in their pockets. Most, though, were trying to get a word in with Shirley. As they thronged around the veiled one, you could tell by his stiff, awkward posture how uncomfortable this petitioning was making him. Shirley's face was covered but his body English was speaking volumes.

It was a bizarre tableau: the inarticulate attempting to charm the unapproachable. Almost all of them tried to press a tape on Shirley. Some of them were songwriters hoping that Shirley would record one of their compositions. Others just wanted him to hear their guitar playing in a more expansive setting. Time after time, Shirley waved a thumb behind him at Raul, who was amassing a pile of cassettes in a plastic Blockbuster bag.

Shirley walked past me like I was a bike rack and glided out the door. He was followed by Raul, Keith and then Slab. The newest member of the band stopped at the exit and turned back to face his rivals. He threw his thumb up in the air triumphantly and flashed them a smile as ragged and rotten as a compost heap.

Another gracious winner.

# CHAPTER
# 20

The concert that night in Nashville was ragged as hell. The band had rehearsed all afternoon. It wasn't enough. Slab gained a passing acquaintance with all the songs but he didn't master any of them. There weren't too many sour notes, but the transitions within songs, the bridges from one section to the next, were mangled all night. And the band couldn't seem to end together for the life of them. There was a lot of spillage.

You couldn't tell from the crowd reaction. They went crazy. Of course, they always do. Rock fans are the most indiscriminate audiences in existence. Essentially they're cheering the fact that the performers are there and so are they. Any act that has achieved arena or stadium status will tell you they disregard the ovations. You can have your worst night: sloppy musicianship, bad acoustics, the drummer passing out. The next night you may be on fire—the band is inspired, you're digging new textures out of songs you've played a thousand times. And the applause is just the same both times. It's a real spur to excellence.

Shirley, to his credit, set more exacting standards for himself. You could see the show in Nashville was killing him.

He winced every time the band stumbled. And when he ran offstage as he did every night, to quickly towel himself off during Gram's drum solo on "Poison Kisses," he vented his frustration, screaming, "Fuck!" into the terrycloth.

If you'd seen the band at its best, the show in Nashville was painful to watch. I was standing next to Paula, who displayed her company allegiance by bopping along to the lumpy music. I ducked out after about five songs, asking Paula to call when she got back to the hotel.

I backtracked through the arena's underground corridors to the door of the players' entrance where I had come in. Stepping into the outer lobby, I saw something that made me stop in my tracks. Over by the will-call window stood Jacinda. She was wearing a black leotard, a torn tartan skirt and her usual Kewpie-doll-gone-psycho mascara. And she was talking with Deacon Jones, the pockmarked subordinate to Reverend Isaacson.

You had to admire Jacinda's feistiness. She was really giving Jones an earful. Then she spotted me staring at her. She nervously put up a hand to cover her face, then turned and ran out of the building. The deacon just glared at me, like I was a drunk who had stumbled noisily into his church in the middle of the sermon. Then he left too.

I returned to the hotel. Under the portico by the lobby, I saw the Blockbuster bag full of audition tapes stuffed into the bottom of a big pebbled ashtray/garbage bin. Raul hadn't even bothered to bring them inside.

I went upstairs, took a shower and called my sponsor, telling him about Tommy's death. He asked me how prevalent drugs were at Shirley's moveable feast.

"Tommy was the only hard-core junkie I've noticed," I said. "Although the guy they hired to replace him today doesn't strike me as a Boy Scout." I described Slab and his coronation that morning.

"You know," Chris said when I concluded, "it strikes me that you've chosen a really peculiar way to make a living."

"Really. I sort of thought it chose me."

"Maybe that's what happens to all of us," he said. "We just prefer the illusion that we're steering the train down the tracks."

I described my dinner with Shirley and the way Jacinda had loitered outside the door. "It was like she really resented him spending time with me. I'm wondering if maybe this chick isn't so pathologically possessive that she might harm anyone who came between her and her boyfriend."

"Like Jake?" said Chris.

"Yep."

"But their friendship goes back way before he met her, right?"

"I get the feeling that Jacinda thinks time started when she and Shirley hooked up," I said.

"How romantic. Like Romeo and Juliet."

"More like Punch and Judy," I said, describing the scratches on their faces, the screaming match they had in Cincinnati and the phantom intruder in their suite.

"Wow," he said. "I always thought Cleveland had the crazies."

That was almost exactly the same observation Paula had. Cleveland must have some civic reputation.

After we hung up, I pulled out Jake's laptop, which had more decals on it than a NASCAR coupe, and powered it up. A quick inventory revealed pretty much what I had expected. Most of the memory was given over to splatter games like Doom and Quake. He had a whole library of pornographic images downloaded off the net. Based on my sampling, it was a pretty sleazy stockpile, dominated by harsh, slatternly chicks who looked like they had never smiled. Pure Appalachian smut.

That was the genius of Hugh Hefner. The Playboy models always looked so fresh-scrubbed and wholesome. He was the Walt Disney of porn.

Among Jake's documents were several attempts at songwriting, in various stages of completion. Most of them were inchoate anthems of frustration and disaffection, lyrics plugged into an alternating current of self-pity and hostility. The most impressive effort was "Preacher's Seeds," three verses and a chorus about religious hypocrisy and the corruption of innocence.

This one really stood out from his other efforts because there was a passion and a conviction sweeping the words along. The rest were out of Songwriting 101: a decent opening line followed by a wobbly, labored attempt to come up with rhymes. "Preacher's Seeds" had a cohesive flow to it (although there was an unfortunate attempt to make a couplet out of "Judas" and "Buddhist").

Jake had also made a fitful attempt at keeping a tour diary. The exultation of the opening entries quickly gave way to despair as he realized he was in over his head and Fisher wanted his scalp. As soon as that crisis passed, presumably after the boys began concocting their death threats, the entries became sporadic. Only a couple of situations motivated him to write: when he got the band to believe something ridiculous (for instance, in Charlotte he informed them that Shirley was terribly noise-sensitive and for three days they all whispered whenever he was in the room) and when he had sex. I won't repeat any of those jubilant jottings.

Then I stumbled across another folder whose contents really jolted me. These documents I quickly realized weren't written by Jake. I was poring over them for the third time when the phone rang.

"What are you wearing?" Paula said in her duskiest voice.

"A luge outfit," I said. "It's tighter than a sausage casing."

She laughed. "Funny. That's exactly what I have on."

"How'd the rest of the show go?" I asked.

"Same old."

"No kidding. When I was there, I thought Shirley was going to blow a gasket, he was so steamed."

"What can I say? He's a perfectionist."

"You wouldn't know it to look at him. Listen, Paula, I came across some posters of Shirley," I said, describing the banners I found in the rock star's closet. "Are those officially sanctioned?"

"I haven't seen them. They could be black market. We're not exactly pushing the I-killed-my-parents angle. But I'll ask our merchandising guy in New York."

"Thanks. I have one more request. Do you think I could speak to Shirley for a few minutes tonight?"

"I wouldn't even try. He's in a foul mood. He's called for a full day of rehearsals in St. Louis tomorrow."

"Would you ask if I can get some time with him before or after the show tomorrow?"

"I'll ask when he's cooled off a little. What did you want to talk to him about?"

"Something I read."

# CHAPTER 21

The next afternoon in St. Louis I managed to cross all the remaining names off my list. I had worked my way through everyone associated with the tour in Portland to ask them if they had seen Jake between the time the show ended and the time he died. I finished up with Pete Bota, a loader who helped break down and reassemble the stage. He answered my questions with keen disinterest while leaning on an empty handcart. Okay, after all my canvassing I still didn't have any helpful responses, but I had finished off my list. Progress, not perfection. That's the AA motto.

It was easy to work through the list that afternoon because Shirley was really cracking the whip after the sloppy show in Nashville. Nearly everyone was present at the arena. The band was getting the worst of it, as Shirley drove them through a rigorous rehearsal of bits and pieces. "Okay, okay," he'd wave them quiet. "Now 'Children's Crusade.' Pick it up at the second chorus. One-two-three-four." They'd play a few bars and then he'd either make them do it over or he'd move on to another song. This wasn't too exacting for Mike or Gram. They had been playing these arrangements night after night for a couple of months. But it was a real workout for Slab. After about an hour of stop-and-go jamming, the curl in his lip was starting to droop.

As I was leaving to go back to the hotel, I saw Legs, Billy and Sandra huddled together backstage. They were arguing heatedly with each other while staring at me. Legs said something emphatically and started to move toward me. The other two seemed to object and Billy even tried to grab him by the arm, but Legs jerked away.

"The fuck is your problem, man?" he said as he approached me belligerently.

"What?" I said, miming difficulty hearing. I had caught what he said but the noise from the band provided a convenient excuse.

"I said, what is your fucking problem?" He was shouting and also moving his lips with exaggerated vigor. Since we were now overcommunicating, I shrugged *and* held up my hands in bewilderment.

"I told you not to bother Joey Stamps," he said. "So what do you do? You call him up and tell him I gave you his number."

"So Joey got my messages," I shouted, as if delighted with the news.

"Yeah," he yelled. "Now here's my message: You bother Joey again and I will fucking body-bag you!"

He lowered the fist that he was brandishing at me and looked around. Everybody within shouting distance inside the arena was staring at us. Shirley had brought the band to another roaring stop, and in the sudden quiet, Legs's threat could be heard in the upper balcony.

"Thanks for the warning," I stage-whispered and walked around him.

I didn't make much of Legs bracing me like that. Aggravation runs downhill as surely as water. Drug dealers don't like getting calls from strangers. Walk-up inquiries are always discouraged. So Joey Stamps had torn into Legs for giving out his number. And Legs had pissed in my ear. I couldn't think of anyone to yell at.

There was a message from Paula when I got back, asking me to come up to her room. "Who is it?" she called out when I knocked. I identified myself and she opened the door. Her hair was brushed back and held with barrettes. She had on a glistening cinnamon-colored lipstick that made her lips, particularly her lower one, look fuller. She was wearing a pearl cable-mesh sweater, blue jeans and a crooked, canny smile that made me blush all over, starting in my chest.

"Come on in," she said, leaning her head against the door.

"I didn't see you at the arena," I said, sitting on a couch that offered an aerie-eye view of downtown St. Louis.

"I had to teleconference with my office," she said, curling up next to me. "We have eighteen other artists on the label and each of them has their own weekly PR crisis. Well, all but one."

"Who's the exception?"

"Stan Howerchuk. He's an old blues guitarist from Maryland. Sweetest guy you'd ever want to meet. Never a problem. Of course, Stan will probably barricade himself in a motel room with a loaded shotgun and a thirteen-year-old boy while I'm out riding herd on Shirley. Everything else has happened."

"Must be hard to manage things from the road," I observed.

"Keith keeps promising I can go back to New York in a few days. But as long as Shirley's tour keeps springing leaks, I'm stuck."

"The little Dutch girl," I said.

"Oh, I spoke to the head of merchandising and licensing. He said they were approached with that poster concept you described but the guy wanted too much money and it was off-message anyway."

"Who pitched it?"

She batted her eyes at me to signal that I was going to love this answer. "The late, lamented Jake Karn." The phone rang and Paula answered it, dealing with the caller in a few brisk sentences.

"Hey, no fair," I said as she hung up. "You got a fruit basket."

"Actually, I ordered it, along with a cheese plate and two bottles of sparkling apple cider." She gestured at a table of goodies across the room.

"Wow, what's the occasion?"

"I wanted to thank you," she said.

"For what?"

"For being here," she said. "Keith is a royal pain in the ass to work for. He's crude and inconsiderate. And Shirley isn't exactly a publicist's dream." She poured a couple of cups of cider and handed me one. We tapped plastic. "These last few weeks have been really difficult. Having you here—someone I can talk to, someone I can laugh with—has made it so much easier. And I wanted to let you know how much I appreciate you. In fact . . ." She walked over and took the phone off the hook.

I looked at her as though stunned. "Can a publicity manager *do* that?"

"She can when she wants to do this," Paula said, crossing the room with her chin lowered and her eyes intently on mine. She knelt on the couch, straddling me. She put both hands behind my head and gazed into my eyes, slowly bringing her mouth down to mine. We kissed tenderly, my heart doing a pretty fair imitation of the frisky star of *Flipper*. The second kiss was hungrier.

I thought that low humming sound was the blood in my ears, but it was me, moaning quietly in my throat. The girl had lips. Paula was unbuttoning the second button on my shirt when her cell phone went off.

"Damn," she said, getting up to retrieve it from the table. "Hello? . . . Yeah. . . . He did what?" She turned and gave me one of those there's-nothing-I-can-do-about-it shrugs. Sprawled on the couch, panting shallowly, I must have looked like a castaway flung up onto a beach by a big wave.

"Did you talk to Pete? . . . No, you have to call his manager. Where? . . . All right, I'll tell him." She hung up and gave me a sheepish look. "I'm sorry, Jim. I have to make a few phone calls."

I got to my feet, jiggling my leg to disguise the rocket in my pocket. I buttoned my shirt back up and cleared my throat. "No problem," I said hoarsely.

She just smiled at me. "Another time?"

"Definitely," I said, heading for the door. I was about ten yards down the corridor when Paula's door flew open. "Jim?" she called.

"Yeah?" I turned back eagerly, ever the optimist. This is where she runs into my arms, right?

"I forgot to tell you. Shirley said he could meet with you tonight after the show. He said to come to his room at midnight."

Then she was gone. And I never even got to sample the cheese plate.

# CHAPTER 22

I didn't go to the show that night. I figured I'd give the band a little time to gel. Instead I had dinner alone at a seafood restaurant a few blocks from the hotel. It was a long way from any ocean, but the fish was good.

Then I spent an hour on a folding chair in the basement of a Methodist church listening to a speaker and gulping down several cups of rancid coffee. I was already feeling drowsy and I knew I had to stay up to talk to Shirley. The coffee at meetings is free but a lot of people feel it's still overpriced. You could use it to strip wallpaper. A big part of the crowd passes on the communal urn and carries in their own takeout cups instead.

Back in my room, I watched *SportsCenter* and the first half of Letterman and then took the elevator upstairs shortly after midnight. I knew Shirley was in because two body-guards were positioned outside his door. When I identified myself, the older one, who had some hard miles on a Slavic-looking face, nodded and I knocked. Shirley, dressed in an ankle-length embroidered green robe that looked like it belonged to a Mesopotamian priest, answered the door himself. There was no sign of Jacinda, although she could have been in the back. The bedroom door was closed. A floor lamp, illuminating a table on which sat a chessboard with the pieces all set up, provided the only light in the room.

"You want to play?" Shirley asked.

"Sure," I said.

The pieces were ivory, carved into thin, elongated men of La Mancha. It resembled a Staunton set as designed by Modigliani. Shirley didn't bother with the ceremony of choosing colors. He simply took black. I tried not to read too much significance into that. I opened on the Queen's side, intending to find out as quickly as possible what caliber of player he was. After a couple of moves, I said, "Listen, I wanted to ask you about—" Without taking his eyes from the board, he silenced me with a finger to his lips, which were coated with a waxy yellow gloss.

For the next hour and a half, we played without speaking ten words. I'm a multi-tasker. I like to chat, comment on the game, glance at the TV, do a crossword puzzle, get up from the board in between moves. But Shirley was completely absorbed. Not even music playing. The quiet disconcerted me. More than once, I felt like I was in an Ingmar Bergman movie sitting across the board from the Grim Reaper. Of course, Shirley's grave countenance and bizarre garb had something to do with that.

I had to admire his focus, though. He stared at the pieces as if he were Uri Geller, willing them to move themselves. He studied every position for minutes and then shifted his piece quickly and decisively. Usually a player that deliberate tends to be conservative, but not Shirley. He was unconventional, almost spontaneous (if you could say that about a guy who took five minutes to make up his mind).

Shirley definitely had game. He created nasty little br'er patches with his pawns. It took patience to penetrate them. What impressed me most was the flair with which he used his knights. And he had a knack for pairing up his bishops to maximize their coverage. We split two games and I won the rubber match. It could have gone the other way, but Shirley never really brought his rooks to bear and his endgame was weak. Our session wouldn't have lasted so long if it wasn't for his stubborness. Shirley refused to resign, even when his position was untenable. I had to checkmate him.

When I did for the second time, he said, "Very good." He sat back away from the lamp's radiance, pressing his hands together and holding them under his nose. "What is it you wanted to ask me?" he said.

"I'm not sure how to phrase this. You're a hard person to get to know," I said. "Magazine and newspaper articles don't tell me much. Even spending time with you can be confusing. The only good source I've found has been a web page written by a someone known as Virgil 62." Shirley regarded me as closely as he had the chessboard.

"I couldn't figure out how this guy knew so much about you, assuming it's all true, or how he was getting access to these personal photos. Then you let me take a look at Jake's computer. All the Virgil stuff was on there, including a brutal story about you and Jake on a YMCA camping trip. As far as I could tell, that entry hadn't even been posted yet. That's when I realized: You are Virgil. You wrote all that stuff."

Shirley stood up and moved to the window, gazing out, his hands clasped behind him. The lights on the exterior of the building shed a dim fluorescence on his face.

"What I don't understand is why," I said.

"It's a long story," he said. Will wonders never cease? I thought. The guy who talks in haikus is about to spin me a yarn. "I was toying for a while with the idea of writing a concept album," Shirley said, after a long pause. "It was going to be my *Tommy*. It was about a kid named Virgil with psychic abilities. He could see into other people's minds, read their motives. He grows up to become a rock star. I thought I could explore all these big themes—deception, alienation. But I abandoned the project because the lyrics were turning out so pretentious." Shirley came over, putting both hands on the back of the chair he had been sitting in during our chess game.

"I go on-line almost every night," he said, "hang out in the chat rooms just to see what people are saying. You know there are more than two dozen websites devoted to me? When Jake died, not one of them mentioned his name, not even what is supposed to be my official home page.

"It was like he never existed," Shirley continued. He looked pained but there was no vehemence in his voice. "You know what everyone was talking about that day? This rumor someone started that I had secretly married some porn star . . . a woman I never met. That's when I resurrected Virgil." Shirley walked over and sat on the arm of a couch. He was facing me but I could see him only as a shadow.

"Telling people about Jake, that I get. But you told so much about yourself. Those Virgil entries are unbelievably revealing."

"So much bullshit has been written about me. So much stuff has been made up, that the truth becomes like a form of disinformation. I'm tugging at the curtain."

"You're pulling the whole damn curtain down. The press, the fans, they're all convinced your real name is Pete Turner. Then you go and tell them it's Irwin Ostertag."

"Irvin," he corrected me.

"And those stories you told about growing up," I said. "You practically admitted your introduction to sex was a circle jerk with Jake. That's beyond confessional, Shirley. Why would you admit to something like that?"

"Because it's true," he said. "It may not be pretty but that's how most people first experience sex. The reality is usually shabby—your underwear is down by your knees and you're being groped in a dirty shed by the bucktoothed kid from down the street. But we insist on romanticizing sex in this country, turning it into some dazzling fantasy. Sex is America's religion."

I grimaced, thinking about how I had been left at the altar that afternoon. "But you gave away your family name and your hometown. Don't you think fans and reporters are going to start knocking on your mother's door?"

As soon as I said it, his chin jerked to the side as if he had been slapped. Could he not have considered that consequence? Or was I merely reminding him? Feeling bad for him either way, I changed the subject.

"The thing about you wanting to start a therapy center for troubled kids—is that for real?"

"Yeah, I've wanted to do that for years," he said. "I think music can heal."

"And you think Jake was killed for encouraging that idea?"

He slowly shook his head.

"I don't get it, Shirley. You're a successful rock star. You've gone to a lot of time and effort to create an image. And then you shred it with these Virgil entries. It's like self-sabotage."

"Exactly," he said with more enthusiasm than I had ever heard from him. "And I'll tell you why." He leaped off the couch and paced over to the window. He looked charged up, like a college professor lecturing on his favorite topic.

"This," he said, spreading his arms wide. "This is all bullshit. All this rock star crap. It's not real. It's a fucking joke. Thousands of kids screaming for me every night, hanging on my every word. Five years ago, they wouldn't even talk to me. Ten years ago they wouldn't let me sit at their table in the cafeteria. My whole life I was this pathetic, fucked-up loser. Then I put on some makeup, write some songs and make a record. And suddenly I'm some messiah? Uh, I don't think so."

"Come on, man," I said. "That's an old cliché. Every glamor queen in Hollywood says she couldn't get a date to her high school prom. You can't blame people because they somehow didn't recognize your potential."

I couldn't be sure in the dim light but I think he was glaring at me. After a pause, he spoke. "I'm not saying I should have been more popular back then. I'm saying I don't deserve to be this popular now. We've built up this ridiculous fetish around performers in this country. Do you think Brad Pitt has any special insights into life? Or Scott Stamp? Or

Shaquille O'Neal? They're all hothouse flowers, leading these totally artificial, sheltered lives. But we treat them like they're the repositories of all the wisdom in the universe. It's ridiculous. A phone repairman knows more about the human condition than Eminem does. Celebrities are mutants, man. Weird, twisted mutants."

"So if I understand you correctly, you resent the fact that people are paying attention to you?"

I watched a smile play grudgingly across his lips. He knew I was fucking with him. "I'm not saying I don't enjoy it," he said, "but it's nothing but ego masturbation. I'm grateful I can write songs, because I have a few things to say and I want people to listen to them. But I'm not gonna last. I know that. I'm no Bob Dylan. In five years, I'll be an obscure answer in Trivial Pursuit—The Gen X Version. So it would be pretty silly of me to take all of this seriously. In fact, I can't believe other people do. Because—did I mention it's all bullshit?" Pleased with himself, he flashed his teeth, making a mock happy-face at me, the yellow unguent on his lips making him look like a jaundiced lifeguard.

"Must have been pretty disappointing for you to see your friend Jake buy into the whole charade," I said. That wiped the grin off his mug.

"You didn't know him," he said accusingly.

"I know he was partying every night with Tommy. I'm sure that didn't sit too well with you."

"Jake liked chronic. And Tommy had good pot. That's the only reason he hung out with him. He said the quality was like night and day. The only pot we ever got in the Falls was ragweed, probably grown in the Poconos. All it ever gave you was a headache."

"He was doing a lot more than smoking pot."

"You don't go to France and not taste the wine. This is a big-time rock 'n roll tour. Guess what? There are drugs. Just because I don't use them doesn't mean I frown on people who do."

"And how did you feel about him trying to capitalize on

your image?" I asked. Shirley frowned at me, a muscle in his jaw clenching and grinding. "The parent-killer posters? You telling me you endorsed that package?"

Shirley took a deep, audible breath, straightening his bony shoulders. Then he turned and walked briskly toward the bedroom. "You can let yourself out," he said, closing the door behind him. He never looked back.

# CHAPTER
# 23

I didn't. Let myself out, that is. Instead I sat for a long time in that darkened room, not because I thought Shirley might come back. In fact, I was pretty sure he wouldn't reemerge. But our tête-à-tête left me feeling like I had just taken a subterranean gondola ride with the Phantom of the Opera.

Looking at the scattered chess pieces, I marveled that Shirley could be miserable when most people in this country under the age of thirty would give anything in the world to trade places with him. What a mindfuck that was! We confer on celebrities like Shirley the ultimate carte blanche. They're like the fortunate souls in fairy tales who get the keys to the cosmos. You know, the guy who reels in the talking fish or the fellow who dusts off an old lantern and a plume of smoke comes pouring out. They are the fortune-kissed creatures to whom nothing is denied. Life, for them, is a catered affair. If someone like Shirley can't be happy, what chance do us sad-sack civilians have?

Sometimes I think the strongest weapon in the human arsenal is our adaptability. We will take absolutely anything for granted. Go ahead—bend and twist our reality. We'll adjust.

Plunk us down in a torture chamber or a pleasure palace and in a remarkably short space of time we treat it like home. But Shirley hadn't been at the fame game long enough to have worn out its delights, to find it so burdensome. There had to be something else bothering him. But what?

I was startled out of my reverie by the sound of breaking glass and raised voices from the inner room. I heard Shirley shout bitterly, "Then do it—just fucking leave!" This was followed by some strident caterwauling that I assumed was Jacinda, some scuffling and another crash. Apparently she had been confined to the bedroom during our chess match.

I quickly let myself out, passing under the wary regard of the bodyguards on the way to the elevator.

I thought about knocking on Paula's door, but it was late and I didn't want to presume too much on our relationship. If I startled her awake in the middle of the night, I wasn't sure she'd be glad to see me. I wish I had taken the chance. It would have been a far more restful night.

When I got back to my room, I discovered I was under sonic invasion. Loud, raucous music blared from the suite next door. I brushed my teeth and tried to get some rest but it sounded like a gang of demented trolls was trying to break into my room with sledgehammers. Mostly what I could hear and feel was the deep reverberation of the bass. Unless I missed my guess, it was a White Zombie CD. The wall was fibrillating like the woofer on a cheap stereo speaker.

I clutched a pillow to my ear but I might as well have been trying to catch some shut-eye on a runway at O'Hare. After a few minutes, I got up, pulled on some clothes and marched down the corridor to the adjoining door. The music wasn't quite as obtrusive out here. Maybe they had the speakers pointed at my bed. I knocked loudly and waited. No response. I pounded with my fist. Again no one answered. Luckily my third assault on the door coincided with the end of the song.

Mike Denny yanked the door open, the rapid movement making him stagger back on his heels in his heavy-lidded, highly inebriated state. "Yo-yo, how's it going?" he said, smiling. His black shirt was unbuttoned, the tails hanging down over his jeans. A black shawl with gleaming metallic threading was looped loosely around his neck. He held a half-empty fifth of Jack Daniel's loosely in one hand. "Come on in, man," he said, gesturing with the blocky bottle. "We're partying."

Mike turned, let out a loud yowl and resumed his place on the couch between two prodigious blondes. One woman had long, limp platinum hair. The other's was shorter and spikier with dark streaks. Both of them had immense, gravity-defying breasts that looked like dirigibles were tethered under their tops, straining to float free. The white-haired gal, whose lips were nearly as puffed up as her chest, was wearing a T-shirt that read "Sugar Shack" with a silhouette of a buxom woman on it. She knelt and faced Mike, giggling, as he flopped back on the couch. The darker one, whose sharp green eyes made her appear a little smarter and crueler and a good deal less drunk than her friend, was wearing a cutoff sweater that revealed her midriff. Mike leaned back against her, and she threw an arm around his shoulder as he gurgled bourbon.

Seated in a high-backed chair a few feet away was Slab. Actually he was so wasted he looked like a melted-down candle. His head lolled almost sideways on his neck and a tendril of drool hung from the corner of his mouth. A bottle of Courvoisier dangled from his hand. He was still smiling. So was the woman sitting across his lap in a red blouse and black miniskirt. She had on an abundant, cascading hairpiece in a lustrous, if unnatural, coppery shade. And she had a body that made Dolly Parton seem dainty.

It was fairly obvious that the boys had paid a visit to a strip club that night after the show. And that meant that the ventilated animal carrier that sat on the floor by Slab's new friend in all likelihood contained a large snake of the constrictor family. I wasn't inclined to check the contents but I doubted that any of these gals would lug their pet schnauzer to work at the Sugar Shack.

Bottles, some full, other empty, littered the room. By the window, on a table that looked just like the one on which Shirley and I had played chess, Billy O'Connor hunched over, chopping lines of white powder with a razor blade. A red-striped drinking straw that had been cut into three sections lay by the pile of drugs.

The throbbing boom box sat on a windowsill, CD jewel cases scattered around it. I wasn't being paranoid: the machine was pointed at the wall that separated our rooms. I sidled over to the stereo, nudged it toward the center of the room and turned down the volume ever so slightly. I tensed, waiting for an indignant objection. No one complained. I probably could have wrestled a twelve-foot alligator on the rug and no one would have noticed—except maybe the snake in the box. Reptiles stick together.

I walked over to Billy and clapped him on the shoulder as he started to hoover a line. He grunted, scattering powder as he exhaled, and jerked upright. He had to turn nearly all the way around to see who had startled him because I was standing on his eye patch side.

"What the fuck are you doing here?" he said belligerently.

"Couldn't sleep."

"Why'd you come here?" he said. "I know you don't party."

"Just checking it out," I said. "I see you brought your camera." I nodded at Billy's camcorder lying atop a stool. He scowled. "You expecting a lot of action tonight?" I asked him. "Because I have to tell you Slab looks like he's about to pass out."

"He'll rally," Billy said, then turned and shouted at Slab. "Get over here, man. Have some blow." Without moving in the chair, Slab waved a hand listlessly at him.

"Have you ever seen his cock?" Billy asked me in a conspirational stage whisper.

"Can't say I have," I said, shaking my head.

"It's supposed to be enormous, big as Tommy Lee's," he said, holding his hands about a foot apart to illustrate. The prospect seemed to excite him. "Get over here, Slab," he shouted. "Flame on, dude."

I wandered over and turned the boom box down a hair. Slab remained inert but the lady on his lap got up and walked toward me, shoulders back, hips swiveling. They didn't teach her to strut like that in convent school. Mike was engaged in a lively game of slap and tickle with the other women.

"Are you with the band?" the bewigged stripper asked me innocently, her dilated eyes open as wide as Little Orphan Annie's. She was standing about as close to me as her tits would allow. Rubber baby bumpers.

"No, I'm in insurance," I said, going with a rejoinder that I assumed she would find stupefyingly tedious. It didn't work.

"Really?" she said, her rising inflection indicating interest. "Some of the girls at the club were talking about having their bodies insured . . . like Jennifer Lopez. I mean, it is our livelihood and all. Would that be expensive?"

"I imagine it would be," I said. "But it's not my field. I'm just a claims adjuster."

She looked puzzled. "Oh. What are you doing here?"

"I really don't know," I said. "Excuse me." I turned back to the boom box. Okay, she was a babe . . . a big, bodacious, drunk babe. So why was I snubbing her? First of all I was tired, too tired to dance. Second I had just seen her draped around Slab, which was a pungent turnoff. She was like a lollipop with hair on it. And I have to admit, staggeringly endowed women like her may make me gawk like a rube at a carnival. But I don't find them sexy. There's something almost deformed about them. Like bodybuilders, they leave me a little uneasy.

And finally I was hoping for a rematch with Paula and I

didn't want gossip getting back to her that I had been screwing some stripper.

I lowered the volume on the stereo one more time and let myself out. Back in my room, I discovered that my efforts at reducing the noise level had been way too subtle. The party and its pounding soundtrack continued in Mike's room until just before six in the morning. That's when I finally drifted off to sleep.

# CHAPTER
## 24

The Triumph of the Antichrist tour moved on to Chicago. As I groggily dragged my ass through the day, I consoled myself with the thought that Mike and Slab were hurting worse than I was. Of course, they were conditioned to handle the punishment. They abused their bodies every night. I was out of practice. If at this moment you were to dump half the chemicals into my system that I used to consume on a daily basis, I would drop like an ox. See what I mean about us being adaptable creatures?

I ran into Paula in the lobby as I was checking out. She looked fantastic, in a shiny emerald jacket, black slacks, with a fetching flush on her cheeks. I wanted to take her in my arms and kiss her but I sensed a certain standoffishness on her part. Her remoteness stung me. I swallowed my enthusiasm and began making some lame-ass small talk.

To my surprise, Paula cut off my inane chatter, yanked me into a pay-phone alcove and gave me a long kiss that melted me like butter in a microwave. I couldn't believe I had misread her signals so badly.

When I opened my eyes, the first thing I saw was Keith

Fisher exiting the hotel. He was talking to someone in front of him, but I couldn't see who it was. Nicky Hagipetros brought up the rear, ducking to enter the revolving doors.

Later, the timing of that kiss made me suspicious. Was it passion or distraction? But at that light-headed moment, I wasn't inclined to look a gift mouth in the horse.

"You going to Chicago?" she asked, using her thumb to wipe away a smear of lipstick from my mouth.

"I'm taking a commercial flight."

"You look tired," she said.

"My room was next to Mike's and he was entertaining a covey of strippers until daybreak."

"Is that what strippers travel in? Coveys?"

"I'm not sure. All I know about them is that they apparently like their music loud."

"You should have bunked with me."

"Believe me, I wish I had."

"Maybe tonight," she said, leaning into me. I kissed her by way of response. Paula smoothed the sleeves of her silky green jacket, winked at me and walked toward the street.

The airport was a madhouse. I bought a *USA Today* and settled in to wait at the gate. Opening the sports section, I saw that Allen Iverson had dropped thirty-eight on the Pistons at the Palace at Auburn Hills but I was having trouble reading the game account. TVs were suspended from the ceiling about every fifteen yards, all of them blaring *CNN Headline News.* And all around me, jerks were barking into their cell phones. The cacophony reminded me of a kennel.

I hope there is a special ring in hell reserved for those people who brazenly conduct their business and personal conversations in crowded public settings. I'd like to see them spend eternity in the Manuel Noriega wing of Hades, being bombarded with deafening marching band music around the clock.

My seat on the plane seemed to have been designed with the Lollipop Guild in mind. I wedged myself in and just before the doors closed, I saw Terry Tisdale, the tour's sound engineer, and Raul Porto, Shirley's stage manager, take seats a few rows up from mine. I admired their blasé approach to flying, boarding at the last minute. With the increased security, the airlines now recommend you arrive at least an hour and a half before your flight. Like a lemming, I do it.

Once we were airborne, I moved up to sit across the aisle from Terry and Raul, who were engaged in a game of gin.

"Hey, how you guys doing?" I said. Raul, who was sitting on the aisle, gave me a brisk Boy Scout salute with two fingers. Terry lifted his head an inch in acknowledgment without taking his eyes off his cards.

"You know, I never heard," I said. "Was there a funeral service for Tommy?"

"They flew his body out to Phoenix where his family lives," Raul said.

"I don't think anyone from the tour went to the funeral," said Terry.

"That's pretty sad," I remarked. I had to sit back in my seat so an attendant could rattle by with the drink cart. Then I leaned back into the aisle. "Shirley didn't seem too shaken up by Tommy's death."

"I didn't see any tears when Jake died either," said Terry. "And that was his best friend. He hated Tommy."

Raul chuckled. "It coulda been a lot worse."

"What does that mean?" Terry asked.

"I'm just saying Shirley has a bigger problem with Mike than the rest of the band. That's what made this whole tour go sour."

"I didn't pick up on any special hostility there," I said.

Raul shrugged. "Not now. Shirley just ignores him, but before you came on board it was really nasty."

"Musical differences?"

"Nah," said Raul. "Mike hit on Shirley's girlfriend."

"Jacinda?" I said incredulously.

"You're kidding!" said Terry, folding his cards together to hear this story.

"You never knew that?" Raul asked Terry.

"No," answered Terry, registering his amazement by stretching the word into two syllables.

"Oh, man. It was about two weeks into the tour. I think we were in San Diego. Anyway, Shirley had to stay at the arena to shoot an EPK and Jacinda ended up riding back to the hotel in a limo with the rest of the band. Mike gets to talking to her and asks her if she wants to come up to his room to party."

"That guy is such a horndog," said Terry without a trace of disapproval.

"Was he attracted to her?" I asked.

"Who knows? He had a few pops. I think he did it mostly to screw with Shirley's head," said Raul. "But according to Mike—and this is the part that freaks me out—she was more into it than he was."

"Whoa," I said. "Every time I see her she seems monumentally pissed off."

"That's because you're usually talking to Shirley. She doesn't like that," said Raul. "Anyway, Mike told me he started as a goof, thinking she would bite his head off. I mean, she never said boo to him before. But he gives her a little of the Denny charm, and suddenly she's all friendly and flirty. Like she had just been waiting for some attention, or something."

"So they go up to his room and what happens?" asked Terry.

"There were some other people there. Friends of Mike's. Everyone is drinking," said Raul. "Mike and Jacinda start fooling around and they end up in the bedroom."

"Yeah," said Terry expectantly.

"And that's when Shirley burst in. He got back to the hotel and couldn't find Jacinda so he sent Jake out to look for her. When Shirley found out where she was, he went storming down there."

"Catch 'em in the act?" asked Terry.

"More or less. They still had most of their clothes on."

"Oooh, I bet Shirley was pissed," said Terry.

"He had a complete meltdown," said Raul. "Dragged her out of there. And she was screaming and scratching at him the whole time."

"How did I miss all this?" asked Terry woefully.

"Then about a half hour later he comes back to Mike's room and he's seething he's so mad. Reamed Mike out up and down, calling him a scumbag and everything. And Mike's like, 'Yeah, whatever, dude.' That's when Shirley went for him."

"He jumped him?" asked Terry delightedly.

"Yeah. I mean, he's not a big guy, but he went crazy. Everyone who was there said it was really scary. Two guys had to pull him off Mike."

"I can't see Shirley freaking out like that," I said. "He doesn't seem like the jealous type."

"Believe me, you catch your old lady in the sack with some conceited rock star . . ." began Terry. Then, seeing both of us looking at him curiously, he waved his hand. "Never mind."

"I don't think Shirley was jealous," said Raul. "I think he was scared. He said Jacinda was on some heavy meds and giving her alcohol to drink was really dangerous. It was like he was her caretaker or something. The booze bothered him more than the sex."

"So why is Mike still on the tour?" I asked.

"Fisher. I don't know what he told Shirley but he got Mike to apologize and promise him it would never happen again," recounted Raul. He and Terry resumed their card game. "Shirley didn't say anything. In fact, that night was the last time he talked to any of the band members. He's been like the boy in the bubble ever since." Raul picked up a card from the pile, quickly scrutinized his hand and laid it back down. "It's a good thing Shirley never found out about Tommy and Jacinda. That would have really sent him over the top."

"What?" Terry and I said in amazed unison. Raul lifted

his eyebrows and flicked his nose, delighted with his secret.

"When was this?" Terry asked.

"I don't know," said Raul, rubbing his earlobe. "More than a month ago. Remember the night the show got canceled in Dallas and Shirley flew off to New York?"

"Why did he go to New York?" I asked.

"Big meeting with the label," said Terry. "I keep up on the business stuff. I just never hear the hotel gossip."

"What was the meeting about?" I asked.

"Fisher and Rocky had a big blowup," Terry said. "Rocky claimed he was getting ripped off. Said he wanted to bring in an outside accountant. So they all went to New York to meet with the bean counters."

"And what happened?" I asked.

"Who cares?" cried Terry. "I want to hear about Jacinda."

"Well, she was supposed to go with him," said Raul.

"Of course," said Terry. "They're like Siamese fuckin' twins."

"Then I guess Fisher told him there was no room for her on the jet."

"He's always doing that to screw with people," said Terry, pursing his lips. "Taking away their seat on the jet. Which may explain what we're doing on this crappy flight."

"Do you want to hear this story?" asked Raul.

"Sorry."

"So, Shirley leaves and he asks Jake to keep an eye on Jacinda. And that's fine, except when he goes to take a dump, she slips out of the room. Jake is frantic. He doesn't know what to do. He's afraid to call Shirley and tell him. He's got me searching with him."

"Get to the good part," Terry said.

"About four in the morning," said Raul, "we run into Mike in the lobby. He's just rolling in from some party. Jake practically attacks him. 'Have you seen Jacinda?' And Mike gets this sly look on his face. 'Why don't you try Tommy's room?' he says. That had never occurred to us. So we hustle up there and pound on the door. Tommy finally opens it in his underwear. Jake barges right past him and there is Jacinda in Tommy's bed, wearing only a sheet."

"I don't get it," I said. "Why would he get involved with Jacinda?"

"What are you *talking* about?" Raul asked emphatically. "Who wouldn't want her? She's a fox."

Terry and I both looked at him in astonishment. "What?" he spouted. "She is."

"Was Jake furious?" I asked.

"No," said Raul. "I thought he was going to tear into Tommy but he didn't. All their reactions were ass-backwards. Tommy was all guilty. I think he just woke up and realized what he did the night before. But Jacinda is smiling like she just won money. And Jake has got this little smirk on his face too. It was weird."

"So what'd Jake do?" I asked.

"He told Jacinda to get dressed," he said. As Raul talked to me, I could see Terry craning over to peek at his cards. "Then he had me take her back up to Shirley's suite. And he stayed and talked to Tommy for . . . I don't know how long. When we got upstairs, Jacinda went right in the bedroom. I sat down on the couch and turned on the TV. The next thing I know, Jake is shaking me awake. And he says I shouldn't mention to Shirley what happened, that it would upset him too much."

"And Shirley never found out?" I asked.

Raul smiled. "Oh, I think I would have heard something if that happened."

Maybe you already did, I thought, picturing Tommy curled up on the hotel floor.

"That's why I love this business," said Terry expansively. "You're always surrounded by a warm family atmosphere."

"Is this the weirdest tour you've ever been on?" I asked.

Terry snorted derisively. Raul said, "Hell, no."

"Remember the Tubes?" Terry said.

"They did 'White Punks on Dope,' right?"

He nodded. "And 'Don't Touch Me There.' I once went

coast to coast with them," he said. "Man, they drew a bizarre audience—transvestites, punks, glitter queens, sadists, survivalists, sniper-types, all mixed together. You have never seen parties like the ones they threw in their hotel rooms. It was like a Fellini movie every night."

"Yeah? I spent one winter with the Cramps," said Raul, pretending to shiver. "I still get the willies thinking about it. Lux Interior was like a bargain-basement Iggy Pop. Nastiest venues I've ever seen. It was an endless succession of shit holes with blood on the walls. I don't know how those places got a liquor license. Forget Fellini; it was a Quentin Tarantino movie every night."

Terry reached to draw a card, pausing to muse as he separated it from the pile. "You know, in terms of maintaining a purely poisonous mood on tour, no one in my experience can touch Roger Waters."

"The guy from Pink Floyd? He tough to get along with?"

"You can't imagine," Terry said. "Going on that fucking tour was like being shanghaied by Blackbeard."

A woman in the row in front of Terry turned around and frowned at him. "I'm traveling with my eight-year-old daughter," she said. "Could you please watch your language?" He raised his hands in mock-surrender and smiled self-deprecatingly at her. She turned back around. We had been cursing all along but as the guys started to swap war stories, their voices had gotten a little louder.

"I hear Pat Benatar was a real horror show to travel with," Raul said. "Her sound guy told me she had permanent PMS."

Terry made a show of examining his cards and laid them down faceup on the tray table. "I'm bumping with seven," he said.

"Shit!" Raul exclaimed. The woman's head popped up back over the headrest, a look of anger and consternation on her face. Looking penitent, Raul said, "Sorry, ma'am. Slipped out." He glared at Terry as he laid down his hand.

"You never go out with over five," he said. "You looked at

my hand." Terry smiled, toted up the score and jotted it down on an airline barf bag.

"The band I would never work for is Oasis," Terry said. "Those arrogant little—" Both Raul and I simultaneously shot out a hand to cover his mouth and stem the imminent obscenity. He held up his palms to indicate he was cool. "They put out a CD I wouldn't use for a coaster and compare themselves to the Beatles? I don't think so."

Raul dealt a new hand. "The guy I would never hire out to is Marc Anthony."

"The salsa guy?" I said. "How come?"

"There's just something about him that really spooks me," Raul said. "He looks to me like a serial killer. I keep seeing him running around in the woods with camouflage paint on his face and a nasty sawtoothed knife." Terry and I stared at Raul with bewildered expressions.

For the rest of the flight, the conversation veered off into a three-man plebiscite on the scariest-looking rockers of all time. In the end, I held out for Lou Reed, the God of Piss and Vinegar. Terry favored Gene Simmons from KISS. "Under all that makeup is a carpet salesman just itching to get out," he said. Raul voted for Bjork. "Maybe it's her eyes," he said. "I keep thinking she's a cannibal. Like she'd gnaw on your kidney." Terry placed his cards facedown on the tray when he heard this. "You should consider getting some professional help, Raul," he said. "You are seriously twisted, man."

"Come on," Raul replied. "You never thought that about her? She's just like Roseanne."

"The comedienne? Roseanne Barr?" asked Terry.

Raul nodded, saying, "Now, there's a gizzard gobbler if I ever saw one. I could never watch her show, man. Even the reruns. Every time that broad would cackle, all I could see was her incisors. She terrifies me." Terry looked over at me quizzically.

After landing, we shared a cab over to the hotel on the North Side. During the ride, Terry confided that he felt fortunate to still be working. "I really thought the tour was going to end after the show in Memphis," he said. "I still think Rocky might pull the plug any night."

"Why do you say that?" I asked.

Terry shrugged. "His heart just isn't in it," he said, fluffing his ponytail. "Since Memphis, he's been using more and more pretaped vocals in the mix. He told me to bump it up again tonight. And this guy was a stickler for live performance. It's like he's on autopilot."

"Have you been using prerecorded stuff all along?" I asked.

"We started about two weeks in. Come to think of it, it would be right after that incident with Mike and Jacinda," Terry said. "But only because Shirley lost his voice. That happens to a lot of singers on their first tour. They hit a wall early. But there's nothing wrong with his voice now." He glanced out the window and exhaled deeply. "It's a shame, really, because the one thing I respected about Shirley was his craftsmanship. He really cared about his music."

After we arrived at the hotel and checked in, I walked to a Happy Hour meeting down in the Loop and then took a taxi over to the arena. I saw the bus from the Church of the Divine Light, taking up about eight prime parking spots right by the building. The proselytizers must have arrived early.

I walked over and spotted the Reverend Isaacson standing by the door talking into a cell phone. He saw me approaching, frowned, turned away from me and hunched over to keep his conversation private. I waited.

After a moment, he clicked off and faced me. "Evening," he said.

"Hello, Reverend," I said. "How are you?"

"I am doing God's work." He gestured over his shoulder at the arena. "That always lifts my spirits."

"Maybe you could help me, Reverend. I know the Lord works in mysterious ways, but the other night I saw something that truly baffled me."

He stared at me. Either he sensed the sucker punch coming or he knew exactly where this was going.

"I was leaving a Shirley Slaughterhouse show early and I stumbled upon your deacon wrapped up in a conversation with a young woman."

"That's our mission at these concerts, Mr. McNamara—reaching out to young people." The reverend's tone didn't give it away, but I could tell from the hostile narrowing of his eyes that he knew exactly which incident I was referring to.

"I don't think so," I said. "The girl in question is named Jacinda. She happens to be the girlfriend of the rock star you are constantly vilifying."

"I don't know anyone named Jacinda," he said firmly.

I tilted my head skeptically and stared at him for a few seconds. Then I sighed. "All right," I said. "I guess I'll have to take this up with Mr. Slaughterhouse, ask him if he has any idea why his lover would be meeting with an official from your church." To complete the bluff, I started to walk away.

"Wait a minute, Mr. McNamara. That won't be necessary," said Isaacson. "I will explain the situation to you. By the way, I wasn't lying. I don't know anyone named Jacinda. That young woman's name is Hannah. She is the daughter of one of my parishioners."

I whistled a plunging glissando, like a slide trombone.

"In fact, that's what initiated this crusade," the reverend said. "One of my flock came to me very upset because his daughter had begun traveling with a rock musician. But this wasn't merely some debauched young Philistine. My friend showed me pictures of this man, played his music. We immediately recognized Shirley Slaughterhouse for what he is: an abomination."

"How does a church girl from Ohio meet Satan anyway?" I asked.

"I'm trying to have a frank discussion with you, Mr. McNamara. We can do without the sarcasm."

"My apologies. Please continue."

"It's my understanding," said Isaacson, "that Hannah met him during a trip to San Francisco. She called her parents, told them she had fallen in love with a musician and wasn't coming home. Her parents were horrified, doubly so when they found out what this 'musician' looked like."

"Why would she be outside the concert arguing with Deacon Jones?"

"The deacon has been trying to convince her that God has placed her in a unique position," he said. "She could be an instrument of divine providence."

"You mean bringing Slaughterhouse to Jesus?" I said incredulously.

"Yes."

"Does that seem a likely prospect to you, Reverend? Is she at all inclined to help with your missionary efforts?"

"Not in her current spiritual state, no. But we continue to conduct prayer vigils for Hannah. And the deacon, more than anyone, is able to reach through her cynical veneer and speak to her heart."

"Why is that?"

"Because he's her father."

My mouth dropped open. What was it Popeye used to say when he was caught off guard? Shiver me timbers. Consider mine shivered.

"Can you imagine what a victory that would be for Jesus if we could convert Shirley Slaughterhouse?" the reverend said, his gleaming eyes trained on the heavens.

"Like Paul on the road to Damascus," I suggested.

"Exactly."

"Or Ringo on the road to Albert Hall," I ventured.

His eyes came back down to look at me uncomprehendingly. You know it's a tough crowd when even Beatles references go over their head.

# CHAPTER 25

I paid close attention to the performance that night in Chicago. Terry was right. Some of the sizzle had gone out of Shirley's act. Gram was flaying the drums, but he was the only member of the band playing with abandon. The show was still pretty entertaining as theater, but it lacked passion, which is the plasma of rock 'n roll. That's why I went to see Bruce Springsteen's marathon concerts so many times even though I didn't much care for his music. (Maybe it was that sour milk-can sound of Clarence Clemmons's saxophone that turned me off.) But Bruce was a rock 'n roll revivalist, a guy who spilled his guts onstage night after night. He was the second-hardest-working man in show business. As of Chicago, Shirley had dropped out of the top 100.

The audience at the Horizon didn't pick up on it. They were as rabid as every other crowd on the Triumph of the Antichrist itinerary. I could tell how whipped-up they were by the number of EMT teams running on and off the floor, hauling off the fallen on stretchers.

You see this a lot at the rowdier rock shows and at the all-day outdoor festivals in the summer where there's a lot of drinking going on. One guy jostles another or smiles lasciviously at his girlfriend and—drop the gloves, Gordie—it's clobbering time. The paramedics have to carry off the pulped-up loser.

But there wasn't a lot of booze at Shirley's shows. In fact, I'd wager that the drug of choice among his devotees was Paxil. Most of these kids were carted off after fainting dead away. Sure, it was the excitement and the fact that they were dressed too warmly in layers of black clothing. But Shirley's pale proselytes tended to be loners with varying degrees of social anxiety. Being around this many people, even kindred spirits, was overwhelming. The paramedics were busy that night in Chicago.

Back at the hotel after the show, I considered calling my sponsor. I could phone Chris at three A.M. if I was really stressed out and he would spend an hour talking to me ungrudgingly. But this night I just wanted to chat. And given the hour and the time difference, I decided to hold off.

Besides, I had better things to do. I was going to pay an unannounced visit to Paula, give the girl a thrill. After all, she had said this might be the night.

Wrapping myself in one of the hotel's big, fluffy white robes, I grabbed a rose off a delivery cart in the corridor on her floor. I clasped the rose stem in my teeth and arranged myself in Paula's doorway like one of those saucy rogues on the glossy cover of a romance novel. Then I knocked. When the door swung open, I was looking at the carpet, the better to stun Paula with my sultry bedroom eyes as I languorously lifted my head. My gaze climbed slowly up her body, but instead of Paula, I found myself posing in front of an elderly Japanese woman who I had just rousted from bed and was now looking at me with considerable astonishment.

After a series of abashed apologies, I retreated to my room and called the front desk. I had gone to the right room, all right, but Ms. Mansmann had checked out at four P.M. Her suite had been assigned to a late arrival. Despite my unwanted visit, I felt unusually fine when I tucked myself in a few minutes later. After all, it's not every night I get to climb into bed with someone as sexy as myself.

I was still feeling pretty Fabio fabulous the next morning on the trip up to Madison, Wisconsin. In fact, as I walked up to the hotel entrance, I was fighting the impulse to whistle. What stopped me is that most popular music of the last forty years—with the exception of show tunes and Disney anthems—doesn't lend itself to the old lip flute. Have you ever tried to whistle "Smoke on the Water"? Ridiculous. With lips unpuckered, I was crossing the lobby on the way to the elevator when a hand yanked at my shoulder, spinning me halfway around.

It was Keith Fisher in a loose-fitting black and gray shirt with an Attic design, black slacks and black cowboy boots with tan piping and three-inch heels. Standing right behind him, and glowering at me as if I were causing his ulcer to act up, was Nicky Hagipetros. Nicky was wearing blue slacks and a plaid shirt with sleeves that didn't quite cover his elongated wrists. The guy's arms went on for so long, he looked like Reed Richards, the elastic leader of the Fantastic Four. I wondered how I could have missed noticing this Mutt and Jeff tandem as I strolled in.

"Don't bother unpacking your stuff," Fisher said. "I spoke to your boss. You're gone, McNamara."

"Exactly what is it you have against me, Keith?"

"Don't flatter yourself, scumbag," he said. "Getting rid of you is like pulling a tick off my dog."

"Really? Maybe me looking into Jake's death makes you nervous."

"Right," said Fisher with throaty sarcasm. "How's that investigation going there, ace? You pretty close to nailing somebody? I mean, besides my publicist." I could feel myself blushing. Fisher was squinting his eyes and nodding his head. "You think anything goes on on this tour that I don't know about?"

Fisher's cell phone rang and without taking his eyes from

mine, he pulled it out of his back pocket like a gunslinger going for his holster. "Yeah," he barked into it, then listened for a minute. "We already went over this, Charley. No. I don't fucking care. Those are the terms. . . . If he doesn't like it he can try booking the Box Tops into his sucky little venue. See how many tickets that sells."

That seemed like a curious threat for Fisher to be making, since only a couple of years ago, unless I'm mistaken, he was promoting the Box Tops as part of his Oldies Extravaganza. He concluded the conversation with a brisk, "Fuck 'im," then jammed the phone back in his pocket.

"I can only think of one reason why you wouldn't want me looking into Jake's death," I said.

"Oh yeah," said Fisher, huffing with scorn, "like I killed him. Hey, shit-for-brains, why would I want Karn dead? He was the only thing keeping Shirley's head screwed on."

"What are you talking about?" I said. "You know you tried to send Jake packing months ago."

"Wrong. I wanted to fire him as tour manager because he was so fucking incompetent. But I never said he had to leave. He was welcome to hang with Shirley as much as he wanted. I just wasn't going to pay him for the privilege."

"So why don't you want me looking into his death?" I asked.

"You mean besides having to look at your face? It should be obvious even to you. Shirley's video is in the Top Ten on *TRL* for the seventh week in a row. You understand? That means Carson Daly mentions Shirley's name at least once an afternoon to every CD-buying kid in America." Fisher sucked in a breath and continued. "Shirley's album is selling more than forty-five thousand copies a week. And the numbers spike in every city he does a concert in. All I care about is keeping that big money ball rolling.

"You know what a rock tour is all about? Moving on. You play the show, you count the receipts, you pack up the shit and you go to the next city. And you won't let us move on. You keep asking questions, bothering people. Every time

Shirley sees you it's a reminder that his friend is dead. So guess what?" He yanked his thumb over his shoulder like he was an umpire ejecting me from the game.

"And every time Shirley sees you, it's a reminder he's getting robbed," I said. "I heard about him demanding an outside audit."

Fisher sucked in his cheeks and shook his head. Then he blew out an exasperated spume of air. "You think that was a big deal, huh? Let me tell you, McNamara, I got accountants crawling up my ass every week. It relaxes me. I never signed an artist yet that didn't turn around a year later and scream that they were getting ripped off. So we go to New York, we sit in the conference room and we pull out the contract. End of discussion. That was months ago. Shirley hasn't made a peep about money since.

"I always say there's two types of people in this business—jerkoffs like you who are convinced it's about music. And guys like me who know it's about product." He shot his wrist and studied his gaudy watch. "I figure I made twenty thousand while I'm standing here talking to you. And that's the only reason this hasn't been a complete waste of time." He glanced back at Nicky and they headed for the front doors. "Have a good flight, McNamara," he called out, without bothering to turn his head.

I didn't feel like whistling anymore. But I didn't feel like quitting the case either. First of all I'm a little compulsive about finishing things I started. Second, I felt sorry for Shirley. His best friend's dead. His manager is an asshole. His girlfriend is a major whack job and he's got holy rollers dogging his every step. And there's no one looking out for him. I wanted to help the guy.

Finally, I have to admit that Fisher's insistence that I leave made me want to dig in my heels. I'd do anything to annoy the guy. And if he was connected to Karn's death, I would dearly love to prove it. But if the insurance company had pulled my voucher, I had no choice but to leave.

Up in my room, the message light was blinking. Paula had

called from her office in New York. When I told the assistant who I was, she responded with a very arch, knowing, "Ohhh, Jim McNamara. She'll be right with you." Had Paula told her she liked me or do women just have some sort of intimacy radar?

Then Paula's husky voice came on the line. "Hey, you."

"What happened to you yesterday?"

"We had a PR crisis with one of our touring artists," she said. "I had to fly back for damage control. I meant to call you but the barn was on fire. This little ladybug had to fly away home."

"What happened?"

"One of our rappers, a young white kid from Paterson, New Jersey, who calls himself Hot Pocketz, is in one of these mammoth rap reviews with about ten other rap acts. It's a nightmare. No one performs more than three songs and the shows still go on for about five hours. Fights in the audience, fights backstage. Everybody has a posse. They're all at war.

"Anyway, the Count Yo' Benjamins tour was down in North Carolina two nights ago and a woman who was working security claims that HP pulled her into his dressing room and committed several lewd and unwanted acts on her person. She's about two hundred forty pounds and was wearing a blue serge uniform, but I don't doubt for a minute she's telling the truth. Hot Pocketz is like a dog in heat, G. Put him in a leper colony and he would start humping legs."

"Did you just call me G?"

"Huh? Oh yeah. Sorry, Jim. I've been dealing with rappers all day."

"I wish you had let me know you were leaving. I went up to your room last night and almost committed an act worthy of Hot Pocketz on some unsuspecting Japanese matron."

"What?"

"I'll explain next time I see you."

"And when will that be?" she asked, her voice dipping lower. A number of hairs on the back of my neck bristled.

"Could be sooner than you think, G," I said. "I'm flying east this afternoon." I explained how Fisher had booted me off the tour. "By the way," I said, "he knows about you and me."

"So does everyone here in the office, apparently," she said. "Word seems to be getting around."

"Huh."

"Well, now that we've been outed, maybe I can come visit you in Connecticut for the weekend. Give 'em something to talk about, like my girl Bonnie says."

"That'd be great."

"Where's your place again?"

"Winsted."

"Is that where you're headed this afternoon?"

"Probably not right away."

"Yeah? What's on the itinerary?"

"I'm not sure yet, Paula."

Actually, I had a pretty good idea, but I hesitated to tell her. I guess I didn't want to take a chance on word getting around.

# CHAPTER
# 26

My next call was to Paul Roynton. He confirmed that I was a goner. "I'm sorry, Jim," he said unconvincingly. "I fought for you."

"I know something bad happened to this kid Jake Karn."

"I need something that's going to hold up in front of an arbitrator. Otherwise . . ."

"Just give me a few more days," I pleaded, knowing it was futile.

"No can do," he said. "I can't hold off Fisher anymore. It's just not worth it. We're going to settle it."

"Do me a favor. Don't write the check yet. I have a couple of things to pursue that may open this up."

"Just stay away from Keith Fisher, all right?" he said. "Gotta run."

There was just one loose end I wanted to singe before I left for the airport. I called Raul Porto's room. "H'lo," he croaked. I adopted a phony Spanish accent. "*Buenos dias*, Raul. This is Marc Anthony. I am in the lobby waiting for you." I turned the last word into a singsong dipthong.

I heard the phone fumbled and dropped before Raul came

back on. "What'd you say?" Perplexity, sleepiness and terror mingled in the phrase.

"It's Jim McNamara, man."

"You prick. I was trying to take a nap."

"Do you know where the crew is staying?"

"Don't they give you a fucking itinerary?"

"No, they don't."

"Hold on, man." The phone was dropped again. About fifteen seconds later, Raul returned. "They're at a Ramada on Kenosha Boulevard."

"*Gracias.*" He hung up.

I showered, packed up my kit bag, pulling out a treasured old tape, Donovan's *Open Road,* to listen to during the flight. Then, without ever having ruffled the sheets on the bed, I checked out and headed over to the Ramada. I recognized some of the tractor-trailers parked across the boulevard in the massive lot of a Big Kmart.

It wasn't hard to find my trippy little triad. They were the only ones patronizing the bar in the lobby at nine A.M. Billy O'Connor was standing up from his stool. In his tight black Danzig T-shirt and blue jeans, he was acting out a struggle, squinting his visible eye while twisting and reaching his arm like a man trying to extract something from a stovepipe. As I approached, he resumed his normal posture and said, "The doctor says to him, 'So why are you laughing?' And the guy says, 'Doc, you should have seen the look on that monkey's face'!"

Legs Turkel put his head down on the bar, his shoulders heaving with laughter. Maybe it was the beanie, but he put me in mind of a Muslim saying his prayers. Sandra Blanchard tilted her head back and brayed. Her insubordinate hair was gathered in a towering topknot. It looked like a loosely bound sheaf of wheat was affixed to her head.

"You guys are whooping it up early," I said. They were too lubricated to switch gears from hilarity to hostility that fast. So they registered my presence placidly, glancing at each other and picking up their glasses more or less simultaneously to take a drink.

"Nothing like a reformed drunk to try and spoil everyone else's fun," said Legs.

"Here, here," said Sandra, shaking her head wearily.

"You nearly killed that party in Mike's room the other night," said Billy. "After you left, that cute blonde asked me 'What's his problem?' She was all bummed out. You are quite the horse's ass." The mood was quickly turning ugly.

"If you ask me, he's a wet blanket," said Legs.

"Maybe he's a wet horse's ass," suggested Sandra. They lifted and drained their glasses like a precision drill team.

"He's a party pooper," said Legs.

"A pooper scooper," crowed Billy.

"A super duper stinky pooper," Sandra said with a giggle.

Legs looked at her reproachfully. I guess this wasn't the caliber of capper that their Huey, Dewey and Louie comedy act called for. He turned to the bar, hoisted his empty glass and shouted, "Barkeep. Another round."

"You end up getting some good footage out of that party the other night?" I asked Billy.

"I would have. I should have," he said, with consternation. "Slab was too wasted. He passed out facedown in a pile of coke. First time I've ever seen that happen. And Mike got sick in the bathroom. Actually, on the way to the bathroom. He wasn't too into it after that. But he told the girls to get it on with each other and I filmed that. They were fucking fantastic. I'm telling you, man, this was the real dream team. The best threesome I've ever seen." High praise indeed. His face, which grew more animated as he replayed the night in his mind's eye, suddenly fell.

"When I got back to my room," he said, "the tape was missing. We found out later, so was four thousand dollars of Mike's money and his stash. And Slab lost a jade and diamond ring. Had it soaped off his finger. That's fucking low, man. Ripping off a guy's jewelry while he's passed out. I think it was that spiky-haired chick. She was fucking mean. Nice ass, though."

"So what are you guys celebrating this morning?" I asked.

"Celebrating," scoffed Legs. "This is a death watch."

"For whom?"

"For the tour," said Sandra. "Shirley is about to pack it in."

"The announcement is going to be made any minute," said Billy glumly. "It's all over but the shouting."

"What makes you think so?" I asked.

"My friend April does Shirley's makeup, right?" Sandra said, turning a statement into a question. "And yesterday, while she was working on him, he told her that things were about to change and maybe she should start looking around."

"But it's been pretty obvious anyway," said Legs. "The wheels are coming off this wagon."

"Shirley has been pretty apathetic since . . . well, for a while," said Billy. "Now it seems like he doesn't give a shit at all."

"Doesn't mean the show can't go on," I said. "It wouldn't be the first rock tour to stagger along under its own momentum. I once saw the Cars near the end of their career when they were running on fumes. I thought they were going to expire of boredom right before my eyes on that stage. And they played forty-five dates after that night."

"Well, this tour is over," said Billy.

"*Finito, kaput,*" said Legs.

"Shirley is about to leave the building," said Sandra. "We won't see his like again."

They looked at each other and chimed in unison, "Thank God." Then they clinked glasses and drank.

"So where will you guys go?" I asked.

"I'm headed home," said Legs emphatically. Then he adopted a blank expression. "Remind me where that is again, Sandra?"

"You live in Hoboken, sweetie."

"Right, right," he said, nodding his head.

"I'm going to have to find some other tour," said Billy, "get right back in the harness. You know why?"

I shook my head.

"Keith fucking Fisher," he said, angrily enunciating each syllable. "The next payday.for the crew is Monday. If they pull the plug on this tour today or over the weekend, we're never going to see that money."

"Fisher is notorious for stiffing his crews on their last check, even when the tours run the table," said Sandra. "It's his little parting gift. So you *know* we're screwed."

"Why do you work for the guy," I asked, "if he has a reputation for ripping his people off?"

Legs looked down at his drink and said somberly, "Loyalty." They all laughed bitterly.

"Fisher is a thief," Sandra said. "Big deal. So is everybody else in rock 'n roll, especially the promoters. Billy says it's the only business more corrupt than professional boxing. But in the end some cheese is better than no cheese."

"Here, here," mumbled Billy, and once again they clinked glasses and chugged the contents. "Barkeep," he called, wiping his mouth with the back of his hand.

"I guess my timing is good," I said. "I'm jumping ship today."

"You're leaving?" Legs and Sandra asked, overlapping each other with identical inquiries. I was beginning to think these kids spent too much time together. Maybe it was good the tour was disintegrating. Keep 'em separated.

"Got my bag rye-cheer," I said, patting my valise on the stool beside me.

"Guess you're giving up on that whole Jake Karn thing, huh?" asked Billy.

"Not officially, no."

"What does that mean?" Legs asked, as if affronted. I shrugged and stuck out my lower lip like J. Fred Muggs. Legs eyed me, then looked down into his fresh cocktail. "Where you headed from here?" he asked in a tone that was supposed to be nonchalant. Ho-ho!

One of the trapdoors that booze places in your path is that it deludes you into thinking you can put things over on people. After a few belts, you're convinced you're the world's greatest bullshitter. But unless the person you're trying to snow is just as plastered as you are, believe me, you're not fooling anybody. A drunk trying to be tricky is like a pole vaulter working with a broom handle. In other words, I wasn't buying Legs's feigned disinterest.

"Back East," I said.

"Back East where?" Legs asked with a trace of frustration.

"I didn't know you cared, Legs."

"I don't," he growled. "I just want to know where you're flying. New York?"

"Actually, Bradley Field in Windsor Locks is the closest airport to my house."

"Good," he said, flexing his shoulders in satisfaction. "Just wanted to make sure you weren't planning to go to Boston."

I hefted my bag and bade them take it easy. On to Beantown.

# CHAPTER 27

Not long ago, I would have needed a friend inside the phone company, the motor vehicle department or some other big bureaucracy to track down Joey Stamps. Now I could go on-line and, for a reasonable bite on my Master-Card, get most of his vital statistics. For a few hundred dollars more, I could have his complete credit history and what kind of toothpaste he favored. Guys like Joey, who are operating in the clandestine cash economy, make every effort to fly beneath the radar of official scrutiny. But even drug dealers leave traces in the catch-all webbing of consumer records. In ten minutes, I knew his address in the South End. The downside of this easy exposure is that Joey could, if he so desired, obtain the same kind of information about me. Little Brother is watching all of us.

I rented a car at Logan Airport and banged a left as soon as I got through the tunnel. Actually it would be more accurate to say I ventured a left. I am always a little subdued behind the wheel in Boston because, for my money, the city has the most impatient and aggressive drivers this side of Bangkok. Following the harbor rim past Faneuil Hall and the aquarium, I made my way to Joey's neighborhood. After circling the block four times, I even found a parking space that allowed me a decent vantage of the three-story row-house he lived in.

I sat for a while, settling in, getting the lay of the street. Then I walked up to the market around the corner to grab a turkey sandwich, a bottle of iced tea and copies of the *Globe* and the *Phoenix*. On the way back to the car, I soft-shoed up the steps of Joey's stoop. There were three mailboxes in the vestibule and three doorbells stacked on the wall. The top two had names affixed beneath them in letter-punch plastic. The bottom one was blank. That, I presumed, would be Mr. Stampinato. Recovering alcoholics aren't the only ones who prefer anonymity. Plus it would make sense for him to be on the bottom floor. If you get a lot of foot traffic at odd hours, you don't want your customers clomping up and down the stairs, alarming the neighbors.

After my quick reconnaissance, I walked back to my roost. I considered making a full frontal assault, but the chance of Joey letting a total stranger in his front door seemed remote. And most self-respecting drug dealers have the front entrance well barricaded to protect against either predatory home invaders or a police raid. I could pound on his door and make a scene. He would certainly hate drawing attention like that but he still wouldn't let me in.

So I decided to make like a real detective and stake the joint out. I would stalk this guy like he was a skittish sand crab: waiting for him to emerge from his hole before I pounced. It turned out to be a fairly pleasant vigil, in large part because Boston is one of the few cities left in this country that still has decent, independent-minded radio. The large, restive college population must be holding at bay the ubiquitous programming consultants who have blighted most of the nation's airwaves with their monotonous mall-mentality playlists.

I had just finished my sandwich when a handsome couple in their twenties promenaded out the door. I immediately dubbed them Abercrombie and Fitch. They were vital and robust, with gleaming teeth and expensive haircuts, clearly impressed with themselves and each other. I thought it inconceivable that Abercrombie could be Joey Stamps. First of all, he couldn't possibly be this preppie. And second, I doubted he would be involved in an ongoing relationship, even one this narcissistic. I didn't doubt Joey had sexual partners, but I imagined his affiliations being far more expedient.

Okay, my drug dealer profiling wasn't even up to New Jersey State Trooper standards, but I couldn't roust the whole neighborhood. I had to play the odds.

About twenty-five minutes later, a swarthy young man came out packed in bicycler's spandex and hoisting a ten-speed over his shoulder. His upper body was trim but he had the pneumatic legs of a speed skater. I ruled him out as too athletic. Once you get seriously involved with drugs you become like a whale that shuts off most of its circulation to stay submerged for long periods of time. The nonessential things—sleep, nutrition, family, hygiene, exercise—start to fall away. Besides, I figured if this guy lived on the first floor, he'd be wheeling the bike out; he wouldn't have it over his shoulder.

Just before four, a man in his early thirties stepped outside. He would have been handsome if his sunken eyes and grim expression didn't make him look so wizened. He was wearing a dark blue long-sleeve shirt ringed with white cowboy action figures and pipestem blue jeans. He was clean-shaven and his long, sandy hair was moistened and brushed back behind his ears, but it was obvious he had gotten up a short time ago. He reminded me of those old Merrie Melodie cartoons of a wolf dressed up in a zoot suit: rakish and feral at the same time. He swept the street from corner to corner with his eyes (though not registering me), then put on a pair of black, angular sunglasses even though the day was overcast. Hello, Joey!

I busied myself with the newspaper as he passed me on the opposite sidewalk, moving purposefully. I spotted him nearly a fifty-yard lead before I got out of my car and started to follow. He walked a few blocks toward the Prudential Towers, then turned into a cramped café decorated with zinc and mirrors. Across the street, I browsed a shoe store display, furtively watching him order at the counter, add multiple packs of sugar to his latte and take a seat at an album-sized table inside. I moved down the street to loiter.

When he emerged ten minutes later, turning back in the direction of his apartment, I closed the gap rapidly. "Excuse me, Joey?" I said as I approached.

I gathered he must be wrapped pretty tight, because my mild inquiry jolted him like a car backfiring. He tilted his head down to look at me accusingly over his sunglasses, as if I had been trying to startle him. "I don't know you, man," he said in a voice that was an octave higher than his phone message. He was moving away before he finished speaking.

I kept pace, a development he noted out of the corner of his eye with irritation. "Name's Jim McNamara," I said, walking a stride behind him in tandem. I felt like an insurance salesman pestering a hinky prospect. "I called you a bunch of times. About Legs Turkel and Jake Karn."

"Fuck off, all right?" he said, nanny-goat gruff. "I don't want to talk to you." I could have grabbed his arm and stopped our madcap little march down Boylston, but I had a presentiment that physical contact would really set him off. I was tempted to do it anyway.

"I came all the way to Boston to see you," I said. "I only need five minutes of your time and you'll never see me again."

He stopped in his tracks and turned back to regard me. After giving me a careful twice-over, he craned to look over my shoulder down the street. Then he jerked his head around and peered the other way. I had to fight the urge to bark some phony mobilization order down my sleeve ("Bravo gypsy tango! Move in!") just to spook him.

"Jim, right?" he said, adopting a very insincere tone of chumminess, screwing his mouth into a simulacrum of a smile and taking off his sunglasses. I nodded. "How'd you find me?"

"Reverse phone directory," I said. The lie seemed to placate him.

"I got your messages," he said. "But I got nothing for you."

"I know," I said. "I'm grasping at straws. That's the only reason I'm here. I'm desperate. All I'm asking is for you to talk me through that night and I'll split. I swear this won't come back to bite you."

He blinked his eyes spasmodically. Then he nodded. "All right," he said. "Let's go back to my place. Take our business off the street."

As we walked together, his head on a swivel, he pulled out a yellow pack of Chiclets, chomped on a couple and offered them to me. I accepted. Why not? We were bonding now.

"So what were you—camping outside my house?" he asked with a smile as thin as tissue paper.

"No, I only pulled up a few minutes ago," I said. "Just flew in from Chicago. I was debating whether to knock on your door."

"You have a picture of me or did Legs describe how I look?"

"Neither," I said. "I played a hunch when I saw you come outside."

"Yeah, well, Legs told me about you," he said, and smirked, as if this gave him some sort of advantage. "He's not a big fan."

"He'll like me even less when he finds out I came to see you."

"So you're like the rock 'n roll detective or some shit, huh?" he said, growing more voluble as we turned onto his street. Maybe he was like one of those trail ponies that pick up the pace when they realize they're headed back to the barn. "I hear you worked for Axl Rose and Carlos Santana and a bunch of big names."

"Actually, I never worked for Carlos—" I started to say, but he broke in.

"You ever meet Jeff Beck, man?" he said, tearing off a few notes on his air guitar. I shook my head. "Yeah, well . . ." he said, losing all interest in the conversation as he reached for his keys. He let me in his apartment and double-locked the door behind us. We were in a narrow corridor that ran in both directions from the entryway.

"In here," he said, indicating with his head the door closest to us. The kitchen was to the rear and I surmised that the bedroom was back there somewhere too. I had seen the front parlor of his apartment from the stoop. It was furnished modestly. Joey was clearly keeping down appearances. But the den he ushered me into was lavish—thick pile carpeting, Wilt Chamberlain–sized plush black sofas and an eye-popping entertainment console.

"Nice crib," I said. He ignored the compliment, pulling a transparent blue plastic contraption out of a coffee table he knelt by. The device looked like a tiny water gun. I soon realized it was a coke snifter, dispensing premeasured snorts into its barrel. Johnny whaled on it four times, inhaling so fiercely I thought he was trying to get the drug down into his feet. He didn't offer to share this candy. I guess we weren't bonding anymore.

"You think I'm weak," he said in a voice so high and strangled I wondered if his blow was treated with helium. "Is that what you think?" He began rooting in the drawer. I had a premonition of what was coming even before he hefted out a moose of a large-caliber pistol, pointing it at me and twisting his mouth into a tooth-baring scowl.

I held my hands up in capitulation. I assumed this display was pure bluster on Joey's part, a little sword-rattling, as it were. But I didn't know the guy so I didn't want to make too many assumptions about his sanity or impulse control. I sure didn't like how tightly he was gripping the pistol. The fact is I didn't grow up around firearms so I still have a keenly developed sense of fear around them. When anyone waves a gun in my vicinity, I take it very seriously.

"You think you can fuck with me," he said, turning his head so that he had one eye trained on me.

"No, I don't," I said. "I didn't come here to hassle you."

"You shouldn't have come here at all," he shouted. "You call me out of the blue to ask me about a drug sale? You think I am going to talk about that with you on the fucking phone? Are you fucking *insane*?"

"No, I—"

"And then you come to my fucking house? Unfuckingbe-lievable." He was shaking his head ruefully. "I don't even know you. And you brace me on the fucking street?"

"I didn't know what else to do," I said.

"You respect my fucking privacy is what you do!"

"Hey, I'm sorry, Joey," I said mildly, holding my hands a little higher. "I just want to ask you a few questions. What are you going to do? Blow me away in your living room?"

"Maybe," he said. "This room is completely soundproof."

"Make an awful mess, though," I said. I know it sounds like I was prodding him toward the edge, but really I was hoping to make him see the situation as a *little* bit ludicrous.

"Maybe I'll make a phone call," he said. "I know people who would fucking flush you, no questions asked."

"I swear I don't mean you any harm," I said. "You just happen to be one of the last people to see Jake Karn alive."

"I don't give a rat's ass about Jake Karn," he remonstrated.

"I understand. Not a lot of people did. Could you do me a favor? Put that down. We'll talk for five minutes and then I will be so out of your life forever."

Joey turned his wrist sideways and narrowed his eye as if he were targeting me. Then he lowered his arm. I inhaled for what seemed like the first time in three minutes and dropped my hands slowly.

"You're wasting your time," he said, "but ask your fuck-ing questions."

"Okay," I said. "Just tell me about that night—meeting Jake Karn, what he said, anything you remember."

"Not much to tell," Joey said, sitting down on the central sofa and placing the gun on the table in front of him. "I drove up to Portland, which I wasn't too happy about to begin with." The phone rang but Joey continued talking. "Legs left me some tickets so I watched about a half hour of the show, which by the way sucked."

The answering machine picked up on the third ring and I heard Joey's invisible-man message again. There was a beep and then a filtered voice spoke. "Joey, it's Stu. Pick up. . . . Pick up, man."

Joey reached over the armrest and snared the cordless phone. "Whassup? . . . Yeah. When? . . . No, that's cool. . . . Yeah? I might be into that. . . . You hear anything from Wendy?" Whatever Stu said made Joey smile. Then his eyes drifted up to meet mine and the smile faded. "Hold on," he said, looking at me reprovingly. He got up and moved toward the door. Halfway there, he pivoted so quickly he almost lost his balance. He rushed over to the table and picked up the gun, glaring at me as he did so. Then he went into the corridor, closing the door behind him.

When he returned a minute later, he wasn't brandishing his cannon. He placed the phone back in its charger and resumed his seat. "So where was I?"

"You didn't like the concert."

"It sucked," he said, puckering his gaunt face for emphasis. "So fucking lame. And the crowd looked like they were trick-or-treating." With his remote, he flicked on his giant TV, which had a screen as big as a kiddie pool. CNBC came on with the sound muted, but Joey was content watching the stock ticker crawl. Everybody's in the market.

"So Legs tells me to meet him by the beer stand near the main entrance—which is doing like no business—right after the band leaves the stage. Before the encore. So Legs shows up and gives me my money and tells me to wait there for Jake. I tell him I'm not going to do my business on the concourse and he says, 'Don't worry. He'll take you downstairs.' "

"Wait a minute," I interrupted. "Legs paid for the drugs?"

"Hell, yes," Joey said, wagging his head as if my question was moronic. "Top dollar. Both times. Only in Portland—"

"Wait a minute," I said. "Both times?"

"Yeah, Providence first and Portland a few days later. It was the—"

I butted in again. "You brought stuff to them twice?"

Joey cocked his head. "Are you fucking deaf?" he said. "I just told you that. . . . Can I finish?" I nodded. "So I wait there, and the show ends and this freaky, bug-eyed crowd starts streaming past me to the exits. I felt like I was stuck in a termite nest." Joey looked away from CNBC, turning his attention to me to deliver this witticism. I chuckled dutifully.

"And then Jake shows up and he's overjoyed to see me. Like we're old friends now, right? Slapping me on the back and shit." Joey reached back in the drawer for his coke wand and punctuated his account with two scorching snorts. He made more noise inhaling than Moe, Larry and Curly snoring away in a bunk bed.

"You can tell this guy is really excited to be copping. Like we're in a James Bond movie or something." Joey looked over again for approbation but this time I only granted him a weak smile. "He's got an orange all-access pass around his neck and he gives me one to wear. Then he takes me through the press box and downstairs to this dressing room that no one was using."

"How do you know it was the press box?"

"Because there were two guys in there typing away on their laptops. And 'cause it said 'Press Box' over the entrance." Joey smirked.

"Did he take you backstage in Providence too?"

"No, we met at his hotel. Legs was in the room with us. In Portland it was just me and butterball in this little concrete bunker. That's when I jacked him up. He wasn't smiling after that."

"What are you talking about?"

"I told him I had some great drugs but it was going to cost him."

"I thought Legs paid you."

"He did," Joey said, "but I figure I'm the one humping my ass all over New England. I'm the one taking all the risks. I deserve to get paid twice. He groused about it, but I knew I had him. He was champing at the bit. Plus, I wanted to discourage him and Legs from ever calling me again. I ain't no delivery service. So fuck 'em." He pinched his nostrils and inhaled.

"What did Jake end up buying?"

"The whole combination plate. Two eight-balls of coke, a half ounce of Hawaiian herb and a couple of grams of crank."

"The autopsy said he ingested Ecstasy. You know anything about that?"

"That's right. He got a few tabs of E. I don't think he even knew what it was. If I offered him Ex-Lax, he probably would have swallowed that."

"Then what happened?"

"He paid me and I split."

"You left him there? Did he say anything about what he intended to do with all this shit?"

"No," Joey said, shrugging. "He was practically pissing his pants he was so fucking happy to have this mad stash. It was kind of creepy how jazzed he was."

"Did you see anyone with Jake or talking to Jake the whole time you were with him?"

"You mean all ten minutes? No."

"That's it?"

"That's it . . . except for this," Joey said, executing a quick-draw move behind his back and pulling out a compact Glock. His self-satisfied grin was so broad, I could see his gums. "Admit it—you were sitting here feeling all safe because you thought I was unarmed this whole time. Right?"

"I was kind of hoping. Yeah," I said, leaning away from him.

"I got this little throw-down gun right after that trip to Portland," he said, turning the pistol in his hand and gazing at it admiringly.

"Why?"

"For protection. Because I thought that fat little fuck was trying to take me off."

"I thought you got your money and left."

"After we conducted our business, I came out of the room, and there's this guy who looked like a professional wrestler standing right there, leaning against the wall, staring at me. And I figure this is a setup. This freak is gonna shake me by the ankles and take back all the money I just got from Jake. But he never says boo. I walk right past him. But on the ride home, I decide I got to get a deterrent." He twirled the pistol around its trigger guard with his finger. "Just in case."

"This big guy. What did he look like?"

"I don't know. He was nasty-looking. Built like a fucking Clydesdale."

"Hair color? Clothes? Anything?"

"I don't know," Joey wheedled. "I only saw him for a second. He had on denim, a lot of denim, boots. Long brown hair, I think. I don't know. He's big, mostly. Believe me, you run into him, you'll know it. There won't be any confusion."

The phone started ringing again. Joey studiously ignored it until the machine picked up. "Joey, it's Bart. Pick it up. I'm over in Copley." Joey tucked the pistol behind his back and snared the phone.

"Hey. . . . All right. Make it fifteen minutes. See ya." He hung up, slapped his hands atop his thighs and stood up. "And that concludes our business." Walking in front of him out the doors, I contemplated handing him my business card and asking him to call if anything else occurred to him, but I was pretty sure he would tear it to shreds in front of me. I didn't see any reason to encourage littering.

Just before I reached the vestibule, he called out to me. "Hey." I turned back. He was nestled in the threshhold like a half-moon, the door pulled tight against him. "I'm gonna forget this visit ever happened. You make sure you do the same thing. Understood?" He mimed turning a key in his lips.

"From now on, I will avoid you like the plague," I said. I don't know when I've ever been more sincere.

# CHAPTER 28

I drove home to Winsted. There were practical matters to attend to, like nabbing some fresh laundry and cleaning up the Dead Sea Scrolls, the folded newspapers scattered around my driveway. But mostly I wanted to rack out in my own bed. Whether it's the strange mattress or the incidental noises, I've never been able to get a good night's sleep in a hotel. Not sober, anyway.

I woke up early and, after attending to some minor housekeeping chores, I pushed myself to go to the health club for a workout. I observe the same attendance rule for the gym as I do for AA meetings: the days I don't want to go at all are the days I force myself to. Can't let inertia build up momentum.

As was my custom, I brought a copy of *USA Today* into the sauna after my workout. The newspaper, with its prechewed observations, requires so little attention, it seems to have been designed to read in an inferno. After showering, I rewarded myself with a visit to my friend Ken's diner. One of his corn muffins, toasted on the grill, probably nullified all the sit-ups I had just done. On my way home, I stopped by the post office to pick up my mail. Among the magazines was the latest copy of *Spin*. I noticed Adam Buckman's story, "Limp Bizkit: Pissant Waltzing Across America," was on the cover.

I put in a call to Paula, expecting to get her voice mail. It wasn't even eleven A.M., after all, but to my surprise, her assistant answered and put me right through.

"Hey," I said, "you're in early."

"I had a breakfast meeting with those devils over at MTV," she said. "We're trying to get them to play this video by Thrush 99, our punk-ska band from Carlsbad. The boys like to run around in the all-together, show off their tattoos. Apparently MTV has some sort of rule: You can only appear naked on the channel if you've sold over five million CDs."

"I hope Blues Traveler isn't close to the cutoff," I said. "I don't want to see John Popper with his clothes off."

"I don't even want to see him with his hat off," she said, laughing.

"So . . . how you doing?"

"Hectic," she said. "Where are you?"

"Home," I said.

"In Winsted?"

"Hey, you remembered. I'm starting to think you might make good on that promise to visit."

"How's this weekend?" she asked. "I thought I was going to have to fly out to Des Moines to rejoin the Antichrist carnival, but I just found out I don't have to."

"Uh-oh," I said. "Shirley's tour fold up its tent?"

"No," she said, as if the suggestion were outrageous. "Why do you say that?"

"That was the rumor when I was in Madison," I said. "Apparently Shirley intimated to his makeup person that she should update her résumé."

"I hope she took his advice. Shirley fired April yesterday. But the tour goes on."

"You see how these nasty rumors get started," I said.

"Guess who is going to be applying Shirley's greasepaint from now on?"

"John Wayne Gacy?"

"Close," she said. "The beautiful and charming Jacinda. I spoke to Terry after the show last night. He said Shirley came out onstage looking like Tammy Faye Baker on acid."

"Jeez," I said, "how tough is it to screw up that look? The guy has been wearing the same fright mask for months."

"Typical male," Paula said huffily. "Always underestimating the challenge of makeup. The cosmetics didn't slow Shirley down, though. Terry said it was his best performance this week."

"I'm sure the crew is relieved. They didn't think Fisher's severance package was going to be very generous."

"Probably a safe assumption. But their jobs are secure for now."

"Hey, Paula, can you think of anyone associated with the tour or Keith Fisher who is extra, extra large? Super-sized."

"Hmm," she said. "Nicky."

"No, it's not Hagipetros."

"Some of those bodyguards Keith hired for Shirley were pretty hefty."

"Nah," I said. "They wore business attire. This guy was dressed more like a biker."

"Which guy?"

"Someone who was spotted backstage at the Portland show," I said. "I'm still trying to nail down the last few questions about Jake Karn."

There was a long moment of silence on the line. I thought perhaps Paula was dealing with someone else in her office and had her hand over the mouthpiece. Then she spoke. "No one comes to mind. If I think of any big specimens, I'll call you on the batphone."

"You know, when you think of it," I said. "Rock is really a small man's sport. I mean, Mick Fleetwood was tall, but that's about it. I bet rock 'n roll heaven has low ceilings."

"Sebastian Bach is a pretty big boy," she said.

"How would you know?"

"Goodbye, Jim," she said, pretending to be fed up with me.

"Wait. What about this weekend? Don't you want directions to Winsted?"

"Just give me the address, I'll get a driving map off Yahoo."

After we made some tentative arrangements, I hung up and dialed my sponsor, assuming I'd get his machine too. But Chris picked up on the third ring. I tried to remember if my horoscope that morning had promised anything about my extraordinary success in getting people on the phone.

After the usual pleasantries, he asked where I was. "Sitting in my living room," I said.

"You're not chaperoning Shirley anymore?"

"Got the boot from his manager."

"You're kidding," Chris said. "What can you do that's so heinous it gets you kicked off the—what is it?—'Evil Incarnate' tour?"

"Triumph of the Antichrist," I corrected him. "And apparently all you have to do is keep asking questions."

"That makes you a gigantic pain in the ass in most settings. You get any answers?"

"Nothing concrete," I said. "Aww, hell, who am I kidding? I don't even have anything diaphanous."

"What's your theory, Quincy?"

That's a question I had heard from Chris a hundred times. In my first years of recovery, Chris and I hung out a lot, dividing our time between meetings and movies. We must have hit every AA group and every theater between Eighty-sixth Street and Battery Park.

If the film was a mystery, Chris would lean over sometime in the first twenty minutes and ask, "What's your theory, Quincy?" I would hazard a guess and then he would designate his pick. The loser paid for the concession-stand goodies.

Let's just say I bought him a ton of popcorn. I once asked him how he was able to spot the bad guy before the first reel was half over. "Logic," he said, "instinct . . . and thousands of movies." Now whenever I was locked in a perplexing case, he would pop the question.

"I'm still leaning toward Fisher," I said. "He was determined to have me sent home. And somebody tried to kill me in Catoga Falls. He's the only one who knew I was going there."

"Him and Paula," Chris pointed out.

"I think we can safely rule her out," I said.

"Ah-ha. You two a tag team now?"

"Getting there. She's coming to spend the weekend."

"That's great," he said. "Too bad she works for your primary suspect."

"There's plenty of those to go around," I said. "You know Jake was developing quite an appetite for chemicals near the end."

"Yeah."

"And he might have been extorting people too. I know he had dirt on that guitarist who OD'd. I think he was telling people that if they didn't get him drugs, he would have them fired."

"That's a dangerous game."

"If he squeezed one of them hard enough, maybe they killed him," I said. "So that's my lineup. What's your theory?"

"Umm, I'm sticking with the preacher. Just a hunch."

"There's a lot of bluster there," I said, "but he's never displayed any outright aggression toward Shirley."

"I think the reverend has cards he ain't showing."

"They all do," I wailed. "Did I tell you the deacon in Isaacson's church is her father?"

"Jacinda's?"

"Yes. And she gets rabid if anyone comes between her and Shirley. And I certainly wouldn't dismiss the star of our show from consideration."

"Come on," said Chris. "Jake was his oldest friend."

"Friends that were getting increasingly alienated as the tour went along. Jake was trying to sell tacky posters of him behind his back, for Christ's sake. And you can't imagine how seriously Shirley takes himself, like he's the high priest of song. That must have been an awful betrayal for him. And he still hasn't explained his initial reaction—how he knew it was going to happen to Jake."

"I wouldn't put too much stock in that," Chris said. "Rock stars get used to talking in this obscure burning-bush style because fans and journalists are hanging on their every word. And they want to sound deep. So they say all kinds of crazy shit. I don't think Jim Morrison had any idea what he was talking about half the time." There was a pause during which Chris was evidently reading my mind. "You're still hovering over Shirley. You think he killed Tommy too, don't you?"

"It's the timing," I said. "They have this fight onstage in Cincinnati and the next day Tommy is dead. And I just found out that Jacinda slept with Tommy."

"My, my," said Chris. "This is a busy little tour."

"Shirley's not supposed to know about it but maybe he did. I wouldn't be surprised if Jacinda threw it in his face during one of their arguments. Anyway, I need to focus on Jake, not Tommy. And my trip to Boston gave a whole new take on this investigation."

"I *knew* you were holding out on me," he said.

I gave him the unexpurgated version of my encounter with Joey Stamps. He made no comments until I was finished. "I think you're insane to confront this guy alone in his house. You don't want someone suffering from amphetamine psychosis to perceive you as a dire threat. But Jesus—a coked-out drug dealer who is armed to the teeth? I'm bumping this guy immediately near the top of my list."

"Jake wasn't shot," I reminded him.

"No, but if you're trying to force some guy who is afraid of heights to climb up on a platform two hundred feet in the air, a gun makes a pretty good argument."

"My next priority is identifying this menacing giant who was lingering in the hall when Joey left."

"Shouldn't be too hard to find," Chris said.

"That's what I'm thinking."

"Where do you start?"

"Portland. I'm going back up there," I said. "Whatever happened that night, it all seems to have gone through the press room."

# CHAPTER 29

I stuck around to attend my home group, which meets on Wednesday nights in the basement of the Episcopalian church. I notched another restful night in my bed and got an early start to Maine. It was a pleasant drive up to Portland with the windows open and the tape deck blaring. I worked my way through Steely Dan, Third Eye Blind, the Goo Goo Dolls, the Dixie Chicks and an old Leo Kotke favorite. I had on Pharoah Sanders when I pulled into town a little after eleven A.M.

I went straight to the public library and hunted down some weeks-old copies of the *Portland Standard-Union*. I started with the date immediately after the concert, the day when I had first flown up and met Shirley. Nothing there. But in the following day's edition, the Leisure section contained a six-inch review under the headline:

## SLAUGHTERHOUSE
## FAILS TO SHOCK

I think Ebenezer Scrooge is the patron saint of rock critics. They're always so damn grumpy. This was a typically dyspeptic account of the show, raking Shirley for "a derivative rehash of carnival theatrics that were tried back when Alice Cooper had a fully functioning liver."

I shot up a little prayer of thanks right there in the back of the periodical section of the Portland Public Library. In AA we say that coincidences are God's way of acting anonymously. I had definitely caught a break here. The review was written by Steve Harrington, a guy I had known since Alice Cooper punch lines had currency.

Steve was a journeyman journalist. His career had peaked when he was a rock critic—and a good one—for the *Philadelphia Inquirer.* His downfall was a review of an R.E.M. concert at the Spectrum. It was an innocuous, you might even say generic, description of the performance. The problem was Steve didn't find out until after the article had run in the paper that the group had canceled the show at the last minute after Michael Stipe came down with a stomach flu. I can't recall Steve's excuse—there were extenuating circumstances involving a girlfriend—but his editors were unrelenting. A couple of weeks later he went to work for the *Atlantic City Press,* covering the casino shows.

For the past decade, he had been drifting north, hiring on for shorter and shorter periods of time with papers in smaller and smaller markets. Now he was in Maine. I figured he was one short hop away from handicapping the Juno Awards for a rag up in the Canadian maritime provinces. Yeesh! I enjoyed reading Annie Proulx's novel *Shipping News* but I wouldn't want to live it.

While I had the stack of *Standard-Union*s in front of me, I searched through for more of Steve's concert and record reviews. The writing showed evidence of fatigue but Harrington was still observant. I gave him a call at the paper and got his voice mail. Where was my knack for getting through to people on the phone when I needed it?

I didn't leave a message because I didn't have time to wait or a place for Steve to call me back. Instead I dialed the *Standard-Union* switchboard and asked for the Leisure editor.

"Jane Bykovsky," was the stern salutation. This was a woman with deadlines and no time to waste.

"Yeah, hi, I'm trying to reach Steve Harrington," I said.

"Join the club," she semi-mumbled. Then in a clearer voice she said, "He's not here right now."

"Do you know where I can reach him?"

"Who's calling?"

"This is Craig Cavanaugh from Mercury Records. We're having a special showcase for one of our artists down in Boston tonight and I wanted to invite Steve." I had no compunctions about lying to a newspaper editor. I figured turnabout was fair play. She gave me Steve's home number.

"Hello?" Steve sounded a little groggy when he picked it up on the fourth ring.

"Hey, Steve? It's Jim McNamara. How you doin', man?"

It took him a few seconds, but he managed to locate me on his mental Rolodex. "Long time, man. What's going on?"

"I'm here in Portland. I need to talk to you," I said. "Can we get together?"

"I don't know," he said. "I'm kind of busy this . . . afternoon." I imagined him during that brief pause looking urgently around the room for clues as to what part of the day I had roused him in.

"I'll buy you lunch," I said. "Anywhere you want to go." He told me to meet him in twenty minutes at a restaurant called Gentry's and gave me the location.

When it comes to print reporters, there is no bait more dependable than free food. When I was working at the record company, we used to joke that the most endangered species in the world was the shrimp at a press buffet.

Gentry's turned out to be an upscale steak house. No surprise there. The stunner was Steve's appearance. The years had been merciless. He barreled into the dining room and over to my table when I waved. He was wearing red Keds, tan corduroy pants with patches where the ridges had vanished completely and a short-sleeve seersucker shirt that was so wrinkled it looked like it had been at the bottom of a time capsule. What made it sad is that I was sure Steve had dressed for the occasion. After rooting through his wardrobe, this was the most presentable outfit he could come up with.

He had gained an enormous amount of weight, but it looked like he had accomplished this by eating out of Dumpsters. He didn't just seem fat; he was lumpy. His hair was gray and he had grown a beard, but it couldn't hide his puffy face or his bee-stung eyes. He reminded me of a dialysis patient on welfare. Another grizzled veteran of the rock 'n roll wars.

Steve crashed down in his chair. He didn't bother shaking hands. He was too busy spearing the menu. He flicked his eyes at me and said, "Good to see you, man." Then he devoted his attention to the entrées. Clearly he wanted to get his order in before I asked him for whatever favor I had in mind.

A craggy old waiter approached the table with surprising alacrity. He must have sensed Steve's fervor. With his tired toreador jacket and sour expression, the waiter belonged to the league of steak house servers, an order more ancient than the Knights Templar. His voice was just ingratiating enough to solicit a tip but his eyes and his manner both said, *Let's get this damn thing over with.*

My disheveled luncheon companion ordered a Bloody Mary, stuffed mushrooms and a cut of steak of such massive proportions that Fred Flintstone would have found it obscene. I ordered scallops. We engaged in some dilatory chitchat waiting for the food. Steve described to me his migratory path and the editorial injustices that had driven him from Bridgeport to New London to Cape Cod to here. "I'm just not as willing to put up with the bullshit," he said, scarfing down the mushroom caps. A rivulet of fungal juice ran down from his mouth as he bit into the fourth cap. He dabbed at it with his napkin, but missed the red stain that clung to his mustache thanks to his second Bloody Mary.

I asked if, after all this time, he enjoyed the work. "I still like writing about music, reviewing records. I sometimes wish more people got to read my stuff but . . ." he said, and shrugged. "The hardest part of my job is mustering up enthusiasm for rap. I have to know the names and aliases of every member of the Wu-Tang Clan and keep track of their latest arrests. I feel like a court reporter."

He told me had heard rumors of my activities from time to time, but only after he had tucked into his steak, seasoned and sour-creamed his baked potato and tasted his creamed spinach with evident satisfaction did he ask me what I wanted with him. I explained I was looking into Jake Karn's death following the Shirley Slaughterhouse concert.

"You're just getting on that? It happened weeks ago," he said. At least I think that's what he said. I was having to translate, like a dentist, through a lot of oral blockage. In this case, beef.

"Actually, I've already been up here once," I said. "At this point I'm kind of backtracking, trying to figure out what I might have missed. It would really help me if you could go over that night, tell me what you saw, who you remember passing through the press box."

"I don't know, man," he said, working away on the towering north face of his steak. "I was pretty focused on what was going on onstage. Me and that dickhead from Bath were the only reviewers working that show. There's always a lot of foot traffic in the press box but usually they're passing behind me. I hardly notice them. Sorry, man."

"Did you see Jake Karn that night?" I asked.

Steve ruminated while he chewed. "I think I did," he said. "I mean, I didn't know him or anything but the day after the show, I was in the office and my editor called up a wire photo of the guy to run with his death notice. She didn't end up using it because the quality of the picture was shitty and no one had any idea who he was anyway. But when I saw it, I kind of remembered seeing him come through the box a couple of times."

"Do you remember who he was with?"

"Nah. Like I say, there's always a lot of people passing

through there to get downstairs. I try to screen out the distractions."

"Anything at all that night catch your attention, seem out of place?"

Harrington shook his head. I reflexively shied away, as you would when a wet dog shimmies itself. I was afraid I might catch some spray off Steve's beard. "It was a pretty unremarkable night," he said. "But I thought it was pretty weird to see Jumpy there."

"Who's Jumpy?"

"Oh, man, Jumpy Brown? He's bad news."

"Never heard of him."

"Really?" Steve said, plowing another forkful through the pool of steak sauce on his plate. "You know Keith Fisher, right?" I nodded, a little burst of adrenaline sprinting around my chest.

"Back in the day, Jumpy Brown was a notorious biker. Believe it or not, in the sixties and seventies, they used to hire chapters of bikers to provide concert security. A lot of times the promoters would pay them with beer and speed. It was like asking a pack of wolves to watch over your sheep— all these drunk badasses storming around cracking the skulls of these skinny, peace-and-love hippies. It was like the Democratic Convention in Chicago every weekend.

"Back then, Fisher was managing New Riders of the Purple Sage, or maybe it was the summer he was promoting Ten Years After. I forget. But the way I heard it, he saw Jumpy in action stomping some kid at a racetrack outside Atlanta during a set by the Elvin Bishop Band. Apparently he admired Jumpy's enthusiasm for the job. So he put him on his payroll. Jumpy was Fisher's bodyguard before Nicky."

I was nodding along, following the bouncing ball of his narrative. "There are a lot of stories from that era. Jumpy supposedly beat up a promoter in Cleveland, put him in the hospital. And there was some singer—I can't remember his name but he always reminded me of Eric Carmen—and he wanted Fisher to renegotiate his contract. Wouldn't take no for an answer. So Jumpy depantsed the guy and threw him out of a moving limo on Central Park West. Their little partnership ended when Jumpy raped and knocked around some girl real bad down in Tallahassee and Fisher fired his ass. Or maybe Jumpy just vanished. I heard it both ways."

"That's like, what? Twenty years ago? And you haven't seen the guy since," I said incredulously. "And you recognize him when he walks into a press box here?"

Steve laughed. "Trust me, Jumpy makes an impression that stays with you. And he really hasn't changed all that much." He was prodding the outsized bone that remained on his plate. For a moment, I really thought he was going to pick it up and gnaw on it. "Besides," he said, laying down his silverware, "I didn't say I hadn't seen him."

"You stayed in touch with Jumpy?"

"I caught up with him again a year ago when I was working down on the Cape. Jumpy was a bouncer at this really great funky bar down in P-town. I went out there to see the Incredible Casuals play and there was Jumpy, big and ugly as ever."

"You talked to him?"

"Yeah," Steve said. "We caught up. Turned out Jumpy had been in Massachusetts for a while. Done some time at Walpole for aggravated assault. That's why I was surprised to see him up here in Portland a few weeks ago, because I know he wasn't supposed to leave the state without permission from his PO. They keep convicted felons on a pretty short leash. Unless you're a rapper."

"Did you talk to him that night?"

"Didn't get a chance," Steve said, using his fingers to try to prize out a shred of meat caught between his teeth. "I caught him going by out of the corner of my eye. Like I say, Jumpy is hard to miss. Anyway, I called out to him but the music was pretty loud. I don't think he saw me."

"Was he with anyone? Maybe Jake Karn?" Yes, Your Honor, I was leading the witness.

"Not that I remember."

"You know where Jumpy lives?" I asked.

"Unless he moved, he's in Truro Beach," Steve said. "You want to get some dessert?"

I encouraged Steve to go for the strawberry-covered cheesecake and I happily sat there, sipping coffee, while he ate two pieces.

# CHAPTER
## 30

If my trip to Portland had been a dead end, I probably would have had to drop the investigation. But now I had a thread and I was determined to unravel it. And I knew that Anderson & Finch was about to cut Fisher a fat settlement check and it rankled me that he was going to profit from Jake Karn's death. I drove south.

My reporter friend wasn't off by much. Jumpy was still on the Cape, but he had moved a few miles inland, to a salt-stained shack in a desolate section of East Brewster. I sat in my car, parked in the side lot of a gas station near the bathrooms, sipping Quickie Mart coffee and staring at Jumpy's corncrib.

An Olds 88, patched with orange Bondo, sat on cinderblocks in the sandy turnaround in front of the house. A few yards away, a Harley which hadn't seen much action lately hunched beneath a sloppily arranged drop cloth, the edge of the dark blue tarp snapping in the gusts of a raw northern wind. The only vehicle on the weedy lot that looked halfway serviceable was a funky Chevy Corsica with a broken taillight.

The door opened and Jumpy headed for the Chevy. There

was no doubt in my mind that I had found my man. Unless East Brewster had the distinction of harboring two ogres, which seemed unlikely. Harrington was right: Jumpy created quite an impression.

The guy who lumbered out of that cottage, twisting sideways and stooping slightly to get through the doorframe, was the bluntest object I had ever seen. His legs could have been used as pier piles. He was wearing a blue jean jacket cut off at the shoulders. Of course, it's possible, given the hammy size of his biceps, that his arms had simply atomized the sleeves.

His trunk and chest were so broad and stolid, I was surprised some enterprising kid hadn't tagged them with graffiti. What freaked me out was that his head, which could have served as a battering ram, was proportionally bigger than the rest of him. It looked like a big old janitor's bucket sitting upside down on top of a double-wide refrigerator.

Jumpy had passed the half-century mark. That was evident from the stiff way he had stomped across the yard, stirring up a small dust storm with each step, like some Hell's Angel version of Pig Pen. And the years showed in his face, which was more wrinkled than a ripple tank. But you still wouldn't want to get on his bad side. And from where I sat, he appeared to have nothing but a bad side.

The car belched a big cloud of gray smoke in protest when Jumpy cranked the engine. I don't think Jumpy had much confidence the Chevy would start. He kept the door open and one elephantine leg braced on the ground while he turned the key. Only when the car had stopped hacking and cursing and had established a restless sort of idle did he pull his leg in and accelerate toward the street, the tires spewing sand.

At a discreet distance, I trailed him east on Route 6A. After my last experience in Massachusetts, I wasn't about to corner Jumpy in his lair. If a minor scumbag like Joey Stamps had two guns in his house, I couldn't imagine what kind of arsenal a card-carrying renegade biker like Jumpy would have. Then again, he didn't look like he'd need much in the way of accessories to be lethal. In fact, as I drove, I even shot up a prayer that whatever happened I wouldn't have to get close enough to smell his breath.

Somewhere between Brewster and East Dennis, he jolted into the parking lot of an old weathered roadhouse. I stopped in front of a battered linoleum warehouse next door. Jumpy got out, flexed his neck, which resembled a mushroom stem beneath that massive head, and crossed the wooden porch into the bar. The Chevy, relieved of his bulk, bounced on its springs like a jack-in-the-box.

There were only four other vehicles when I pulled in the lot. And one of them was a van that looked an awful lot like the one that had tried to run me off the road in Shirley's hometown in western Pennsylvania. Except it carried Massachusetts plates. But that didn't stop my heart from beating double-time in my chest as I headed across the lot.

I don't want to give the impression that I was stepping into the lion's den nonchalantly. The previous evening, I had called the Portland police, explained my business and was connected with a Detective Aaron Pressley. After I made a wisecrack about how I bet he got assigned all the rock 'n roll cases, the unamused detective had spelled out his last name for me.

Obviously, this guy had been hearing Elvis jokes his whole life and had yet to find any of them funny. I told him what I had discovered about Jumpy being at the concert, waiting backstage while Jake Karn bought drugs. I let him know that I was planning on looking up the massive Mr. Brown the next day and asked if he would like to accompany me.

"Who are you working for?" he asked me with a rising inflection, as if I were some guy reporting a flying saucer over my dairy farm. I informed him of my proud allegiance to the insurance industry. Might as well have said Priscilla.

The detective reminded me that the case of Jake Karn was now closed, ruled an accidental death, and that all I really knew at this point was that Jumpy had been in the arena that night. Of course so had fifteen thousand other people. No one had even seen Jumpy and Jake together. I tried to extract a promise from Detective Pressley that if I suddenly vanished after my trip to the Cape, he would at least try to remember Jumpy's name. "Yeah, sure," he said wearily.

Going in the door of the Bayview Tavern, I clutched the piece of protection that I had hastily secured on the drive down. At a bait and tackle shop, I had bought one of those metal saps shaped like a miniature baseball bat. Sport fishermen keep them on their boats to bludgeon any big fish they pull in to stop them from flopping around wildly on the deck.

What else was I going to do? Hire some rented muscle? It's strictly against the private eye code to retain bodyguards. We're supposed to take our lumps. But it did raise an interesting question. How many goons would it take to subdue Jumpy? Is two enough? Is three too many?

The first thing that hit me when I walked through the door was the smell, a fetid odor that I hoped was coming from the bay outside, not from the kitchen. A long bar, scarred and scorched, ran along one side of the expansive, low-ceilinged room. Fastened to the wall behind the bar was a grimy, mottled mirror that gave all the liquor bottles arranged on shelves in front of it a dusty, antiquated appearance. A heavyset man with bristly, balding white hair tended the bar with narrow eyes and a scowl. He had the appearance of a superannuated graduate student, taking a double major in disappointment and constipation.

The sightlines in the room were obstructed by a number of wooden pillars arranged in no discernible pattern. Patrons of the tavern had chiseled their initials and various inspirational mottoes into these posts over the years. There was a worn pool table over in the corner farthest from the door, and tables and plastic chairs sitting unoccupied in clumps around the room. Curiously there were no chairs arranged near the long, mullioned window that ran most of the length of one wall, affording a view of a magnificently mildewed wooden deck and the gray water that lay beyond. Apparently customers of the Bayview were not interested in savoring this maritime vista.

Jumpy was sitting near the end of the bar closest to the hanging TV set and the pool table, sipping a beer. The brown, long-necked bottle was nearly eclipsed in his huge, coarse hands. He was the only guy I've ever seen who looked like he could catch Randy Johnson without using a glove.

Sitting next to Jumpy was his physical opposite. Actually the spindly, hawk-faced, hollow-eyed guy with the goatee didn't sit anywhere for long. He was a whirl of constant, nervous motion, leaning over the bar, flipping his drink coaster, orbiting around Jumpy, twitching his head. If he was a kid, you would have pegged him as a candidate for Ritalin. But when you see someone that jittery at his age, you assume they're already self-medicated.

I tried to choose a spot at the bar where I could eavesdrop on this jailhouse Oliver and Hardy but it wasn't easy. Not that I thought either of them would recognize me. But men have to observe very strict rituals of spacing in public settings. We're instinctual proponents of *Lebensraum*. Unless crowded into proximity, watch how far apart we automatically sit on airport shuttle buses, in movie theaters and restaurants. We engage in instant, exacting calculations whenever we enter a busy men's room, to determine the optimal urinal, i.e., farthest from the ones in use.

Because Jumpy and his friend were alone at the bar—a couple of blue-collar guys were drinking at a table near the door—immutable male rules dictated that I bisect the plane, choosing a stool halfway down the bar. To sit any closer would be a clear-cut violation of their airspace and would have immediately drawn their attention and suspicion.

Apparently not one to mince words, the bartender approached me and, with a remarkably economical lift of his head, inquired what libation he might have the pleasure of serving me. I ordered a Coke. I actually wanted a Diet Coke but I was determined to show him I could be almost as sparing of words as he was.

Meanwhile, Jumpy's friend continued to orbit him like an unstable electron, keeping up a running stream of commentary in a thick Massachusetts accent. Patches of his soliloquy drifted over to me. The basic building block of his vocabulary was the word "pisser" which had numerous applications, most of them positive. With his sibilant voice, whenever he said "pisser," it sounded like a snake hissing. But he did confirm I was trailing the right behemoth, addressing his larger companion by name.

Jumpy sat placidly, looking straight ahead, taking pulls on his beer. Finally, he sat back on the stool, stretched and reached into the rear pocket of his jeans. His companion froze the moment Jumpy's hand reached behind, staring at the motion with the fixed attention of a hunting dog. The transaction happened so fast it was almost a feat of prestidigitation.

Jumpy placed a folded manila envelope on the bar. His hot-wired buddy slapped some cash in the biker's mammoth paw, where it quickly disappeared. The thin man had scooped up the envelope and was gone before you could say "pisser." I could hear his van starting out in the lot while the door of the tavern was still swinging shut. It was an exit worthy of Speedy Gonzalez.

Moving with considerably more deliberation, Jumpy drained his beer, belched loudly, pushed up off his stool and rumbled for the exit. I watched him pass me in the germy reflection of the bar mirror. He looked like Bluto heading across a rolling deck in gale-force winds to mash a helpless Popeye. As soon as he was gone, I got up to follow, throwing a couple of bucks on the bar. Instead of appreciating the tip, the bartender snarled at me as if I had insulted him. There's just no pleasing some people.

I figured the parking lot of the Bayview was as good a place as any to confront Jumpy. I was certain the element of surprise was still on my side.

I was wrong.

# CHAPTER
## 31

It had started raining while I was inside. Exhaust was spewing out of the tailpipe on the Corsica, so I pulled up the hood on my sweatshirt and hustled over, jumping across puddles in the pitted parking lot. I wanted to catch Jumpy before he pulled out. I couldn't see what he was doing in the car because all the windows were fogged up. I hoped Jumpy had a good defroster because this guy could steam up a bus. I was parked right next to him so I walked in between our cars to tap on his driver's-side window.

"What the fuck you want?" The voice came from behind me, a deep, raspy growl that sounded like Nick Nolte after smoking a carton of Gauloises. I lurched about three inches straight in the air. After touching down, I turned to see Jumpy looming over me, rain dripping off his scar-bunched eyebrows. He had been waiting behind a latticed screen that concealed the tavern's garbage bins. Guess I wasn't as tricky as I thought.

"My name's Jim McNamara," I said. "I need to speak to you."

"'Bout what?"

"About the Shirley Slaughterhouse tour and the concert you went to up in Maine."

"Fuck off," he said. He pushed me without any real vehemence and I still stumbled back onto the hood of my car. I once saw Wilt Chamberlain get a little miffed with Chicago Bulls' guard Jerry Sloan during an NBA game. Wilt was giving him a lecture, jabbing Jerry in the chest with his index finger for emphasis as he made each point. Sloan was about as tough a customer as ever played in the league but each time Wilt prodded him, he sprawled backward like he was on ice skates. Jumpy's shove had the same impetus.

He opened his car door and started to lower himself in. "I didn't think cons were allowed to cross state lines without informing their PO," I said. "Did you check with yours, Jumpy?"

Jumpy glared up at me. I felt like a kid chucking rocks at an angry polar bear, like I was biting off way more trouble than I could hold in my mouth. I heaved another one anyway.

"What's the name of your friend with the van?" I asked. "Do you think your parole officer would like to hear you're dealing crank?"

It was an educated guess based on his customer's hummingbird mannerisms. Coke doesn't make you that fidgety.

Jumpy clambered up faster than I thought he could. I stepped back involuntarily. "Let me get this straight," he barked. "Are you threatening me, you fucking asswipe?"

Okay, bear with me a sec, because I'm not sure what came over me at this juncture. One of those doltish stud-rock bands from the nineties—I think it was Warrant—had a hit with a song called "I Saw Red." Well, when I heard that hoarse voice bellow that particular curse, I knew immediately where I had heard it before. And I actually did see red—like a crimson curtain lowering over my eyes. Pulling out the truncheon I was gripping in the pouch of my sweatshirt, I whacked Jumpy on the head.

Swinging from my heels, I hit him a good deal harder than I would have liked. The club made a sickening, hollow *klonk* against his skull, like the sound of someone going deep in the College World Series.

I have to say Jumpy took it well. In every sense. His knees didn't even buckle. He blinked a couple of times and shook his head. But he never went down. I stood there watching him with trepidation, waiting for his rage to boil up. I assumed I was about to get a thorough stomping. But Jumpy didn't get mad. If anything, he seemed calmer after I walloped him, as if a savage shot to the head had improved his mood.

That's not to say he didn't react. He reached over and grabbed my hand, lifting it over my head and squeezing it so tightly that I couldn't drop the club, although I was trying to. But holding my service hand appeared to be more an act of reflexive preservation than a prelude to retaliation. Standing there in the rain, we must have looked like a victorious flyweight boxer having his glove held in the air by a very large referee.

Jumpy looked at me and said, "What the fuck?"

"You shot at me," I shouted, hoping that indignation would restore me to equal footing with this giant. "In Pennsylvania!"

"I know I shot at you, you dumb fuck," he said, lifting my arm a little higher, forcing me to lift my heels off the ground. "I recognized you as soon as you came in the bar. But what was that for?" As he said that, he wriggled the club in my hand, mashing my fingers painfully on the barrel.

"When people try to kill me," I said, spitting the words out through lips constricted with pain, "I get a little bent out of shape."

"I wasn't trying to kill you."

"No?"

"No way," he said, releasing my arm. "Look, if you want to talk, get in the car." He shook some of the rain off his hair, opened his door and climbed in. I tossed the metal bat in the back seat of my car, reasoning that nothing short of a bazooka was going to help me if this guy got angry. In any event, I had the answer to my earlier question: Three. It would definitely take three goons to subdue Jumpy. Satisfied with my math, I walked around to the passenger side of the Corsica and climbed in.

The process of settling into the front seat entailed some minor landscaping. The upholstery covers were just tattered remnants, held together by a few stubborn strands. Rapidly decomposing foam cushioning bulged out. The rear window on the passenger side was gone and opaque plastic was taped over the frame. Fast-food wrappers, empty beer cans and other refuse were scattered everywhere. As I shifted piles around, I banged my shins against the glove box door, which was hanging straight down. Jumpy was grappling with something under the dash, turning his face toward me.

"The wipers short out sometimes," he said, before giving up and sitting back. "What's your deal, McNamara?"

"Explain to me again how you weren't trying to kill me with all those bullets."

"Don't be a pussy," he scoffed. "I was backing up about thirty miles an hour. I was just squeezing off shots . . . firing blind. I wasn't trying to hit you."

"Well, you came awfully close," I protested.

He shrugged.

"That van you were driving," I said. "Is it the same one that guy just pulled out in?"

"Yeah," he said. "I borrowed it from Rodney."

"But it had Pennsylvania tags."

He looked over at me as if I were a little slow. "Like I'm going to drive around with a loaded pistol and out-of-state plates? I swiped 'em off a minivan."

"That brings us to the bonus question: Why were you shooting at me at all?"

"Keith asked me to."

"Keith Fisher? Why?"

"He said there was trouble with his Shit on a Shingle-house tour. That you were there 'cause you had some dumbasses convinced you were a detective. He said he wanted to give Columbo a real mystery to worry about."

"So you were supposed to scare me?"

Jumpy shrugged. Then he drew in a deep breath, threw his shoulders back and disgorged a burp of startling volume. In the confines of the car, it sounded like a thunderclap. "He told me to peg a few shots at you, said he didn't care if you got hit."

"What?"

"You gotta understand Keith," he said. "That meant he didn't want you hurt."

"How much did he pay you, Jumpy?"

"It's not about money with me and Keith. We go way back."

"How much?"

"Two hundred."

"You borrowed a van and drove from the Cape all the way to some remote town in western Pennsylvania. Then you stalked me and—"

"Believe me," he interrupted. "You weren't hard to find."

"—ran me off the road and fired six shots at me all for a lousy two hundred bucks?"

"Come to think of it, Keith never did pay me."

I threw up my hands in dismay. "So this was a recreational trip for you."

"I don't get you, man," Jumpy said, kneading the back of his neck with his right hand. In the process, he gave me an unobstructed view of the gnarliest armpit I have ever seen. "Would you feel better if I got paid more?"

"Forget it," I said. "Tell me about Portland."

"Tell you what?"

"What were you doing there?"

Jumpy shifted, sitting forward to hunch over the steering wheel. The seat complained loudly. "I'll tell you what went down, McNamara. Because I don't give a rat's ass. But if I'm asked to repeat any of this in front of a cop or in a courtroom, I will deny every single word of it. And if any of this does come back," he said, looking over at me for emphasis, "you will have made a very bad enemy. Got that?" I used my middle finger to cross my heart.

"Keith asked me to come up to Portland. He wanted me to lean on the talent."

"Shirley? Why?"

"He was threatening to quit. Right in the middle of the tour. Spoiled little prick. And Keith wanted me to convince him that it wasn't a healthy option."

"You were going to beat him up?" Jumpy just smirked. "But why would he bring you in to intimidate Shirley? Why not just use Nicky?"

Jumpy sat back and folded his massive arms over his chest. "I do scary pretty well," he said smugly.

"Did you?" I asked. "Scare Shirley?"

"Didn't have to. Keith called me at the arena. Told me it was taken care of."

"I don't understand."

"Keith had the guy's girlfriend on his payroll. She talked him out of quitting before I got there."

I marveled at what a busy girl Jacinda was, working all sides against the middle. "So there you are in Portland—all dressed up and no one to terrorize. What'd you do?"

Jumpy looked at me and smiled thinly. "Somehow I think you already know the answer."

"Humor me."

"I partied with what's his name—Jake."

"Where'd you know him from?"

"The show played Providence a few days before that. Keith got me some backstage passes, like he usually did when he had a tour coming through town. After the concert I was hanging out with some of the crew. It was a pretty wild scene. Anyway, that kid Jake was there and I turned him on to some crank."

"You just gave drugs to a stranger," I said skeptically. "Why so generous, Jumpy?"

"It's a calculated risk. Most dealers do it. You give guys a taste or two and fifteen minutes later they want to buy every last gram you're carrying."

"Is that how it played out with Jake?"

"It would have. But he said he had a big stash waiting for him back in his hotel room. He invited me to go back. Said we could party with the band's guitarist. He was trying to impress a couple of chicks who were there. I couldn't go."

"Why not?"

"I had to meet somebody," he said. "Anyway, when Keith asked me to lean on his rock star, I called up Jake to let him know I was going to be at the show in Maine. He was like, 'Great, I'll take care of everything. I owe you for last week.'"

"Did you know that Jake and Shirley were tight?"

"You kidding? He must have told me ten times in Providence. Every word out of his mouth was Shirley this and Shirley that."

"So you were going to party with the guy and then slap around his best friend?"

Jumpy shook his head. "Nah, I would have leaned on the talent before we started getting high. Business before pleasure, man. Besides, I tend to lose track of time when I'm partying."

"So Jake came through for you?"

"Yeah. He had the full party pack. Copped it from some guy after the show—pot, coke, Ecstasy, you name it. We even had a refrigerator full of beer."

"Sounds like a good time."

Jumpy jerked up one corner of his mouth to indicate ambivalence. "It was all right," he said grudgingly. "He kept saying he asked some girls to join us but they never showed. We were at the arena for like four hours . . . just the two of us in this room. The drugs were good, though."

"So what happened?"

"Nothing. We went at his stash hard. By the time we went through everything, it was just before three. I told him I was going to drive down to Revere to see this chick I know. He said he was going to head back to the hotel. I asked him if he wanted a ride. He said no. So I split."

"Did you see anyone on your way out?"

Jumpy thought about it for a second. "No. The place was like a graveyard. I was pretty wasted anyway."

"After all that crank?"

"Yeah, but I was drinking pretty heavy too. Yin and yang, man." He scoffed, as if this idea were amusing.

"You know Jake died there that night. Right around the time you say you were partying together."

"I heard," he said without a trace of guilt, or any other emotion, for that matter.

Sitting there in the car with the windows all fogged up, it felt like Jumpy and I were suspended in some limbo. I suppose we were sort of floating in a cloud of the big guy's funk. I noticed the steady patter on the roof had stopped. I rolled my window down an inch.

"Stopped raining," I pointed out.

"Yeah," said Jumpy. "So you want to buy some crank?"

# CHAPTER
## 32

The ride home from the Cape took me through Fall River, the ancestral home of Lizzie Borden, another person who, like Shirley, was renowned for killing parents. That got me thinking about Jake and his macabre posters. I took stock of everything I knew about Jake's final hours, a mental inventory I finished before I got to the Rhode Island state border. There wasn't much to mull over.

I had Jake stoned and alone in the arena at three in the morning. I wondered why he had turned down a ride back to the hotel. Maybe he was meeting someone at that ungodly hour. Maybe there was no logical explanation at all. Jake's brain was probably limping in circles after the chemical smorgasbord he shared with Jumpy. But I knew that someone with acrophobia wasn't going up on that catwalk willingly—no matter how stoned he was. And I figured that fact alone might be enough to persuade Detective Pressley to reopen the case. Outside Providence, I decided that first thing Monday I would lobby the policeman.

First I had to prepare for Paula's visit. For me that meant a couple of hours going through my library of CDs and tapes, preselecting the music I wanted to have playing. Sure,

I might have made more profitable use of my time by
straightening up: vacuuming, changing the sheets, all that
junk. But I figured I could scrub from now 'til Tuesday and
never approach the exacting standards of hygiene adhered to
by the female of the species. Anytime a girl visits a guy's
crib, it's something of a Margaret Meade expedition. When
it comes to domestic maintenance, me Tarzan, you Jane.

Besides, I've always thought ambience was far more important than decor. That could be why I still live alone.

Anyway, I took a second pass through my selections,
weeding out the pretentious (jazz and classical) and the obvious (James Taylor and Rickie Lee Jones). That left me
with a strong, flavorful lineup, cocaptained by those crafty
old veterans Van Morrison and Stevie Wonder.

I was sure Paula had an active itinerary planned for us. I
don't know why it is but New Yorkers seem to get all fired
up when they visit the country. They want to get outside,
wear sweaters, get dew on their Timberlands, breathe in lots
of fresh air, mingle with the natives. Anything outside the
five boroughs they treat like some sort of rustic theme park.

If I had my druthers, we would have never left the house.
I looked upon the weekend as a chance for us to get reac-
quainted physically. I envisioned one long stretch of snug-
gling interrupted only by foraging for snacks.

We didn't get a chance to implement either plan. Shortly
after she arrived in a snazzy green Saab convertible, we were
chatting in the kitchen while a Wallflowers' CD played.
Then Paula's cell phone rang.

"Damn," she said with annoyance. "I'm sorry, Jim." She
looked down at the display. "I told my office not to contact
me unless it was an emergency. . . . Hello? . . . Okay, give
me the number." With her hand, she pantomimed scribbling
and I gave her a pad and pen. "Right. 'Bye."

"It's Shirley," she said as she punched in the number she
had just written down. She listened for a moment, then
spoke into the receiver. "Yes. Room 1402, please." There
was a brief pause while she was connected. "Hi, it's Paula."

As she listened, she looked up at me, a look of deep surprise on her face. "It just so happens I do. Yeah." Frowning, she proffered her phone to me. "It's Shirley. He wants to talk to you."

I took the phone from her. "Hello?"

"Hey. It's Shirley. Someone sent me a death threat. Could you help me? I don't know who else to turn to." Shirley's voice sounded anxious and scared, but I wasn't buying it. Hell, I wasn't even kicking the tires.

"Come on, Shirley," I said. "I don't know what stupid game you're playing but I'm not in the mood."

"I'm not making this up," he said. "Somebody is trying to kill me. For real."

# CHAPTER

## 33

I pointed out to Shirley that my ability to help was greatly hampered by my banishment. I had been drummed out of his bugle corps.

"I talked to Keith," he said. "You're back on board."

"Just like that?"

"Please, Jim," he said importunately. "I'm asking for your help here." That was the first time he had used my name. It occurred to me that he really must be desperate.

"Shirley, you've already got bodyguards. What am I going to do?"

"Do you want me to beg? Is that what you want?"

"No. I want you to level with me for once. Why do you want me out there?"

"You don't . . . Because I trust you. Is that so hard to understand?"

I was struck again by his awful isolation. But what decided me was the possibility that I might actually be able to solve Jake's murder.

"This better not be a joke, Shirley," I said.

"It isn't. Please hurry." He hung up.

I handed the phone back to Paula. We gazed at each other

with mutual confusion for a moment—*What the . . . ?* written all over our faces. Then we started to speak at the same time. Finally, completing our little Marx Brothers routine, we halted together too.

"You first," Paula said.

"How did he know you were with me?" I asked.

"He didn't. He called my office asking how to get ahold of you. They didn't have your number, so they called me. What did he say?"

"He says he got a death threat. The genuine article."

"He sounded pretty shaken up, Jim."

"Yeah," I said. "I think Shirley is capable of making up stories, but I don't think he would pretend to be scared. He has a weird kind of integrity."

"What are you going to do?" Paula asked.

"I'm going out to see if I can help him." I hesitated for a moment. "You know, Paula, I was really looking forward to this weekend as a chance for us to get to know each other better."

"Me too."

"Doesn't look like it's going to happen now. But something's really been weighing on my mind. So I'm just going to put it out there." She was looking at me with concern. "You remember that morning in St. Louis in the hotel lobby, when you pulled me into the vestibule and kissed me?" She bit her lower lip and nodded. I noticed she was blushing. "Were you . . . trying to keep me from seeing who Keith was with?"

"Why do you say that?"

"Because you were acting so oddly," I said. "One of the things that I find attractive about you is how self-possessed you always are. But that morning, you seemed really rattled when you first saw me. And then the next minute you were so passionate. It just wasn't like you."

She looked down and exhaled audibly. "This is so embarrassing." She lifted her gaze to meet mine, appeared to screw up her resolve and then continued. "Keith was fuming about you from the day he heard you were hired. I don't know why he has such a bug up his ass. That morning, he calls me up to his suite and tells me to go down to the lobby and make sure you're not hanging around. If you are, he says, get rid of you.

"I'm sorry, Jim. I know it sounds sleazy. And normally, I would insist that something like this is not in my job description. But Keith hates to be contradicted. Especially in front of someone he's trying to impress. So I come downstairs figuring, What are the chances Jim is going to be in the lobby? And of course, there you are, right by the front desk.

"So now I'm thinking of all these excuses of why you have to leave the lobby with me right away. And then I start feeling really guilty. Because I can't lie to you. Not for Keith." She sighed as she approached the final hurdle in her confession. "But I'm keeping one eye on the elevator bank and when I see Keith and his friends come out . . . I planted one on you. I couldn't let him run into you face-to-face without . . . uggh. Anyway, that's what was going on. Can you please forgive me?"

Actually my affection for her had risen several degrees while she was telling me that story. As a child of divorce, I understand divided loyalties. In AA we tend to be a little fanatical about honesty. That's because once you start lying to yourself or to others, you're about one foil cap away from a full-blown relapse. Mendacity is addiction's roadie. But civilians like Paula don't have to be as rigorous with the truth. So I really respected her decision to come clean with me.

"Who was Fisher meeting with?" I asked.

"Reverend Isaacson," Paula said.

Okay, maybe you saw that one coming but I sure didn't. In fact, remember Quickdraw McGraw's alter ego—El Kabong? I felt like he had just splintered a guitar on my head.

I think it's called cognitive dissonance when you can't reconcile two things in your mind. I simply couldn't fit Isaacson and Fisher—the shepherd and the fleecer—in the same frame. Why would a rock promoter meet with the guy who was trying to shut down his tour?

Lost in thought, I stalled by invoking my generation's default expression: "Wow." Then I asked, "What were they talking about?"

"I don't know," Paula said. "They had already wrapped things up by the time Keith called me in."

At that moment, her cell phone rang again. For the next several minutes, every time she finished one call, it would chime again. I guess the ripple effect from Shirley's crisis was spreading quickly.

While she talked, I went on-line. After clicking the print icon, I looked over at Paula. She had just hung up and was facing out my kitchen window, distractedly tapping a fingernail on her front teeth.

Sensing my observation, she turned and smiled at me. I've never been in a tanning booth, but I imagine the sensation is similar to having Paula look at me that way—all warm and radiant. I found myself grinning back.

"What are you doing?" she asked.

"Making flight plans for Des Moines."

"I'm coming with you," she said. "When do we leave?"

"Depends," I said, consulting my findings. "If we go right now there's a two-thirty to Chicago we could just make. Then it's a crop duster down to Iowa."

"What are you waiting for?" she asked. "Start packing."

"Well," I said, drawing the word out. "There's also a flight at six o'clock that gets us in just after ten local time."

Paula looked at me quizzically. "Why would we consider that?"

"Because," I said, "the six o'clock leaves us time to fool around."

"Jim, I'm surprised at you," she said sternly. "A man's life may hang in the balance. Is there anything around four-thirty?"

# CHAPTER

## 34

We drove to the airport in my car. Even though all our luggage was carry-on, we barely made that first flight. Because we were cutting it close, Paula put both of our tickets on her credit card. We thought doing two transactions might be too much to handle for the ticket agent, who seemed to be heavily tranquilized. When the airlines made their cutbacks after the hijacking scares, they seem to have based their staffing decisions on the demerit system. Only the incompetent survived.

"I'll write you a check," I said as we ambled to the gate. "But you better make sure Fisher doesn't see your expense report."

"If you're good I might even buy you a snack during our layover in Chicago," she said. "I was hoping to get some magazines for the flight, but I guess we don't have time."

Once we were buckled in our seats, I reached over and took Paula's hand in mine. Maybe I was holding it too tight. She looked down at our hands and back up at me and asked, "You're not afraid to fly, are you?"

"No," I said. "I just like you."

"Good," she said, and leaned over to give me a quick kiss.

"Look, it's not like I don't appreciate your company, but why did you decide to fly out with me?"

"This tour is springing leaks right and left," she said. "And that was before Shirley's life was threatened."

"So you're going out to put a positive spin on all this?"

She laughed mirthlessly. "Sometimes I think of my job as being like the official apologist for a klutz," she said. "You know, the client walks face-first into a pole, and the publicist prompts him to say, 'I meant to do that.'"

"So what poles has Shirley been hitting lately?"

"Mostly logistical problems," Paula said. "The show in Lincoln, Nebraska, Tuesday night was canceled. That worked out okay because this radio station in D.C. has been begging him to take part in their annual rock festival. Now he can. It's a good gig.

"But then Shirley announced he's staying on the east coast. He wants to cancel the next four dates because he's booked a recording studio in Philadelphia. What Shirley doesn't seem to grasp is that when he takes a night off, forty other people can't do their jobs either. Needless to say, Keith is freaking out over the lost gate."

"But not over the lost show in Nebraska? That doesn't bother Keith?"

"Nothing we can do about that," Paula said, flipping quickly through the airline magazine and slamming it back in the seat pouch. "The mayor pulled the plug. He was getting heat from religious groups. No biggie, anyway. Ticket sales were pretty slow."

"Hmm," I mused. "Paula, can you get the figures on advance sales for the Antichrist tour?"

"I guess so. Why? What's up?"

"Just something rattling around in my head."

"I'll have my office fax them to Des Moines," she said. "If Keith finds out I'm feeding you inside information, he'll lock me in a car trunk and drive me off the Chelsea piers."

I scoured the overhead bins for blankets and pillows and we cocooned into our seats. When we were settled in, our heads almost touching, Paula said, "That's not the real reason I'm flying out with you."

"Really?" I said, instantly alert, thinking she was about to reveal something further about Keith to me. "What is it?"

"I didn't want to spend the rest of the weekend alone in that dust bowl you call a house. You ever hear of a vacuum?"

"Sorry," I said. "My cleaning lady called in sick this week."

"You might want to check on her condition," Paula said. "Judging by your kitchen, I think she might be dead."

"All right, Ms. Finicky. Maybe we should only get together in hotels."

"Not in Des Moines," she said, pulling the blanket up to her chin and shifting into a comfortable position. "I'm already getting teased about us. I don't want to give them any more ammunition."

"Fine," I murmured. And the truth is, by the time we arrived at the hotel in Des Moines, I was so groggy, all I wanted was to crawl into a bed of my own and snooze. I didn't even have dinner. Maybe it was oxygen deprivation from breathing the recycled air on the planes.

When the phone rang, I was certain I had only been asleep for an hour. But I looked over at the clock and it was after eleven. "Hello," I croaked, and then, adjusting the phone so that the speaker was actually near my mouth, I repeated myself.

"Jim, it's Shirley. Could you come up to my room, please?"

"Five minutes," I said. "Order me coffee."

I had left a message at the front desk to have Shirley call me. Since the last time I had seen him, he had adopted more stringent screening measures. He was now employing a policy favored by many celebrities: No direct calls put through to his room and no messages taken unless you provide the password. No exceptions. Paula had furnished me with Shirley's magic word: Mudhoney.

I threw some water on my face, ran a comb through my hair and headed up to Shirley's suite.

He opened the door, holding an acoustic guitar in one hand. His clothes lacked their usual flamboyance. The plain black T-shirt and jeans made him look drawn and vulnerable. The room service waiter, a trim young guy who reminded me a little of Rob Lowe, finished arranging things on a table. "There you are, sir," he said. He smiled and nodded as he passed me on his way out.

I smelled coffee. Thank you, Lord. Shirley sat on a low couch, the guitar cradled in his lap, several loose pages of notes spread on the table in front of him. I made a beeline for the coffee, but before I could get there, someone shot out of the bedroom, startling me.

It was Jacinda. Dressed in a lavender peasant blouse and ragged cutoff jeans, she scurried to the food, shooting warning glances across my bow. She grabbed up a heaping plate of french fries and hugged it to her chest. Scowling at me as if I were trying to snatch it away, she backed toward the bedroom, then turned and hurried out.

I looked at Shirley to see his reaction. But the whipped-dog expression he was wearing didn't have much to do with Jacinda's hoarding instincts. I poured a cup of coffee and sat down across from him.

"You all right?" I asked. He shook his head. "Anything else bothering you besides the death threat?"

"That's not enough?" he asked sardonically, propping the guitar up on the sofa.

"May I see it?" He gestured at the papers on the table. Most of them were legal-sized, covered with lyrics and chord notations. The one he had been working on had the initials "P.S." at the top. Two stanzas below, my eye picked out the word "Buddhist." Shirley was working on an arrangement of "Preacher's Seeds." I was glad to see he had crossed out the subsequent line, ending the couplet with "nudist" instead of "Judas."

Closer to me on the table was a memo sheet, inscribed with a thick black Magic Marker. I picked it up.

> ***Drop it or you're dead by Wednesday! This is your only warning.***

I read it several times. "Drop what?" I asked.

Shirley shrugged. "I don't know."

"You have any idea who sent this?"

"No."

"But you're taking it seriously?" He nodded forlornly. "When did you get this?"

"Yesterday. Slipped under the door."

"How come there are no bodyguards out there?" I asked.

"Keith had them pulled," he said, slouching over and hugging his elbows.

"Why?" I asked with consternation.

"Tit for tat. He's angry because I decided to take a few days off to record. So now he's punishing me. He said he's not going to shell out money to protect a selfish ingrate like me."

"Did he see this?" I asked, holding up the note.

"Yes. That's when I told him I wanted you to come back. We fought about that too." That's me, all right. *Casus belli.*

"While we're on the subject of arguing with Fisher," I said, "could you clear something up for me? Did you threaten to quit the tour? Just before Jake died?"

"No," he said emphatically. "Never." His denial shot the hell out of Jumpy's story. I hadn't even been back with Shirley ten minutes and already things were getting murky. It would be comforting if there was one thing on this case that I knew for sure.

As I walked over to pour more coffee, I weighed my options. I opted for bluntness. "This note," I said. "It makes a very specific demand. What is it warning you not to do?"

"I told you," he said. "I have no idea."

"I think you do, Shirley," I said sternly. "I think you know exactly what it refers to."

We stared at each other for a long time. "I'm asking you to help me," he said plaintively.

"Then tell me who wants to kill you and why."

"I can't."

There was an even longer silence as we regarded each other closely. Finally, I said, "What happens Wednesday? Why does it specify that day?" He shrugged.

Again we fell silent. I looked at him. He gazed at the floor. For some reason, I thought that things were going to be different between us because he had practically begged me to return. But here I was again—trying to get a mule to climb a ladder. "What do you want me to do, Shirley?" I asked.

"Stay close," he said. "Watch over me."

As I was considering his request, out of the corner of my eye I saw Jacinda scoot furtively into the room, grab the ketchup bottle off the table and beat a hasty retreat.

# CHAPTER 35

There was no show that night. Rock tours generally observe the Sabbath. Not out of any sense of propriety. It's just that the union workers who run the arenas get time and a half on Sundays.

So I spent much of the next day and a half sitting in Shirley's anteroom while he and Jacinda kept company in the suite's inner sanctum. Paula came by a few times to visit and every once in a while Shirley would venture out to refresh the pile of CDs he had provided for me. It was an eclectic program: Temple of the Dog, Rufus Wainwright, Sun Ra, Kelly Joe Phelps, Marianne Faithful, De la Soul, Chet Baker, Toni Child, Fela Anikulapo Kuti, and a lot of obscure reggae artists I wasn't familiar with.

Mostly it was quiet. I felt like Horton the elephant sitting on that couch. I kept my vigil until the eleven P.M. *Sports-Center* was over and then went back to my room, making sure Shirley latched the intruder bar on his door behind me.

I resumed my post in the morning, and after a few hours of drinking coffee and reading newspapers, I called Raul and asked him to spell me for a while. I spent the afternoon doing on-line research in my room, gleaning as many details as I could about the Reverend Isaacson's activities.

Shirley called when he was ready to leave for his show at the convention center. I went up to his suite, where Raul opened the door. "Any problems?" I asked.

"Nah. Except Jacinda got out a deck of cards and insisted I play War with her. She cheats," he said, shaking his head and heading for the door. "See you at the show."

When Shirley emerged from his bedroom, Jacinda hovering behind him, he was stage-ready—in full makeup, with leather pants and a Valentine-red sequined jersey that hung loosely off his thin frame. Before we walked out the door, he slipped on a pair of big oval sunglasses and wrapped a long black shawl around his head. Nothing like being inconspicuous.

On the limo ride over, Jacinda amused herself by sticking her head out the sunroof and screeching. In an odd way, it was fitting, since she was dressed like she was going to some debauched prom, in a blowsy black satin gown, long black gloves and a black feather boa.

The gown was slit almost up to her hip. I couldn't help but notice, as she stood on the seat beside me, howling at pedestrians, that even the bruises on her legs were color-coordinated. Shirley paid no attention to her, staring into the distance with his mouth open as if he were in a trance.

Backstage, I made sure I stayed near Shirley, mostly because I could see that my presence was absolutely bugging the shit out of Keith Fisher. Every time I leaned in close to the singer, I could see Fisher grind his jaw ferociously. I remained right at Shirley's elbow.

At Raul's prompting, we walked silently to the wing of the stage. It reminded me of a boxer headed for the ring, trailed by his entourage. The snake charmer music was blaring. Two stage hands stood by to escort the band to their places on the blacked-out stage. Raul handed Shirley a headset so he could communicate with Terry.

Shirley peered intently out at the audience. "Shit," he said. "These people are dead." His assessment surprised me. The crowd looked and sounded to me as if they were about to tear the roof off the building. Shirley studied them for another minute, then grimly said into the bean-sized microphone, "Okay, do it." He immediately pulled off the headset and strode toward the stage, the band in cold pursuit.

Before Slab had even pounded out the shattering opening chords of "Blood Money," I was hurrying toward the exit. Only stragglers were left in the parking lot. The protesters from the Church of the Divine Light had already laid down their placards and were standing around chatting. I walked up to the Reverend Isaacson as he was concluding a call on his cell phone with a hearty, "God bless you, sister."

"Excuse me, Reverend," I said. "Could I talk with you for a minute?" He turned to me, his face registering neither surprise nor annoyance. With a slight lift of his eyebrows, he indicated his ambivalent assent.

"Do you think we could chat on the bus?" I asked. "This is rather confidential."

He frowned and started walking toward the vehicle. "I can't imagine what you and I might have to talk about, Mr. McNamara, that could be considered confidential."

I waited until we were on board to speak. It was a comfortable rig, with plush reclining seats. We sat across the aisle from each other in the first row. Just as I was about to start, a wide-eyed Simon Jones came tearing onto the bus. Someone in the congregation must have informed him that I had pigeonholed the boss. He stood, panting, on the platform by the driver's seat, glaring up at me.

"It's all right, Simon," Isaacson said soothingly. "I agreed to talk with Mr. McNamara. Briefly." He turned to me.

It was a little disconcerting to chat, with the deacon focusing all that hostility on me from short range. I pretended to ignore him. "You haven't been honest with me, Reverend," I said. It was a harsh opening gambit. Purposely so. Isaacson's eyes narrowed to slits. Jones gripped the partition bar by the driver's seat tightly, I think to keep from flinging himself on me.

"I don't know what that means, Mr. McNamara. But there are people outside waiting to board this bus. I don't have time for nonsense."

"You told me that on the night Jake Karn died, you left Portland as soon as the concert started and drove straight back to Ohio," I said. "I don't think that's true."

Isaacson regarded me, frowning. Before he could respond, Jones erupted. "You don't have to answer him, Reverend," he said, as tightly wound as Steve Buscemi on a bottle of Vivarin. "Let me handle this."

Without taking his eyes from mine, Isaacson lifted a pacifying palm in his lackey's direction. "I'm curious, Mr. McNamara," he said. "How did you arrive at this conclusion?"

"I've been studying your schedule closely, Reverend," I said. "You're a very busy man."

"A busy *clergyman*," he insisted.

"On the evening after Karn's death," I continued, "you were to be honored by the Christian Council of Greater Ohio. You didn't show up at your own two-hundred-dollar-a-plate testimonial." Isaacson smiled, not the reaction I was hoping for. I suddenly felt like I had called out a grid location during a game of Battleship and my opponent had gleefully shouted, "Miss!"

I finished making my point. In for a penny, in for a pound. "That really stood out," I said. "Over the last four months, even while driving all over the country to demonstrate against Shirley, you never missed a single appointment. Not even a prayer breakfast. Except for that one day. And I think that's because you stayed in Portland many hours after you originally planned to."

Isaacson's grin was undimmed. "Yes, well, I admire your diligence, Mr. McNamara," he said. "But once again, you don't have your facts straight."

He was drawing it out, enjoying the moment. "During our

previous conversation, I did tell you the bus departed soon after the concert began. That is our customary practice, one which you are currently upsetting." I started to respond. He raised his voice, trumping me. "*But* . . . I never said we drove directly back to Ohio. The fact is, our bus driver took ill. We ended up pulling over in a rest stop off the turnpike in western Massachusetts. That's why I was forced to cancel." He batted his eyes at me triumphantly.

"No offense, Reverend," I said. "But I'd like to speak with the bus driver if you don't mind."

"That won't be a problem," he said, flicking his head. "He's standing right in front of you. Before Simon became my deacon, he was a driver for Trailways. I'm sure he'd be willing to answer any questions you may have about that night."

I glanced at Jones. He was still regarding me like a pit bull trying to gnaw his way through a fence. Apparently, he didn't think any corroboration was necessary. "Get off this bus now," he said with staccato emphasis.

When I arrived backstage again, the band was in the middle of a full-throttle version of "Cold War." Paula was there, her head bobbing to the sledgehammer beat. We carried on a brief conversation by screaming into each other's ears.

"Hey," she shouted.

"You just get here?"

She bobbed her head a little faster. "I slept all day." She looked around to see who was near us. "I got the numbers you asked for." She passed me two pages that tracked advance sales for every stop on the Antichrist tour. From my pocket, I took out a list of all the reverend's far-flung protests against Shirley that I had printed up earlier. I placed the two itineraries side by side on a speaker cabinet and compared them.

"Goddamn!" I exclaimed.

"What?" said Paula, pointing at her ear.

I leaned in closely. "They have three songs left, right?" She nodded. "I'll be back soon," I said, sprinting back to the parking lot with the sheets of paper in my hand.

There had been a brief shower since I had last been outside. The asphalt was glistening. A couple of T-shirt salesmen were getting ready for the crowd to stream out. A pretzel vendor was rolling his stand up to the exit. But the Divine Light bus was gone.

I wondered when I would get a chance to confront Isaacson with my discovery. It wouldn't be the following night in Nebraska. That show had been canceled. The reverend had already seen to that.

# CHAPTER
## 36

"They were in collusion the whole time," I said vehemently into the phone. "Ripping you off."

I had already escorted Shirley back to his suite. Jacinda was in a far less manic mood during the return, withdrawing into a state of surly aggravation. This chick had some nasty mood swings. After locking them down for the night, I visited Paula to explain why I had run off like that.

Then, back in my room, I called my boss Paul Roynton at home. I was trying to infect him with the sense of outrage I felt the situation called for. But he was taking my news with remarkable calm.

"Don't you get it?" I asked. "Fisher and this preacher had it rigged. Every time the gate was soft, the minister would lobby city officials to shut the show down. Then Fisher would bilk you with a phony claim for lost revenue."

"It's certainly a new scam," Roynton said, chuckling.

"What am I missing here? Why aren't you upset?"

"Because I figured something like this was going on," he said. "I mean, I didn't know Fisher was arranging all these lost shows, but it was obvious he was anticipating them."

"You've lost me," I said.

"There was an unusual rider in Shirley's policy. Fisher insisted on it. Shows canceled for reasons outside the artist's control—other than an act of God—would get reimbursed. Not just their expenses but average gate receipts. That's a figure we won't have until the tour ends in two weeks, but it looks to be hefty.

"That clause should have raised a red flag for us. But everything we do is based on statistics. And Fisher's request seemed harmless because rock concerts never get canceled. They go on hell or high water 'cause no one wants to do make-up dates. I can't remember a rock act that had this many dates yanked. Maybe the Sex Pistols."

"It's still insurance fraud, isn't it?"

"Look, Jim," he said, like he was trying to calm a flustered parakeet banging around in its cage. "I appreciate your bringing this to my attention. Really, I do. And I will alert our legal department. But I doubt we'll take action on this."

"Why not?" I said indignantly.

"Lot of reasons," he said, ticking them off. "What you have is a suspicious coincidence. We'd still have to prove Fisher and this preacher were actively conspiring to defraud. And Fisher's middle name is litigation. Any suit we bring against him turns into a long, bitter siege. And finally, it would be bad for our image. We charge a lot to cover these tours. When we take a hit, our customers expect us to pay up without a peep. Nobody likes a sore loser."

"Really? You should talk to my HMO."

"Those guys are pickpockets," he said. "My company occupies a unique niche in the business, Jim. With rock promoters like Fisher, it's a cat-and-mouse game. We've got them over a barrel and they know it. They continually come up with shady new schemes to recoup their money. And these are *very* resourceful people, Jim. They stick it to us, we close that loophole and raise their premiums. 'Round and around. Fisher got us this time. But he's got a new act going out on the road in three weeks. Wait until he sees his bill for that one." Over the phone I could hear Roynton's laugh followed by the tinkle of ice. I think he was toasting himself.

"Where are you calling from, Jim?" he asked.

"Des Moines," I said. "I'm back on the tour."

"I thought I told you to stay away from Fisher."

I filled him on Shirley's desperate summons and the threat to his life.

"Jesus! Keep a close eye on him," he said. "That kid's got life coverage up the wazoo. Don't let anybody punch his ticket for the next two weeks and I'll double your fee. There's only like a dozen dates left on this tour."

"Less than that," I said. I explained Shirley's plans to skip several shows.

"We're not paying for that," he said huffily.

"No, but you're going to pay for tomorrow night's," I said. "The mayor canceled it. Fisher's scam strikes again."

"Price of doing business, Jim. Price of doing business."

At least Paula had been impressed with my discovery. When I explained Fisher and Isaacson's little arrangement, she said, "Wow! How did you put that together?"

"There were a bunch of things that didn't make sense," I said. "First Paul Roynton, the guy who hired me, told me he was losing his shirt on this tour. Insurance companies don't lose money. That's a law of nature.

"Then I couldn't figure out why Isaacson and his flock would drive these enormous distances—all the way to Maine, for Christ's sake—to stage their stupid protests. No one was paying any attention to them. But when they lobbied city officials, they got dramatic results. So if they really wanted to shut down this tour, why wouldn't they use that approach everywhere? Why some cities and not others?

"The real puzzle was why Fisher would meet with Isaacson. Was he trying to patch things up? Get him to lay off Shirley? No way. Fisher doesn't have a diplomatic bone in his body. All he cares about is money. So—this was a stretch—I figured he must have found some way to make money with the reverend. Then you popped it into focus for me."

"I did?" Paula said with surprise.

"Yeah, on the plane out here you told me Fisher was furious about the four missed shows, but not the one that got canceled. What's the difference? Then you said it: weak ticket sales and pressure from church groups. Anytime it looks like Fisher is going to take a bath, he gets the reverend to hector the city council into pulling the plug. Then he gets paid for a sellout."

"Amazing," said Paula, shaking her head. "Every time I think the people in this business can't get any more crooked, someone like Keith Fisher comes along and lowers the bar." She put her hand up. "Wait, not someone *like* Fisher. Usually it *is* Fisher."

"This guy could have given lessons to Elvis's crooked manager—Colonel Parker," I said.

"Well, congrats on figuring it out," she said. Then perplexity clinched her face. "I wonder, though—what does the reverend get out of this?"

"Who knows?" I said. "A kickback? No matter what it is, he's guilty by association."

"But like you said, why drive all over the country to stage these ineffectual protests?"

"Maybe he loves show business," I said. "Anyway, I'm going down to my room to call Roynton and tell him how he's getting screwed."

"Don't forget: you have to be up early tomorrow. At least by rock 'n roll standards. I assume you're flying to Washington with Shirley. Your plane leaves at ten-thirty."

"That's right," I said. "Tomorrow's the big festival. Aren't you going too?"

"Yeah, but I'm on Fisher's jet. The radio station arranged a charter for Shirley. It's just him, you and Jacinda."

"Oh, God," I moaned. "Two hours in a confined space with Little Miss Demented?"

"It's such a shame what's going on with her," Paula said. "She used to be so nice."

"When?" I asked skeptically.

"Let's see," Paula said, looking up as she rewound her memory. "I first met her after the record was finished. That's nine months ago now. Just a quiet, pleasant kid. Clung to Shirley the whole time but I think that was shyness. They were so affectionate with each other back then."

"Are we talking about the same Jacinda?" I asked.

"No, that's what I'm saying. She's a completely different person now. I saw her again during rehearsals for the tour and she was dressing more like a rock chick. But . . . still sweet. When I came back about two weeks later, I swear I could hardly recognize her. The girl had slipped completely off the tracks. She was out of control, raving, cutting herself. The tour had started by then and Keith wanted to have her committed. Hell, we all did. But Shirley wouldn't hear of it. He said he was going to take care of her. And I guess he has. But it must be rough."

"Do you know what happened to change her that radically?"

Paula shook her head. "Whatever it was, must have been weird."

"One thing I learned on this tour," I said. " 'Weird' is a very relative term."

# CHAPTER
## 37

The next morning, I ordered a continental breakfast from room service and called my sponsor. I hadn't spoken to Chris since Saturday, when I got back from Cape Cod. I brought him up to speed on the events of the last few days, including Shirley's Wednesday expiration date.

"Uh, Jim," he said. "You are aware that this is Tuesday, right?"

"Yeah, I knew that."

"That means that today or tomorrow—or who knows, maybe both—someone is going to try to kill Shirley."

"Not if I can help it," I said, with all the leather I could muster.

"So now you're a bodyguard. This job gets better and better."

"Actually, it does," I said. "Paul Roynton just doubled my salary."

"I wonder why," Chris said.

"Maybe I'm just that good."

"You have any idea who sent the note?"

"No. But I'm pretty sure Shirley does. The problem is he won't tell me."

"You have to pry it out of him, man. It makes it a lot easier to protect him if you know which direction the danger is coming from."

Hearing a knock, I said, "Hold on a sec, Chris. My breakfast is here." I conducted a brisk exchange with the waiter, a jowly young Mexican, signed the check and picked up the phone again.

"Sorry."

"I was just going to warn you to be careful," he said. "I've noticed you're getting more and more protective of Shirley."

"I can't help it," I protested. "He's so helpless and he's so alone."

"Just remember this is just a job for you. It's not a sacred trust."

"Don't worry," I said, "I have no intention of taking a bullet for Shirley. I don't even like his music that much. All I intend to do here is limit his exposure if I can."

"What's on the immediate agenda?"

"In a couple of hours," I said, "I'm flying with Shirley and his wacko girlfriend to Washington for some big concert."

"The Gag Reflex Festival?"

"Yes. Wow," I said, genuinely impressed. "How did you know that?"

"A couple of the kids on the adolescent ward at work were going to go over the wall yesterday and hitchhike down to D.C. We had a long talk about it. They said it's the rudest show—all the bands that are too nasty for Ozzfest."

"No wonder they wanted Shirley," I said. "He should be the headliner."

"I think you're in a for an awakening. Shirley is mild salsa. There's a whole horror show genre out there now—guys who were inspired by professional wrestling and snuff films. I swear, some of these masked bands make Shirley Slaughterhouse look like Christopher Cross."

Cross was something of a bugaboo for my sponsor. The year that Risen Angels was nominated for two Grammys—the only year they were nominated—the squeaky-voiced singer of "Arthur's Theme" had won every award in sight and promptly vanished into obscurity.

"Well, after today's musical journey into Sodom and Gomorrah," I said, "Shirley is planning to spend a few days in Philadelphia."

"I thought Sodom was a neighborhood in Philadelphia. What's he doing there?"

"Recording," I said.

"He's going in the studio? Is the tour over?"

"Not for a few weeks. Why?" I asked.

"It's really unusual to take time out to record," he said. "Even if he finishes a song, what could he do with it? The whole business is geared toward selling and promoting albums. Unless he was invited to record a song for a soundtrack. But even then, he'd probably just give them a reject that didn't make it onto his CD."

"All I know is his label and the tour staff are pissed off as hell about him shutting things down."

"That may be all the reason Shirley needs," Chris said. "Listen, I have to get going. We have a staff meeting this morning before first session. But you call me tonight after the show—no matter what time you get in, all right?"

"Okay."

"And you keep calling me until I tell you to stop."

" 'Bye, Chris. Have a good day."

I walked down about two blocks to a Rite Aid Drugstore. I only needed shaving cream, but I left with a plastic sack crammed with crap. Ever wonder why they have those piled-up sale displays at the end of every aisle? It's for me. I'm the ultimate impulse buyer. Marked-down items sing to me. The fact that they're bargains apparently outweighs the consideration that I have virtually no use for the stuff. In the basket it goes.

Back at the hotel, I tended to my ablutions, packed my belongings and headed up to Shirley's suite, all set to jet. In fact, after my Rite Aid spree, I had enough Tic Tacs for a flight to Pluto.

A bored and cynical-looking guy in a flying monkey's suit was leaning against the wall by Shirley's door, his foot rocking a baggage cart back and forth.

I had promised Chris I wouldn't be foolhardy about protecting Shirley, but as the deadline approached, I found I was far more vigilant, eyeing everyone with suspicion. Bellhop or assassin? I wondered as I approached the hall loiterer.

"I hope you're the guy he's waiting for," he said.

"Did you knock?" I asked.

"Yeah," he scoffed. "He wouldn't let me in. Told me to wait."

It took me a few seconds to remember the syncopated pattern Shirley had established for me the night before, making me tap on his coffee table until I could perform it to his satisfaction. The bellhop eyed me skeptically as I banged out our secret code.

Shirley threw open the door immediately. I know he was rattled by what was happening to him, but I suspect part of him was enjoying the cloak-and-dagger precautions.

He looked ghastly—or rather, ghastlier than usual. Under a floor-length black regulator's coat, he had on a black sweatshirt with the hood pulled up. There were bags under his eyes and a haunted expression on his face.

He nodded at me and wearily pointed the bellhop at the pile of gear stacked by the entry closet. Jacinda minced over and reclaimed one of the smaller bags. She was wearing a pink vinyl raincoat buttoned all the way up and knee-high white vinyl boots with splayed toes and thick heels. Her makeup was garishly overdone and her hair was arranged in two lateral ponytails. Standing there with the bag clasped to her chest and a look of lunatic expectancy on her face, she looked like Marlo Thomas having a nervous breakdown.

As we exited the elevator, I swept the lobby without seeing any threats. Shirley promenaded toward the exit holding Jacinda's hand high, almost at chest level. They looked like the homecoming couple at a psychiatric institute, taking their coronation stroll past the nurses' station.

The limo took us in silence to a private airfield. I considered breaking the ice a few times, but I couldn't figure out what would pass for chitchat with this pair.

The driver loaded the luggage into the jet's baggage hold while the pilot stood by the boarding ramp in his uniform and hat, smiling at us. With his alabaster teeth and erect bearing, he looked like one of those impossibly handsome male models who used to adorn cigarette billboards.

The pilot welcomed us aboard, although I was the only one to shake his proffered hand. As he pointed out the plane's amenities, he kept a nervous eye on Jacinda, who was walking down the aisle, merrily flinging open the overhead bins above the four rows of seats. Shirley ignored him completely and took a window seat in the front row. Jacinda threw herself into the adjoining seat as if they were playing musical chairs.

Without dimming his cordial delivery, the pilot gave us a quick flight plan, snapped shut the overhead doors as he walked toward the front of the jet, saluted us and disappeared into the cockpit, closing the door behind him. I heard a distinct click, so I think he locked himself in too.

I took an aisle seat two rows back. I was secretly hoping that Shirley might have administered some sedatives to Jacinda, to cut down on her in-flight turbulence. But it looked like he was the one who had been slipped a Mickey. Shirley was out like a light before the engines warmed up while she ran around like a hyperactive four-year-old. In fact, when the plane took off, she was standing by the bulkhead, rifling through a rack of magazines, tossing the ones she didn't like over her shoulder.

As the nose of the plane lifted, Jacinda was thrown backward. She tried to get her footing, but skidded on one of her discarded magazines and sprawled shoulder-first into the seat bracketing in front of me. And this was a girl without any padding to cushion a fall.

I knelt by her, asking if she was all right and offering her a hand up. The plane was still climbing. She looked at me accusingly and pulled herself into the seat, wincing as she did so. I stood over her, not sure what to say.

Finally, without looking up at me, she said in a pinched and pitiful voice, "Ouch."

"Come on," I said. "Let me help you." She looked up at me, her eyes puddling. I reached across to lift her by her un-injured arm, but didn't touch her until her surrendered body language indicated she would accept it.

We shuffled our way to the back of the cabin, where there was a wet bar. I helped her slowly peel off the raincoat. Underneath it she had on a transparent burgundy blouse and a green tartan skirt. There was an indentation in her collarbone where she had hit the metal bar and it was beginning to discolor.

I sat her down on a jump seat by the bar, put some ice in a double-wrapped paper towel and applied it to the bruise. She inhaled sharply through her teeth.

"Hold it there," I said, scouting some ibuprofen out of the first-aid kit. I poured her a cup of water and helped her take the caplets. Her attitude had become very meek. I led her back to the last row of seats so she could lean back and nestle the ice pack against her shoulder. I took the seat across the aisle.

"You should have a doctor look at that when we land," I said.

"Stupid," she said. "Stupid, stupid."

"Do you want me to wake up Shirley?"

"We're not talking," she said. She started to slump down in the seat but a stab of pain brought her upright again.

"Would you mind if we talked for a while, Jacinda?" I asked. "Or do you prefer Hannah?"

She swung her head to face me with birdlike alacrity. "Jacinda rocks," she said after a moment. "Not Hannah. Jacinda totally rocks."

I nodded as if this were all the explanation a rational person would need. "Look," I said, "I'd like to help Shirley if I can. Do you know who's trying to hurt him?"

"Our father who art in heaven," she said, looking up. I thought she was going to recite the prayer. Then she said, "I told him. I'm not worth it. Loose lips." She held a finger to her mouth as if to hush herself.

"If you tell me who it is, maybe I can protect Shirley," I said.

"Shhhh. Shhhh."

"What do you mean, you're not worth it?"

"I'm a slut," she said, pinching the hem of her skirt with both hands and lifting it to expose her panties. "Party girl."

"That's enough, Jacey." It was Shirley. He had taken the hood off and was kneeling backward on his seat, looking back at her without anger. "Come sit with me."

"Can't," she said. "I'm hurt." She turned to me. "What's your name again?"

"Jim."

"While Mr. Rock Star was sleeping," Jacinda said acidly, "Jim was knocking me around. Weren't you?" I looked at Shirley. His eyes never left her.

"Come up here," he repeated. She secured the ice with her opposite hand, stood up gingerly and joined him in the front row. They began talking quietly. I couldn't hear them over the incidental noise in the cabin. I pulled out my earphones and put on the latest CD from Shelby Lynne.

A few minutes later, Shirley walked past me to get a soda. He stopped by my seat on the way back. I pulled off the headphones and looked up at him.

"Thanks for helping her out," he said.

"Sure."

"I wish . . ." he said, then looked away from me.

"Shirley, I want you to know, I've been around the funhouse a few times," I said. "There's nothing you could say that would shock me." He looked at me as if I were incredibly dense. "Tell me what's going on. I want to help you."

"Just get me through today," he said, and returned to his seat.

I don't know when I dozed off but when I woke up, the

music had stopped playing and something was tugging at my scalp. I looked back and there was Jacinda, with a fractured smile. Her fingers were still poised above my hair. Apparently she had been grooming me.

"I guess you're feeling better," I said, lowering the headphones.

"Right as rain," she said. "Down the waterspout." She rested her forearms on the back of my seat, so I couldn't see her without turning all the way around. I faced forward and we conversed like a pair of toboggan teammates. Shirley was nowhere in sight.

"Tell me about you guys," I said. "How did you and Shirley meet?"

"At a picnic," she said. "I was an ant."

"You're too pretty to be an ant."

"You're right," she said, giggling. "I was a bluebird."

"Where was it? San Francisco?"

"Somewhere around there."

"They tell me you looked different back then," I said.

"I was going through a phase. That's what my parents said."

"What phase were you going through?"

"Confused," she said, pecking at my hair again. It hurt more than you might imagine but I ignored it. "I was a very confused young lady."

"How did you end up in California?"

"Sent away," she said. "All that confusion. Then, poof! It vanished."

"When you met Shirley?"

"No," she said with a spooky rising inflection. "The doctor made it go away. He's a miracle worker."

"How old are you, Jacinda?" I asked.

"Not old enough." As she said it, she twisted a lock of my hair around her index finger and started yanking.

"Oww, that really hurts," I said, rising up in my seat to relieve the pressure.

"Jacinda!" Shirley's voice came from the front row. She

unwound me and then darted her head around the side of my seat like a cartoon mongoose, her lips right by my ear.

"Nobody listens to a confused girl," she said in a whisper. "But everyone will listen to Shirley." Without moving my head, I looked at her out of the corner of my eye. "That's why they're trying to stop him. Because my rock star boyfriend talks LOUD!" She shouted the final word, jolting me sideways. Then she ran up to the first row, curtsied to Shirley and took a seat.

I spent the rest of the flight worrying. I had a feeling we were heading into a situation that not even Jacinda's doctor could make go away.

**T**he rock star travel plan beat the hell out of being a commercial flier. No sooner had the jet landed and taxied up
to the hangar than a limo glided up and parked ten yards
away. An airport employee wheeled over a step ramp. The pilot emerged and threw open the door, smiling brilliantly, delighted to see us go. A jovial but jittery young man from the
radio station was waiting on the tarmac to usher us to the car.

"Hello," he crowed, "I'm Ed Bauer from the promotions
staff at WTTP. Huge fan, Shirley. This is such a thrill for me."

If Shirley acknowledged his existence, it was in a manner
too subtle for me to detect. The singer and his girlfriend
claimed their seats in the back. Ed and I sat facing them
across a yawning gap of carpet. Ed kept up a steady line of
chatter while the airport guy and the driver loaded Shirley's
gear in the trunk. As we drove toward the city, he kept talking about how great today's show was going to be, how all-
out the station had gone and how ticket sales were steaming.

As we crossed the Fourteenth Street Bridge, Jacinda
opened up a pack of corn nuts from the limo's cabinet and,
frowning with the concentration of a dart champion, began
tossing them one at a time at Ed's head. At first the barrage

distracted him. He'd trail off in the middle of a sentence, not sure how to react. Eventually he fell entirely silent. At that point, Shirley, who had been staring out the tinted window the whole time, turned to Jacinda and gave her a proud little smirk.

The limo rolled up to the players' entrance on the side of the MCI Center. The driver walked around to open the door. Ed clambered out first to pave the way. I followed. As Shirley exited, the driver informed him he would take his luggage over to the Willard Hotel.

Two hulks in matching blazers and gray slacks flanked the entryway. I saw them look at each other and raise their eyebrows as Shirley and Jacinda slouched through the door. The two doorkeepers had probably exchanged that look—a blend of amazement and amusement—numerous times already that day.

Inside was bedlam, as the most flagrantly outrageous groups on the planet mingled and clashed. Ed Bauer led us into the central holding area under the stage, which resembled the Frat Party of the Damned. Sum 41 was blaring away on a steroidal stereo system. Two corpulent tattoo artists had set up shop at either end of the room and were doing turn-away business. Booze was flowing everywhere, a goodly portion of it on the flypaper-sticky cement floor. There had also been a buffet set out. The platters were empty but their contents were still abundantly evident. By the looks of it, we had missed a wicked food fight.

The radio station had thoughtfully set up a low wooden half pipe, decorated with WTTP decals, for recreational skateboarders. Apparently someone had taken a sledgehammer to the ramp. Jagged craters were smashed out in a random pattern. Beside it lay a heap of skateboards, broken in half, looking like a campfire-in-waiting. A bank of pinball machines had met a similar fate, with stools and other wieldy objects still protruding out of their shattered faceplates. And it wasn't even three in the afternoon. I shuddered to think what this room would look like by midnight.

Having vandalized everything in the room, the rowdies had turned on each other. People were running around slamming into each other, some fueled by youthful high spirits and booze. Others exhibited an angrier aggression. The big space had the vibe of a stirred-up nest of hornets trapped in a bottle.

The flyer I held in my hand boasted a lineup that included Slipknot, Mudvayne, GWAR, Mushroomhead, Hatebreed, Death Warmed Over and Shirley. Most of these bands wore freaky fright masks, but in the buzzing chaos, it was impossible to tell who were musicians and who were merely emulating their grotesque style. So many people in the room had on distorted disguises, it looked like Halloween in Freddy Kruger's imagination, like a mosh pit in the ninth circle of hell.

Stunned by this tableau, I turned to Shirley, expecting, I suppose, that he would share my trepidation. Instead he wore an expression of happy wonderment. "God," he said loudly, looking around, "Jake would have *loved* this!"

At that moment, I let go of all my suspicion that he had had a hand in Jake's death. He still loved the guy. I looked past Shirley at Jacinda, who was so excited by the pandemonium unfolding in front of her, she resembled a Labrador straining desperately at its leash to get inside a dog park. I stepped over to restrain her. Too late. She bolted into the center of the room and was immediately lost in the punk maelstrom.

Shirley started to follow. I got a firm grip on him. "No, Shirley," I shouted in his ear. "It's not safe." He frowned but didn't try to pull away, merely craning over my shoulder to look for Jacinda. I turned to Ed Bauer. "Is there a dressing room for Shirley?"

He nodded his head emphatically and pointed down a corridor to his left. "All the bands have their own dressing rooms," he said.

I led Shirley away from the madness. With all those masked crazies storming around, the room was a security nightmare. The Justice League and the X-Men together couldn't have protected Shirley in that setting. I needed to stash him somewhere relatively secluded.

We passed the areas designated for Mudvayne, Mushroomhead and Slipknot and there was raucous partying going on in each of them. Finally we got to a door with Shirley's name emblazoned on a star. Someone had hocked a loogie on the sign and the spit was hanging by a tendril from the right arm. I inspected the handle on the door carefully before reaching to turn it.

Inside Linkin Park was playing loudly. A skinny guy in overalls and a crimson demon's mask was spray-painting the wall. The mirror on the dressing table had been smashed and two guys on the couch were hunkered over a piece of it, snorting powder through the nose holes in their zippered, black leather head wraps. They looked like hacky sacks with a drug problem. One took a ferocious inhale, threw back his head and roared, "Oh, shit, that burns!"

I kicked the plug for the boom box out of its wall socket and they all looked up when the music stopped. "Out," I said sternly. Devil boy ran for the exit, cackling loudly. The Tootsie Pop guild looked at each other for a moment, then rose and walked with sullen truculence toward the corridor.

As I started to close the door behind them, the mirror shard they had been carrying came scything through the air, striking the door about a foot from my head. I reflexively turned my head away from the shattering glass. There was a loud, defiant rebel yell from the hall. Still crouching, I pulled the door shut.

I leaned back against the wall and took a deep breath, thinking of an old Randy Newman lyric, "This is the wildest party that there ever could be/ Don't turn on the light 'cause I don't want to see."

"Did you see the guys from Mudvayne in their room?" said an animated Ed. "Are they stoked or what? They've been here since noon. I'm telling you, those guys are up for anything."

"Shut up!" Shirley and I shouted at the same time. We looked at each other. "I have to get Jacinda," he said.

"I'll get her," I said. "You stay here." He nodded. I reached for the handle again. "You promise you'll stay put?" He nodded again.

"Don't worry," said Ed. "I'll keep him company."

"Shut up," Shirley and I mumbled at the same time, both of us frowning. I walked back down the corridor, ducking a group of guys who were drunkenly chasing each other while brandishing sticks. It was a like a prison yard Mardi Gras.

The main room was even more crowded and cacophonous than before. Cypress Hill was thundering on the sound system and human cannonballers were taking turns climbing up on the banquet tables and hurling themselves into the crowd.

Jacinda wasn't hard to find. There weren't many females in the room. I spotted her in a knot of people surrounding a green nitrous oxide tank on wheels. For decadent people on the go. They were passing around an inhaler attached by a tube to the tank. Jacinda had just taken a hit and was standing there, sloshing a half-full drink cup, laughing and swaying, her eyes ecstatic and glazed. Two beefy guys with buzz cuts and starter beards were eyeing her like hyenas.

I didn't think the gentle art of persuasion was going to work here, so I walked up behind her, grabbed her around the waist and started pulling her through the crowd. First she gasped, then whooped with delight. Finally she twisted around, saw who was yoking her and began to struggle, hissing with anger.

Jacinda flung her drink, missing me but splashing a group of revelers. They immediately volleyed back, drenching us with five cups of spiked punch. One caught me right in the back of the head and cold liquid began running under my collar. The unpleasant sensation froze me for a moment and Jacinda took advantage, reaching up and raking my cheek with her fingernails.

That threw me back in gear. Unfortunately, it was reverse

and backing through this throng meant I kept bumping into people, most of whom responded with a shove or a body slam of their own. I felt like a crash test dummy. It surprised me that no one objected or tried to stop me as I dragged a woman, fighting and cursing, out of the room. In fact, I got some boisterous encouragement from a few bystanders. I guess caveman tactics were just this crowd's speed.

It was a struggle every inch of the way, but I finally pulled Jacinda into the dressing room, barring the door with my body. She tried to get past me a couple of times before Shirley wrapped his arms around her, sat her down on a banquette and began whispering urgently to her. Jacinda's eyeballs were still ping-ponging around in their sockets, but she stopped wrestling to get away.

Ed Bauer was staring at the two of them with timorous astonishment. I went over to the sink, turned on the water, grabbed a few paper towels and began trying to clean up from my messy abduction of Jacinda. As I was putting my soaked shirt back on, the door flew open and the Slaughterhouse entourage piled in—Keith Fisher, Nicky Hagipetros, Paula, Raul, Gram and Terry.

"What a fucking zoo," Fisher said, shrugging off his leather coat. He looked around the room, taking in Shirley's huddle with Jacinda. He frowned at me and then at Ed. "Who are you?" he asked belligerently.

"Ed Bauer. I'm with the promotions staff at WTTP."

"Really? Smooth operation you guys are running," Keith said sarcastically. "Which reminds me, if we're going to be hostage in here all afternoon, we're going to need a big assortment of food and drink. And I mean big. Soda, beer, water, cold cuts, snacks, fruit." Ed stared at him blankly. "Let's go," he said, waving Bauer toward the door. "Chop chop."

I took a seat next to Paula. "Hey," I said.

"What happened to you?" she asked, tapping her cheek to indicate my claw marks.

"I made the mistake of acting as Jacinda's chaperone."

"Ouch."

"Where are Slab and Mike?" I asked. "Didn't they fly with you?"

"Yeah, Legs is with us too," she said. "He took off. Said he needed to buy some equipment. But Slab and Mike are out in the rumpus room. Happy as clams."

"Never really understood that expression," I said. "Shell-fish always struck me as kind of gloomy creatures."

"It's not easy being a delicacy," she said.

"You would know," I said. She smiled at me.

Around the room, people were settling down. Raul was picking up the pieces of the mirror and depositing them in a trash can. Jacinda seemed somewhat ameliorated, though Shirley was still pouring words in her ear.

The door opened and Ed stepped in. "Just wanted you to know," he said to Keith. "The food is on its way. All taken care of. If there's anything else you need—"

Suddenly the air exploded. Bang! The sound echoed madly in the confines of the tight, cinderblock room. Two more stinging explosions followed quickly. I dove sideways, luckily in the same direction as Paula, so I ended up blanketing her instead of having our heads collide. I looked around apprehensively and everyone was supine. Except Nicky, who was standing erect and unphased. Either he had terrible hearing or nerves of tungsten.

"What the hell was that?" asked Fisher, rolling out from under a bench, his pygmy ponytail in disarray.

"Nothing to worry about, folks," said Bauer, giggling nervously as he stood back up. "It's just the crew from Mush-roomhead. They've been tossing firecrackers into all the dressing rooms. The band's been touring down South and they brought back these humongous boxes of fireworks."

There was another boom from the doorway, albeit more muted. "How's everybody doing in here?" a voice said. An overweight guy with long, floppy hair had leaned half his body into the room. His beard couldn't hide a beveled chin. He was wearing a white turtleneck, tan cords and a disarming smile. "I'm Dave Kovens, the program director at WTTP," he said, stepping inside.

Spotting Shirley, he said, "Wow. I am so glad you were able to make this gig, Shirley. Huge fan. Really. Having you on the bill really legitimizes the festival. Now it's about the music, not just a freak show, you know?" Shirley stared at him openmouthed. I noticed all of us wore a similar shell-shocked expression. "Ed, you taking good care of these people?"

"I sure am, Dave," Bauer said, doing a fair impersonation of a bobble-head doll.

"Good. Good," he said, his restless eyes settling on Fisher. "You're Keith, right? Shirley's manager?" Fisher just glared at him. "Listen," he said, pointing his thumb toward the corridor, "could we talk for a minute?"

"Stay here, Nicky," Fisher growled, following Kovens into the corridor.

Terry plugged the stereo back in and put on a Jane's Addiction CD. I guess he had been traveling with Shirley long enough to anticipate his musical tastes. Anyway there were no complaints. Shirley was sitting back, his foot wagging to the music. Jacinda was leaning into him, an arm around his shoulder, a tight, smug smile on her lips. The ceiling was throbbing, which meant the opening act, a local monster metal band named Road Kill, had taken the stage. And over all that, I could still hear Fisher screaming through the wall. Lots of crisp, Saxon curse words.

He came back in, scowling and alone. "What's up, boss?" Raul asked.

"That prick wanted us to move down two spots," he said. "Don't worry, Shirley. You're still third billed." Shirley didn't look worried. In fact, he didn't look like he was listening to the conversation at all.

"Wait," said Terry. "This was the program manager's idea? He wanted to shift around the order on the day of the show?"

"Nah, it's those scumbags from Mushroomhead," said

Keith, slumping into a chair and folding his arms across his chest. "They got the cover of *Blender* this month and now they think they're Aerosmith."

"But you said two spots," Raul reminded him.

"Yeah, Hatebreed heard about Mushroomhead demanding to be moved up and they told this radio dildo that they weren't going onstage unless they got a bump too."

"What did you tell him?" asked Terry.

"I told him Mushroomhead could stick it where the sun don't shine."

That observation made me smile. Even a boor like Fisher could evoke poetic justice from time to time.

This backstage wrangling was completely typical, by the way. Musicians always try to give reporters and fans the impression that they're one big happy family, but behind the scenes there's more backbiting going on than you'll ever see on *Animal Planet*.

At festivals like this the bands fight bitterly over pecking order. And that's nothing compared to the wars that go on at awards shows like the Grammys or the VMAs over who gets face time. But then musicians have always been status-conscious. Dig up a copy of the first great rockumentary, D. A. Pennebaker's *Don't Look Back*. There's a young Bob Dylan in the back of a London limo, cool and inscrutable as can be. Someone off-camera casually mentions Dylan's position in the Top 40 and the singer immediately offers up a grave and detailed correction of his chart position. If the Buddha of pop music is keeping score that closely, you know the rest of the pack is too.

Kovens came back to the room twice more to try to negotiate, but Fisher wouldn't budge. Shirley kept his spot, which meant we had several hours to while away. A nice spread of food was brought in. Terry and Raul played cards. Gram had a portable DVD player and a few people gathered around to chuckle at *Glitter*.

Out in the hall, things seemed to be getting wilder and wilder, and a few times marauders burst in with the usual marauder agenda: rape and pillage. Then Fisher instructed Nicky to stand outside the door and there were no further disturbances.

Finally it was time to perform and Raul was sent out to round up Slab and Mike. Kovens led us all up a back staircase to the curtained-off platform behind the stage. Legs was scurrying around setting up the band's equipment. Terry and Raul went out to help him.

Because of the festival format, Shirley couldn't do his elaborate opening. No snake-charming music. No smoke bombs. One of the WTTP jocks would announce him, the band would launch into "Blood Money" and then Shirley would spring onstage to sing the first verse.

At least that was the plan. The introduction was delivered in the usual stentorian circus ringleader's tones. ("Please give a strong D.C. welcome to the duke of disaster . . . the navigator of nightmares . . . the unchosen one. Ladies and gentlemen, I give you . . . SHIRLEEEEY SLAUGHTERHOUSE!!") As the spots hit the stage, Slab lifted his arm, puffed up his chest and twisted his face into a mighty grimace.

It was good windup for that first power chord but he shouldn't have closed his eyes, because at that second, a sneaker came flying up out of the crowd, spinning slowly heel over toe. Whoever threw it had style. It was an old Chucky, a Converse high-top. He also had a hell of an arm. The sneaker whacked Slab right in the forehead, staggering him back a couple of steps.

The crowd began to laugh and jeer, infuriating Slab. He slung the guitar around to his side and angrily walked up to Shirley's microphone at the front of the stage, flipping the audience the bird.

"Fuck—" And that was as far as he got. With his other hand, he reached out to grab the mic stand, and as soon as he did, Slab went incandescent. He began spasming violently. The hair on his head stuck straight out. He was silhouetted by a bright, crackling aura. And almost right away, there was an acrid burning smell in the air.

At first the crowd cheered, thinking it was a bit of show-manship, a gimmick to kick off the performance. But then Slab collapsed on the floor and everyone in Shirley's retinue rushed out onstage. The cheering stopped and you could hear people in the audience talking to each other, trying to figure out what was going on.

It was awful. Slab lay there, still twitching. He looked charred. Small patches of smoke curled up from his head. But no one knew what to do until a pair of paramedics rushed onstage. One of them knelt by him and tentatively touched him with the back of his hand, I suppose to make sure Slab wasn't still conducting electricity. He felt for a pulse and then they lifted Slab onto a stretcher and rolled him off, stage left. I thought Mike would run after them to check on his buddy but he just stood there dumbfounded, still holding his bass. I saw Legs jogging along beside the stretcher, a look of fear and dismay on his face as he looked down at Slab. Then he ran off into the crowd.

The audience was growing more voluble. Some began shouting things at Shirley. It struck me how exposed he was, standing there in the bright lights. I took him gently by the bicep and led him off in the direction we had come. Obviously, he wasn't going to perform. Not without his guitarist. Not on a stage where someone had just tried to fry him.

# CHAPTER 39

As I pulled Shirley away, I heard Fisher shout behind us, "Everybody downstairs now!" And we all clattered down the metal steps, like an army in full retreat. As we approached the dressing room, I saw Ed Bauer staring at us flabbergasted, wondering why the band that had just been introduced was fleeing the stage.

"Call Shirley's limo right now," I ordered him. "Have it waiting outside the players' entrance." He didn't say anything, only nodded.

We all piled in the room. "Holy shit," Raul kept saying.

Shirley looked around. "Where's Jacinda?" he asked. Everyone did a quick visual inventory. She wasn't there.

"Where's Legs?" asked Terry. Another absentee.

I walked over to mollify Paula, who had a hand over her mouth, as if she were about to be sick. Out of the corner of my eye, I saw Shirley bolt out the door. "Shit," I said and tore off after him.

It occurred to me later that Shirley was probably one of the easiest men in America to tail. I could pick him out on a Manhattan rush-hour subway platform, follow him through a crowded terminal at LAX, stalk him at Disneyland on the busiest day of the year. The guy would stick out in just about any setting. Except in this delirious playground under the MCI Center. He vanished.

I hurried down the corridor toward the open funhouse. It was tough sledding, moving against the traffic. The organizers from the radio station had rousted Mudvayne and were herding the band and their entourage toward the stage before the crowd rioted.

Things in the pit had gotten murkier. Every light fixture that wasn't covered with metal screening had been smashed. The music had been turned up even louder—the punishing scourge-metal sound of Celtic Frost. Several people had passed out and were crumpled on the floor. I had to step around bodies as I circled the perimeter. Judging by the odor, guys had taken to pissing against the walls. I spiraled concentrically toward the center of the room. No Jacinda. I began to worry that she had fled the building. Jacinda floating around on inner-city streets—that was a calamity waiting to happen.

Then, as I walked back toward Shirley's enclave, I saw him emerging from Slipknot's dressing room, pulling Jacinda behind him. He looked angry. I rushed over to intercept them.

"Shirley," I said, stopping his progress. "The car is waiting. Let me take you back to the hotel." He looked back at Jacinda, frowned and nodded his head. We threaded our way back through the crowd and out to the street. The driver was standing by the car's rear bumper. He threw open the passenger door as soon as we emerged. A few young fans, corralled behind a line of sawhorse barricades, yelled Shirley's name. He paid no attention, keeping Jacinda on a very short leash.

I felt relieved when I piled them into the back of the limo, but Shirley was obviously still distressed. "We'll call the hospital and see how Slab is doing," I said. He said nothing, tugging fitfully at his hair. I tried again. "Slab's a tough character. He's probably sitting up by now, asking the nurses to bring him tequila."

Shirley turned his head away from me, as if to escape my annoying comments. I deduced that Slab's welfare wasn't his paramount concern. "What's wrong, Shirley?" I asked.

He looked accusingly at Jacinda. She widened her eyes in mock innocence. "How long were we onstage?" he asked. "Two minutes? Less? That's how long it took her to sneak downstairs. I found her rubbing up against one of the guys from Slipknot in their dressing room."

"Not the guy in the clown mask?" I blurted out. I could feel my face wrinkling with anticipatory revulsion as I checked Jacinda for signs of secondhand greasepaint.

"No," said Shirley. "The one who looks like the Elephant Man with dreadlocks." Thank God for small favors, I thought. But I could see it wasn't much consolation to Shirley. We passed the rest of the drive in silence. Jacinda was audibly humming, I think just to show Shirley she wasn't remorseful. I don't know what tune it was but I'm pretty sure it wasn't one of his.

I made them sit in the car while I retrieved our key cards from the front desk. He was registered under the name H. P. Lovecraft. I assume he selected it ironically. The author's pseudonym is something of a front desk cliché for rockers.

The tension in the elevator was particularly strong as I led them up to their suite. As soon as we got inside, Jacinda bolted for the back room and slammed the door. After we made plans to leave for Philadelphia early the following afternoon, I stuck around for a while, sitting on the couch, while Shirley stood by the window, looking forlornly out over the city. Not a word was spoken. Finally, he said, "You can go."

"You sure?" I asked. He gave me a weary, dismissive gesture with his hand. "See you tomorrow," I said.

When I emerged from his suite, I saw Terry and Raul conferring outside a room just beyond the elevator bank. Both of them looked up as I closed the door behind me. I waved and walked over.

"What's the word?" I asked.

"Slab's in intensive care," said Terry. "Paula called from the hospital. She says he's not out of the woods but the doctor is 'guardedly optimistic.'" He quote-bracketed that last phrase with his fingers.

"If he lives through this," said Raul, "he's a lucky bastard."

Terry bounced his head in assent. "Definitely," he said. "The doctor told Paula it was bad shoes that saved him. Kept him from being grounded. If he had had on rubber soles, the current would have killed him. Said he got hit with more voltage than an electric chair."

"Whoa," said Raul, shaking his head. "I believe it, though. Did you see his fucking shoes? They were blown out. Like sandals, man. You could see his feet. Dude's got ugly feet."

"Do you know how it happened, Terry?" I asked.

"I talked to the sound guy for Mudvayne," he said. "They tore the stage down right after we came off. He said they unhooked a double-circuit wire from the mic stand and traced it under the stage. Found an industrial generator all hooked up and cooking. He said the first guy to grab that microphone was toast."

"You guys set up the equipment, though."

They both shook their heads vehemently. "Not the mic," said Raul. "I did Gram's drum set. Terry had the guitars. And Legs taped down the wires and handled the sound system. He was the first one on and the last one off the stage."

"And what does Legs have to say?" I asked.

Terry shrugged. "He gone. Disappeared right after the accident."

"That was no fucking accident," said Raul. "That was meant for Shirley. He's the only one who ever touches that mic."

"What about the DJ who introduced him?" I asked.

Terry shook his head. "He did it from backstage."

"Did the police get called?" I asked.

"I don't think so," said Raul.

"I'm sure they didn't," said Terry. "They had Mudvayne onstage ten minutes after Slab got lit up."

"What are you guys going to do?" I asked.

"Keith is on the phone," said Terry, flicking his head at the door we were standing in front of. "We're waiting to hear what he decides."

"Do you know how to get in touch with the rest of the crew?"

"Yeah," said Terry, "they're still in Des Moines. The label decided it was cheaper to just keep them in a hotel than to fly them all home and fly them back five days later." Raul sorted through some sheets of paper he had in his pocket and wrote down the phone number for me.

"I'll talk to you later," I said, punching the bottom button for the elevator. "Let me know if you hear anything about Slab."

As soon as I got to my room, I called Des Moines. I thought I would have to try every hole-in-the-wall bar in town, but I lucked out. Billy O'Connor was in his motel room. I could hear Sandra Blanchard in the background asking who was on the phone. When he told her, she urged him to hang up. "Wait, Billy," I said. And I plunged into the story of what had happened at the MCI Center.

"Oh, shit," Billy said several times. Each time, I could hear Sandra pestering him to tell her what was going on. He never did.

"Why would Legs do that, Billy?" I finally asked.

"I don't know, man," he said forlornly. "He really kind of lost it the last few days. You know that drug dealer in Boston he told you about?"

"Yeah, Joey."

"He got arrested a few days ago. And I guess he gave up Legs's name to the DEA. Told them he was big supplier or something, the rat fuck. Anyway the guy who sublets Legs's loft called and said a detective came by looking for him. So now the tour is ending and he doesn't have another gig lined

up. He has no money and he can't go home. He really
freaked out."

"Was he angry at Shirley?"

"He was pissed off at everybody. Your name came up several times during his rants," Billy said.

"Well, if he gets in touch with you," I said, "tell him to
call me. Maybe I can help him out of this situation."

"I'll give him the message," said Billy, hanging up.

I was still sticky from the booze bath I had taken while
reeling in Jacinda, so I took a hot shower and changed my
clothes. I meditated for a few minutes, but I still felt agitated
and restless. I tried Paula, but there was no answer, so I
called Chris.

"Checking in," I said, "as ordered."

"You all right?" he asked.

"Yeah, I'm okay."

"I thought maybe something happened, because I asked
you to call me after the concert."

"That's what I'm doing. Show's over," I said.

"You're kidding. What was it, a matinee?"

"More like an ambush," I said, describing what had happened to Slab and then backtracking through the day.

"You know," Chris said when I finished, "I was once
backstage for a triple bill at Max's Kansas City. I forget the
occasion but it was the New York Dolls, Johnny Thunders
and the Velvet Underground. All kinds of weird shit going
on. Andy Warhol was filming the whole thing. I looked
around that room and I thought, This is it. Life cannot get
any more surreal than this. But it sounds like the show you
were at today may have set a new standard."

"I'm thinking of having T-shirts made up that say: 'I survived Gag Reflex.'"

"I hope that poor guitarist gets to wear one. Is he going to
be all right?"

"I don't know. The doctors say he's lucky to still be
breathing."

"Sounds like Shirley's the lucky one. Any other night, he would have been electrocuted onstage."

"I know. I feel bad," I said. "Like I didn't do a very good job of looking after him."

"How in the world could you have prevented that?" he asked. "At least now you know who was after him."

"I'm not sure on that score either," I said.

"I thought you said Legs hot-wired the mic stand?"

"He did. But I can't help thinking he did it on someone else's instructions."

"Why?"

"I could be wrong," I said, "but the whole setup just seemed a little too dramatic and ambitious for Legs. And if it was Legs who was making these latest threats, I think Shirley would have told me that. I think somebody else is behind this and I don't think it's over."

"Well, the tour is certainly finished," said Chris.

"What do you mean?"

"There's only like four dates left, right?"

"Yeah."

"What guitarist is going to take that gig? It's like signing on as Spinal Tap's drummer."

"I hadn't even thought about the rest of the concerts," I said. "But if there's a buck to be made out of those shows, Fisher will put Shirley out onstage with a kazoo player."

"Is he still coming to Philly?"

"That's the plan," I said. "We're heading up tomorrow to Sygma Studios. You ever been there?"

"Not since Harold Melvin and the Blue Notes were making records. But if you're still there Friday, I have the day off. Maybe I could come down and visit."

"That would be great. I haven't told Shirley I know you, but I bet he would be thrilled to meet you. I'm sure he's familiar with your records. The kid's a real student of music."

"You know, the nicest thing anyone ever wrote about me," said Chris, "was Don McLeese in the *Chicago Sun-Times*.

He said I was a musician's musician. I'm not a hundred percent sure what it means but I like the implication."

"You should definitely come down."

"I will. But you have to promise me. No booby-trapped amplifiers or exploding drums."

"No," I said. "This is definitely a more controlled environment. Small enclosed space. Not many people around. After all that chaos today, protecting Shirley in a studio should be a snap."

There are many gifts that come with being in recovery. Obviously, psychic ability is not one of them.

# CHAPTER
## 40

I've always admired people who can make sense of dreams, who can tease the thread of significance out of those whirling images. My own dreams are as decipherable to me as sign language. That night I was beset with a series of unsettling and violent sleep visions. I assume they were brought on by witnessing Slab get vaporized onstage.

As soon as my eyes opened, I rolled out of bed, eager to put some tracks into the day. I pulled open the curtains to minimal effect. Nature had drawn her own set of curtains: dark gray clouds boiled low in the sky, sealing out the sunlight.

After attending to the morning rituals (pray, stretch, shave), I sauntered down to a Starbucks about four blocks from the Willard. Along with my first latte, I got a pocketful of quarters to feed the kennel of newspaper boxes out front. Then I settled happily in a stool by the window, flipping pages, sipping coffee and glancing at the grim procession of office workers. Watching rush hour never fails to make me grateful that I have an unconventional job.

Basically, I was just killing time until I could rouse Shirley. Returning from Starbucks, I hung out in my room, flicking around the TV dial, but the only choices were *The*

*View, Judge Joe Brown, Maury,* a rerun of *The Nanny* and some saccharine PBS cartoon that featured talking animals with big globe-shaped heads. All of them made my flesh creep.

The same song had been rattling around in my head all morning: the title track from David Gray's *White Ladder*. So I got out my CD player, pulled a comfortable chair up by the window and watched the clouds roil.

Just before eleven, I packed up my stuff and took the elevator down to Shirley's suite. I rapped out against the door the complicated pattern he had taught me. No answer. I tried twice more, a little louder each time. It was hell protecting someone as acutely vulnerable as Shirley. All kinds of scenarios were shooting through my mind, none of them pretty.

I began pounding—a steady, urgent beat of my own devising. Finally, the door swung open and there was Jacinda, squinting at me sleepily. I was vastly relieved to see her. "Sorry to wake you," I said. "Will you tell Shirley I'm here?"

"He's gone," she droned.

"What? Gone where?"

"I don't know," she said, aggrieved. "He packed his shit and left." She turned and started slumping toward the bedroom. "I have to go back to sleep. We were fighting all night."

This wasn't good. I picked up the phone and asked to be connected to Raul's room. He picked it up on the third ring and shouted, "What?"

"Hey, man. It's Jim."

"What is this—wake up Raul day?" he said with exasperation.

"Sorry. I'm trying to find Shirley."

"Can't you two get your shit together without bothering me?"

"Do you know where he went?"

"I assume he's on his way to Philly," Raul said, some of the attitude draining away. "He called me about nine o'clock and told me to have the band—what's left of it—meet him in the lobby." He coughed into the phone and I pulled my end away from my face, irrationally trying to shield myself from his germs. "I had to tell him they weren't coming."

"I'm not following, Raul."

"Don't you guys talk? Shirley wanted the band to back him on this record. But Keith torpedoed that idea last night. Had me tell Gram and Mike that if they go, he'll make sure it's the last session they ever work. Shirley is now officially a solo act."

"How'd he take that news?"

"How do you think?" Raul said. "He was pissed. Actually he wasn't in too good a mood to start with."

"Did he tell you what he was going to do?"

"I know he's going to Philly because he asked me to bring Jacinda up there tonight," said Raul. "I said I would, even though Keith is going to have my ass in a sling."

"You're a good guy, Raul," I said.

"Yeah." He yawned. "Can I go back to sleep now?"

Contemplating Shirley's options, I left the suite and took the elevator to the lobby. The guy behind the concierge desk looked remarkably like Anthony Edwards, the actor on *E.R.* He gave me a friendly smile as I approached.

"Good morning," he said. "May I help you?" The voice wasn't far off either.

"Yes, I wonder if you've seen one of your guests this morning? He's registered in room 1523 under the name H. P. Lovecraft?"

"I'm sorry, sir," he said cordially. "So many guests come through the lobby—"

"Oh, I think you'd remember this guy," I said.

Recognition dawned in his eye. "You mean Mr. Slaughterhouse."

"Yes, I work with him. But he left unexpectedly this morning for Philadelphia. Do you have any idea how he was traveling?"

"He came down to the lobby at nine-twenty. Inquired

about renting a car. I told him I could take care of that. But when I asked for a driver's license and credit card, he seemed distressed. Then he asked about hiring a car." The concierge tilted his head to indicate this is where the story got interesting. "I explained that would be a pricey way to travel to Philadelphia. There are cheaper options available, I told him. But he asked me to arrange it. Paid the driver in cash too."

He continued talking, although his voice grew fainter as I picked up my bag and jogged to the exit. "That's not the longest livery ride I've ever arranged, by the way. We once had a guest who took a car to—"

Out front I grabbed a cab to Union Station and just made a northbound Acela Express. I was so worried on the ride up, I barely registered the Chesapeake rolling past. My mind was swirling. Why had Fisher forbidden the band to go to Philly? Was he trying to isolate Shirley? Why had Shirley taken off without calling me? And why was this recording session so damn important to him?

The train had almost reached Wilmington when things swam into focus for me. The death threat had read: *Drop it or you're dead by Wednesday.* The one anomaly in Shirley's schedule—the *it*—had to be today's trip to the studio.

And the song he was working on was "Preacher's Seeds." The only person I could see being mortally offended by that particular message was Isaacson. There was some powerful, personal grudge going on between the rock star and the reverend. Why else would they go to such lengths to antagonize each other? Jacinda was the sole link I could establish between them. But what about her had them both so fired up?

If the idea was to stop Shirley from cutting the song, then someone had jumped the gun by trying to hot-wire him onstage the night before. Unless they already knew that he was determined to keep this appointment no matter what.

It was raining hard when we pulled into Philly. I grabbed another taxi outside Thirtieth Street. An Ethiopian gentleman drove me over to Callow Hill. His last name, spilling all

over his hack license on the dash, boggled my tongue.
Through the scratched plastic shield, he established eye contact with me as he gave me my change and said, "Please take
care." The deliberate way he said it gave me the creeps.

There was no one behind the desk in the lobby. That's
odd, I thought, because there must be so much expensive
equipment in the building. On the wall was a scheduling
board. Jaguar Wright was due in Studio One at six P.M. S.
Slaughterhouse had reserved Studio Two at noon. It was already going on three.

I walked down a hallway decorated with commemorative
gold records and opened the door into the studio. With all
the glass walls it felt like stepping into a carpeted squash
court. Shirley was sitting alone on a stool, hunched over his
black acoustic guitar, strumming away quietly.

"Hey, Shirley," I said. He looked up and nodded at me.
"You all right?"

He smirked and hit a purposefully sour chord. "Things
haven't really been going my way today."

"Why did you take off without calling me? I thought we
were traveling together."

"I never went to sleep last night. Jacinda and I were really
scratching and clawing. So I thought I'd get an early start. I
was going to call you. Then Raul told me Fisher wasn't letting the band travel with me. And, I don't know, I just got
pissed off and left."

"Are you the only one here?"

"Yeah."

"In the whole building?"

"No, there's a guard out front."

"Not now there isn't. Look, man, we gotta get out of
here."

"Not until I record my song."

"Don't be stupid. Whoever tried to kill you yesterday is
coming here. Who cares about some crappy song?"

"I do," he said heatedly. "I'm sending a message."

I heaved a sigh of frustration. "I have been as patient as I know how to be with your cryptic bullshit. But the time has come for you to level with me, Shirley. What's going on between you and Isaacson?"

He carefully leaned the guitar against his stool and then began to speak, so quietly at first I leaned forward to hear him.

"You can't imagine what she was like. I can barely remember it myself—things have gotten so fucked up. She was so beautiful, so radiant, so . . . liberated. Like a prisoner walking into the sunlight."

A current of resentment crossed his face, darkening his expression. "Then he came back. And she fell apart. Which is what he wanted. That's why he started arranging those lame protests of his. So once or twice a week when we'd drive up to an arena, she'd have to look at that sanctimonious bastard standing in front of his stupid bus. And every time it would devastate her. You could actually see her soul collapsing piece by piece. Can you imaging anything crueler than doing that to someone intentionally?"

I knew he was referring to Jacinda and Reverend Isaacson. Still, I had a hundred questions. I limited myself to one. "What was the connection between them?"

"Rape."

"Rape?" I echoed.

"He seduced her," Shirley said. "But she was a teenager. That makes it rape. All those prayer sessions and youth retreats. Talking to her so gently, touching her. She idolized him. Even after he got her pregnant."

"Why didn't her family have him brought up on charges?"

"Because dear old dad was offered the job as deacon." I gave an involuntary grunt of distaste as I realized how deeply betrayed Jacinda had been. "They packed her off to California to have an abortion. That's when we met—when she was recovering. She was so happy, just to finally get away from that hypocrite and her family.

"But when he found out she wasn't coming back, that she was living with me, he came after her," Shirley continued. "Couldn't even let her have that much happiness. This whole crusade against me and my music? It was just a way to torment her. All of it."

"I'm sorry, Shirley," I said. Both our heads slumped a little. "But . . . how does that get us to Philly?"

"I thought I could help Jaz," he said. "But I couldn't. She just kept getting worse and worse. Me and Jake kept encouraging her to expose him, tell people in her hometown what he had done. But that terrified her worse than anything. She got really frantic. So we backed off. Then Jake came up with the idea of writing a song, just to stick it to the guy, you know? We used to talk about what the video would be like—how we'd get David Spade to play the reverend."

I should have read the lyrics more carefully. "Preacher's Seeds" wasn't a metaphor. It was an indictment.

"But Jaz told her father about the song." He shook his head in dismay. "I can't believe she talks to him at all. When the sinister minister heard Jake was writing a song about him, he freaked. Which was the point. So Jacinda's father calls up Jake. I think we were playing Albany that night. And he threatens him. And Jake being Jake—he laughs at him, calls him a scumbag, tells him the song is going to be a huge hit. And then a week later . . . he was dead."

"And you think Isaacson arranged it?"

Shirley shrugged. "I knew somebody dragged him up there. Jake wouldn't even go out on a hotel balcony. He was terrified of heights."

"Why didn't you tell the police all this?"

"Jacinda begged me not to," he said.

"Shit," I said. "So you decided to finish the song and now you're going to record it?" He nodded. "And Jacinda tells her father about your recording plans and that's when you got the death threat?" Shirley nodded once more, reaching down to lift the guitar back into his lap. "Why, Shirley? You knew they already killed Jake. Why rattle their cage again?"

"I don't know," he said. "A gesture of defiance, I guess. For Jacinda. And for Jake too. That's what all my music is for—providing a voice for people who don't get to speak."

I pondered that for a moment. "So how do you plan to do this?" I asked. "Don't you need a producer?"

"I'm going to produce it," he said. "But I need the engineer. And the musicians. They were supposed to be here an hour ago. My friend Kenn Kweder arranged it. He's the only guy I know in the music business in Philly. I called him from the car this morning. I should call him back. They're really late."

"Listen, why don't we wait for them outside? I don't like how deserted this place is."

Suddenly a gruff amplified voice resounded through the room, startling Shirley and me.

"If it's company you boys want . . ." said the voice. It was like an angry God admonishing us from the clouds. We looked around nervously for the source.

A single track light flicked on in the darkened control room, which overlooked the recording floor like a luxury box at a stadium. Illuminated in the bright column of light was Jumpy Brown.

He didn't look like he was there to sing backup.

# CHAPTER
## 41

Jumpy stepped away from the light, vanishing from our sight. Shirley and I looked at each other, both of our mouths hanging open. Deer in headlights are more decisive than we were. Jumpy stepped into the room, executing his distinctive duck-and-twist to fit through the doorway just below the control room.

He straightened up and stared at us, a wolfish grin on his face. "Well, ain't this cozy," he said. Glancing around, he grabbed a crate-sized Marshall speaker, lifted it with two hands and wedged it firmly against the door he had just squeezed through. Then he stomped over to the door that led in from the corridor, grabbed an even bigger speaker cabinet and corner-walked it backward until it covered the doorframe.

He turned to us, dusting his huge, rough hands against each other, and said, "Okay, who's first?" Now that Jumpy had sealed off our exits, my feet came unstuck. Great timing, fellas! Appreciate the help.

I began moving laterally toward the Steinway piano to my left so at least he couldn't grab both of us at the same time.

Jumpy advanced on Shirley. "Look at you," he said, marveling. "You're shaking like a chihuahua." And, in fact, Shirley was quivering in his boots. "Boo!" he shouted in Shirley's face. Shirley's eyebrows shot up so high, he looked like the character in Edvard Munch's painting *The Scream*. His limbs, however, stayed frozen. Jumpy started to laugh, a low, rolling rumble that sounded like a freight train pulling away from a dead stop.

He turned to me. "All right, frisky," he said. "Let's cash you out first." As he moved toward me, I sidled around the piano, keeping its wide body between us.

"Those musicians could come by any minute, Jumpy," I said, more in hope of distracting than dissuading him.

"Don't think so," he said. "I had a little heart-to-heart with the security guy in the lobby. He sent 'em all home when they showed up an hour ago. Told 'em the session was canceled."

"Someone else will come by. This is a busy studio," I said. "And the street door is wide open."

"Not now, it ain't," said Jumpy. "I bolted it shut right after you showed up."

"The security guard?"

"In a Dumpster behind the building."

That answer lent wings to my feet. "How did you know I was coming?" I asked. As we talked, Jumpy and I performed a clumsy crab dance. He would start to slide one way or the other around the piano and I would move in the same direction, trying to keep us on an axis. Except for the vibrato, Shirley was stationary.

"Didn't," he said. "I decided to give you a half hour. See if you turned up. I figured I still owe the reverend your miserable carcass." With his Massachusetts accent, that last word came out sounding like "khakis."

Jumpy made a rush and got fairly close because I had stopped in my tracks, dumbfounded. Quickly reestablishing the distance between us, I said, "I thought you were working for Fisher."

"You made that pretty clear when you visited me," he said, circling to his left. "So I told you what you wanted to hear. But the fact is I have a much higher calling." Jumpy had seemed a lot dumber on his home turf. But maybe he was playing to my assumptions there too.

"So all that stuff you told me sitting in your car . . ." I said.

"Made it up on the spot," he said, grinning. "You know, you're surprisingly naive."

"You *were* trying to kill me."

"Hell, yeah," he said. "Would've got you too. But you slammed on your brakes before I could force you off the road And that embankment you went down was a little too steep and slippery for me."

"But Fisher was the only one who knew I was going to Catoga Falls," I said.

"I followed you all the way from Pittsburgh, dumbshit," he said. "Naive *and* unobservant. Not a real good combination for a guy who's supposed to be a detective."

"You're piling up a lot"—as I was talking, he lunged across the piano, grabbing for my shirt and missing by about six inches; I backed up—"of bodies, Jumpy. They're going to put you away for a very long time."

"After the first one," he said, getting his footing back, "it really don't matter. Besides, soon as we get done here, I'm moving to Mexico. Permanently. You guys are my retirement fund."

"You did all this for Isaacson?" I asked. "How much did he pay you?"

"What is with you? You're always so interested in my fee," Jumpy said, reaching inside his denim vest and pulling out a gnarly-looking .44, which he banged against the piano lid. "But I definitely don't get paid by the hour, so it's time to wrap this up."

"One more thing, Jumpy," I said desperately, still stalling. "Was it you that hot-wired that microphone yesterday?"

"Naah," he said. "I never been too good with electrical

shit. I had that skinny prick with the beanie do it. Man, he was pissed off after too. Guess he was friends with the guy who got grilled. And since you seem to be keeping track, him I put down for free."

"You killed Legs?"

He didn't answer, merely fanning the gun barrel between us. "C'mere."

I shook my head like a five-year-old stubbornly refusing to get into the bath. Jumpy walked over to Shirley and pointed the pistol point-blank at his ear. If it was possible for Shirley to get any paler, he did at that moment. He seemed to turn opalescent.

"Get your ass over here," Jumpy said, "or I will splash his brains all over that wall."

That threat shouldn't have worked. I knew that Jumpy wasn't going to let either of us walk out of that studio. But I started walking toward them anyway. I suppose I couldn't bear to watch Shirley get killed in such a brutal fashion. Apparently, I'd rather die first.

When I was a few feet away, Jumpy said, "That's better," and reached out to grab me with his steam shovel of a hand. I cringed as he clamped my shoulder, pain flaring up to my neck and down my right side. He walked me backward, tucking the pistol inside his vest.

"You know, when you were playing keep-away, I was thinking this piano would make a pretty good coffin, huh?" Jumpy said. He shoved me down and off balance, cracking the back of my head against the curved side of the instrument. He let go and I slid to the floor, the pain pulsing in waves with my heartbeat. "I think I'll stuff both of you in there and then shoot you. That's a good way to send off a musician, huh, Shirley?"

As he was speaking, he lifted the lid on the piano and propped it open. Then he reached down and picked me up by the shirt. I dangled like a rag doll as Jumpy surveyed how best to jam me into the Steinway sarcophagus.

Over his shoulder I saw a sight I will never forget: from

across the room, Shirley was running at us, brandishing a metal microphone stand over his head. His eyes were huge with terror and adrenaline, his legs bowlegged, probably with the exertion of carrying the stand's round base, which must have weighed nearly thirty pounds. As he charged at us, he looked like Ichabod Crane trying to pole vault.

I shouted out, "Not in the head!" But it was too late. Shirley mashed Jumpy right at the base of his skull. It was a neatly delivered blow, staggering Jumpy. He grunted and released me. But he didn't buckle. Turning around, he regarded Shirley, who was slumped over disconsolately, the metal stand dragging on the floor. Jumpy looked at him with bemused annoyance, as you would a pesky bug.

He slapped the pole out of Shirley's hand and then picked him up by the throat. There were some sickening pops, snaps and gurgles as Jumpy tightened his grip. Shirley didn't struggle, although his countenance grew livid—the first time I had ever seen color in his face. Jumpy studied Shirley's expression as he held him up, manipulating his head from side to side as if he were a marionette.

There was a moment when Shirley had the same vacant, abandoned expression as he did when the spotlights first hit him at the opening of his concerts. Then his eyes rolled back in his head. Jumpy shook him once. Getting no response, he casually flung him into the piano, setting off a muffled jangle of chords. The bouncing body dislodged the wooden bracing arm and the lid came down, slamming shut.

Jumpy's tossing motion also yanked the gun out of his belt and I pounced on it. When he turned and saw me holding the weapon on him, Jumpy's face fell. But only for a moment. He smiled and began moving toward me. "Come on," he said. "You ain't going to shoot old Jumpy."

I squeezed the trigger. In the acoustically perfect room, the explosion was searing.

"Shit!" screamed Jumpy, his hands clutching both ears. "Don't do that again." My ears were throbbing too, the sonic aftershock reverberating endlessly.

"Sit over there," I said, pointing at the chair by Shirley's guitar. He sat down and I trained the gun on him, my back to the piano. "Now you're going to answer some questions. If you try to get up or if you don't tell me what I want to know, I'm going to shoot your knee. You understand?"

"Don't you think you should get your friend an ambulance?" he asked, poking his chin at the piano.

"Wrong answer," I said, aiming at his left leg.

He held his hands up. "Fuck. All right."

"How did Isaacson find you?"

"He asked Keith Fisher if he knew anyone of a 'hard nature,' " he said, flicking the hair by his ear. The bullet I had fired had come so close it had actually singed a path through his mane. "That's how Keith explained it to me. Isaacson told him there had been incidents at some of their protests and they wanted to hire some protection. So Keith calls me up, explains the situation and asks me if I'll meet with them.

"Course, when we get together, they tell me they have another job in mind entirely and they lay out their problem. And I'm thinking, All this over a fucking song? But the reverend says he wants me to get close to the Karn kid, feel him out, see if he's serious. That didn't sit too well with that wormy deacon of his. I could tell he wanted me to put the kid down."

"Who introduced you to Jake?"

"What's his name, Legsy."

"So you went to meet Jake in Providence," I prodded.

"Yeah. The reverend asked me if I could ply him with drugs. I said that could probably be arranged for a price. So off I go, and the funny part was me and the kid hit it off. It wasn't that phony suck-up thing I get when guys are intimidated by me. We got along good."

"He invited you back to the hotel and you didn't go?"

"That's right."

"He offered you a pile of drugs and you turned it down?" I said dubiously.

"I had a meeting to get to. The lab I buy from is outside

Providence," Jumpy said. "I figured I'd take the reverend's money and that would be the end of it."

"You never talked to Jake about the song?"

"Not that night, no. I called the deacon and told him a bunch of shit. Jake was no threat. There was no song. Blah blah. I thought it would end there."

"What happened?"

"Like two nights later, Legs is in the drummer's room and he hears him and Jake trying to demo the song. The song I just told them doesn't exist. Legs calls the deacon and now the altar boys are really pissed at me."

"How did Legs get involved in this whole thing?"

"Straight cash transaction," Jumpy said. "He was an informant. The reverend and his flunky knew everything that went on, on that tour."

"So now they know Jake is working on the song."

"Right. And they want me to go back and finish the job. So I call up Jake. He's real happy to hear from me, asks me to come up to Portland. I feel bad 'cause I like the guy. We end up getting totally shitfaced and one thing led to another."

"Why'd you take him up on the catwalk?"

"The deacon told me he was afraid of heights. So I thought that would be a clincher. He was really out of it. But as soon as we came through that door and he saw how high up we were, he started to bolt for the stairs. I grab him by the collar and drag him out on the ramp. He's begging me to let him go.

"That's when I mention how I have friends who want him to forget about the song. See, I'm thinking I can convince him. And the guy gets pissed. Starts fighting with me. And this platform starts swaying back and forth. I'm not too crazy about heights myself and this is starting to get hairy."

"So you pushed him over?"

Jumpy shrugged. "I felt bad about it, but I've killed guys I liked a lot more for less money than I got for that." We looked at each other. "I ain't such a bad guy," he said. "Why don't you tend to your friend and I'll just sneak out of here?"

"When did they sic you on me?"

"You visited Isaacson's church, right?" I nodded. "As I understand it, the deacon was on the phone to me before you left the parking lot."

"And Tommy Freeze?"

"Who?"

"Shirley's guitarist. Did you give him a hot shot?"

"Never even met him."

Holding the gun had my nerves stretched pretty tight. There was a crashing thump behind me. Badly startled, I turned to look even as I realized it was Shirley, flipping in the piano. Before I could recover, Jumpy leaped over and swatted the gun out of my hand. It spun skittering across the floor into the far corner and Jumpy moved into the path I would have to take to get to it.

I turned and ran in the opposite direction, to the door leading to the control room. Heaving the speaker cabinet out of the way, I ran up the stairs, slamming the door behind me. I grabbed what I had seen behind Jumpy's head when he first revealed himself: a wall phone. On my second try I got an outside line. I dialed 911 and breathlessly reported my situation. "My name is Jim McNamara," I bellowed at the operator. "I'm at Sygma Studios on North Sixth Street. I need police and ambulance right away. There is a madman with a gun who has barricaded us in here. He's already killed a security guard."

I couldn't hear her response because there was an explosion. A bullet slammed through the plate-glass shield behind me and dug into the wall over my head. I dropped the phone and slumped to the floor behind the mixing console, hoping the sound of the gunshot would convince the operator of the urgency of my situation.

I saw another door at the far end of the booth. Staying low, I skittered over and tried the knob. Locked. Another shot rang out; another gouge high on the wall.

I crouched there on the floor, listening intently. The sound when it came was not subtle. The door banged hard against its hinges and Jumpy began to climb the stairs, yanking on the banister. I looked around desperately for anything I could use as a weapon. From my vantage, I spied a toolbox under the mixing console and pulled out a screwdriver.

Each of Jumpy's footsteps resounded in me like a gong. Then he was on the landing, looking down at me, frowning, holding the pistol in his hand.

"I could shoot your ass," he said, advancing on me. "But guns are so impersonal. Don't you think?" He tucked the .44 away.

"I called 911, Jumpy. Police are coming."

"Then I better make this fast," he said, reaching to grab me. I hopped sideways and, with my back against the wall, stabbed him in the side with the sharp Phillips head I was holding against my thigh. It slid into his flank all the way up to its yellow plastic handle.

He roared in anger and pain and a look of perplexity crossed his face. It was chased by an expression of murderous rage. "Son of a bitch!" he yelled. In one continuous motion, he grabbed my hair, yanked me up and flipped me over the console, face first into the top half of the window.

I actually felt the glass bow for a second. Then it shattered and I dropped onto the large jagged shard still wedged in the frame. The window stalagmite impaled me just below the ribs and I hung there, pinioned in place. I couldn't rise up off it. Any movement caused excruciating agony. I tried to stabilize myself with one arm and leg against the sill. Blood was coursing out of my side.

I was facing out over the recording floor. Behind me I heard Jumpy grunt and then rumble down the stairs. I couldn't seem to breathe, my skin felt like it was on fire and I was fading out of consciousness as I watched Jumpy make his way to the door. He was holding his side and swaying from side to side as he limped. He put his free hand on the big speaker cabinet blocking the exit and then paused. He turned and looked at me. "You know what?" he said, putting his hand inside his vest and extracting the gun again. "Why fuck around?"

I had to depend on other people to reconstruct some of the details of what happened next. I do remember vividly my vision going to black and white. It was the weirdest thing. All the color bled out of the scene, like one of those fader programs on a camcorder.

No sooner had Jumpy taken his hand off the speaker than it began to rock as someone battered against the door over and over, trying to push into the room. There was a brief silence and then a crash, as the window facing the corridor collapsed.

Nicky Hagipetros was standing in front of the fractured frame, holding a fire extinguisher. At least I assumed from his size it was Nicky. I could only see him from the chin down. He used the extinguisher to sweep the remaining glass out of the window's margins and then stooped down and stepped sideways into the studio, like someone squeezing through the slats in a horse fence.

He took in the situation in the room and then strode right at Jumpy, ignoring the gun pointed at him. Jumpy fired and it hit Nicky in the shoulder. The impact slowed him down, in the way someone poking you with a bamboo pole might impede your progress. But he kept advancing.

Two more shots went off rapidly, one after the other, before Nicky tackled him. I hate to admit it, because it was like having a front row seat to see Godzilla fight King Kong, but just as they slammed into each other, I passed out. I know who I was rooting for, though.

# CHAPTER
## 42

When I came to, I was lying on an inclined stretcher in the studio's lobby. Police and emergency medical personnel were swarming through the room. They must have hit me with some drugs because the pain felt pretty manageable. Nicky was over in a corner, still upright. His shirt was hanging off one shoulder. A female medic, her dark hair bound in a French braid, was standing on her tiptoes on a chair, taping bandages on his wound.

Holding my hand and smiling at me was Paula.

"Shirley?" I asked in a harsh whisper. Trying to talk brought the hurt back in a hurry.

She nodded. "They found him," she said. "He won't be singing anytime soon. But he's alive and on his way to the hospital. Your ambulance should be along any minute."

"How did you know?" I rasped.

"The D.C. police found Legs in Rock Creek Park this morning. His neck was broken. But he still had his backstage insignia on from yesterday. They tracked us down at the hotel. Raul told us that Shirley left for Philly and that you were on his heels. So we drove up as fast as we could.

Sorry we didn't get here sooner. Nicky lifted you off that window, by the way. He might have saved your life."

I could hear another set of sirens whirl up to the entrance. A chunky paramedic with glasses over a spaniel's face trotted over. "Okay, we're ready for you," he said. Paula held my hand until they started to roll me away. "I'll see you at the hospital," she said, and blew me a kiss.

Holding open the door to the street was Keith Fisher. He looked down at me and smiled, much as I imagine a vulture would. "So," he said, "the rock 'n roll detective solves another case. Good work, Sam Spade." He clapped me on the shoulder.

"Hey," warned the guy pushing the gurney.

"You thought it was me all along, didn't you, slick?" Fisher said, walking beside me, the spinning lights from the police cars and ambulance splashing over his face.

"You lost your act," I said with difficulty. Trying to rub it in.

"Ehhh," said Fisher, waving his hands downward as if it were no big deal. "You look at the pop charts next week, you'll see Shirley's album dropped thirty-five spots. He's over. But your insurance agency is going to pay for every date left on the tour." He grinned. That shabby little victory obviously meant far more to him than Shirley's well-being.

"Anyway, I got a new singer, McNamara. Looks like a fucking witch doctor, breathes fire onstage. He's a total pyromaniac. And he has a voice like Satan. I'm telling you, he makes Screamin' Jay Hawkins look like Bobby Vinton. His album breaks next week. The kids are going to eat him up. Wait until you see him."

My voice had stopped working, but I remember thinking as they closed the ambulance doors: I can hardly wait.